CHIHUAHUAS OF THE ZOMBIE APOCALYPSE

Steven L. Hawk

Chihuahuas of the Zombie Apocalypse

Copyright © 2013 by Steven L. Hawk

First Paperback Edition – November 2013

ISBN-13: 978-1493557271
ISBN-10: 1493557270

Cover art: Keri Knutson
Editor: Laura Kingsley

www.SteveHawk.com

This book was previously released under the title, "Creeper Town."

This book is dedicated to my father,
Lee Vernon Hawk.

Also by Steven L. Hawk:

The Peace Warrior Trilogy
Peace Warrior
Peace Army
Peace World

The Justice Trilogy
Son of Justice
Stranded Justice
Final Justice

Others
STUCK
Summer Solstice (Contributing Author)

CHIHUAHUAS OF THE ZOMBIE APOCALYPSE

Personal accountability—that's what it all comes down to. Accept responsibility for your actions, your failures, and your life. Don't blame others when your personal decisions cause you grief. Learn from your mistakes and get on down the road. Shit happens to everyone. It's how you respond to the shit that makes all the difference.

-- SSgt. Cody Wilkins

Prologue

The words refused to flow and the tip of the Montblanc Agatha Christie fountain pen quivered anxiously an eighth of an inch above the blank page. The instrument strained against the invisible leash of anticipation. The hand wielding the pen waited...waited...waited. It wouldn't take long—it never did—but the seconds that preceded the euphoria of divine inspiration always felt like years.

Finally, a pathway revealed itself and the tip stabbed the page. Finally having delivered its first mark, the pen sprinted across the emptiness, eager to fill the void. *Bliss!* The addictive exercise that converted flowing, swirling, dotting, looping, slashing motions into a series of coherent, written thought was his addiction, his obsession, his reason for being. The words slammed heavily against the page and their newborn presence immediately transformed his latest experiences, deeds and thoughts into a compelling documentation of written history—his History. Much like the proverbial tree falling in the woods, the man knew his greatness—his larger than life being— would be nothing unless it was available for the world to marvel upon.

...scalp peeled away from her skull and the inevitable screaming began. It was an interesting development...

The Montblanc slashed an unceasing path through the white void, rapidly eliminating the blank space, filling the ever-present void. No matter how much he scribbled, he doubted he would ever fill all the white. When he filled this notebook, there would be another.

Then another.

Then another.

The neatly stacked, black and white composition notebooks that lined the shelves to his right bore testament. Arranged by year and month, they showed progress against the white, but not nearly enough. The empty journals to his left were further proof. Since the world went to Hell, the shelves that had previously held his unfilled notebooks had been topped off. In addition, the shelves were now buried under a near-mountain of boxes, each of which contained a seemingly endless supply of unfilled pages. No longer constrained by monetary concerns, he had emptied every local office supply store of their stock on hand—and he hadn't limited himself to the black notebooks. Future history would still be recorded on white, lined pages, but those pages would be protected by red, green, blue and purple covers. He thought they would make an appropriate change of pace to his usual black. After all, it was a new world, one full of exciting new challenges and opportunities.

Chapter 1

The rumbling of the garage door alerted Cheech to Mama's arrival. She was home earlier than usual, and he rushed to the door, eager to greet his pack leader.

Daisy—ever anxious to be the first one seen and heard—pushed past the older dog and blasted the uninhibited *yap-yap-yap* that accompanied every new arrival. Her tail whipped furiously, and her body bobbed up and down with joyful glee and anticipation.

The unmistakable *thunk* of Mama's car door closing informed the two dogs that their human would be with them soon. Daisy's bark, already annoying in its intensity, reached fever pitch with the needless announcement.

The small space was filled with sound, which is why Cheech nearly missed Mama's moan of... hurt? Pain? He cocked his head sideways and focused his ears toward the sound. Even through his excitement and Daisy's clatter, he detected a faltering movement in Mama's footsteps. A moment later he heard her issue a ragged cry—definitely hurt—as she fumbled to open the door. Cheech nipped at Daisy to silence her nonsense and warn her that something was wrong, but she merely sidestepped and kept barking, too excited to heed the rebuke.

Mama burst into the house—her aura and smell a broiling cloud of fear, pain and anxiety. Instead of issuing her standard, joyful greeting of "*my-babies-how-are-my-babies*" she slammed the door and rushed past the two eager Chihuahuas without the tiniest glance in their direction. At last, Daisy stopped barking and paused to consider something might be wrong.

The two small dogs followed their human quickly but warily as she passed through the kitchen. Their excitement at her arrival had been replaced by a mutual sense of concern, hesitation and foreboding. Cheech smelled blood. He also noticed that she was cradling one of her hands closely to her body.

Mama led the small group into the room where *Mama-go-potty* and began an anxious search. The trailing pair kept their distance and quietly observed as she retrieved items from various locations and placed them on the counter. Apparently satisfied with her collection, Mama then used her uninjured hand and made the water flow. With a sharp intake of breath and a gasp of pain, she put her injured hand under the flow. Although he couldn't see the act from where he sat, Cheech understood she was cleaning the wound, which was good. After a few moments, the water stopped and Mama began rifling through her collection of items.

When she was finished, Mama stumbled backwards until her back met the wall behind her. The hand was still cradled against her body, but was now wrapped in some type of cloth. He watched quietly as she slid down the wall and sat on the floor with an anguished groan.

Cheech took that as his signal to approach.

Mama's uninjured hand lay limply at her side and he offered it a slight, tentative lick to alert her of his presence. He was finally rewarded with acknowledgment.

"My babies," she mumbled as she lifted the hand to stroke him tenderly from head to tail. The feel of her fingers on his coat sent a cascade of warmth through his being and

he sought out her hand to offer another lick. Daisy quickly
trotted forward and pushed her nose into the caress, anxious
for her share of attention. The three of them remained there
for some time, enjoying shared caresses and the comfort that
comes with the closeness of a happy pack.

"Okay, who's ready to eat?"

Cheech bounded to his feet at the offer of food.
Happy times! He couldn't help but show his excitement and
spun around in a circle to the left. Mama liked it when they
turned circles for food, so he happily complied, eager to
please. He noticed that Daisy turned her own circles, hers
going in the opposite direction. Mama laughed at their show
and Cheech felt a wave of relief at the sound.

The relief was short-lived, however. Mama cried out
with the pain of pushing herself to her feet. She bent over
and took several long, tired breaths before stumbling slowly
from the room and down the hallway.

She seemed to regain strength when she reached the
kitchen because she fell quickly into the routine they all knew
by heart. The water and food bowls were picked up and
moved to the counter where they were quickly filled. Before
sitting them down, though, she retrieved the bowls for the
feline that sat on the other side of the room. Except for the
irritation of having to wait to eat while the feline was also
served, Cheech was indifferent to the other animal, and barely
gave the creature a glance. It kept to itself, for the most part.
It shared their living space, but wasn't part of the pack.

Mama placed the water bowl in its place without
incident, but nearly fell when she leaned over to put their
food bowls on the floor. Cheech was already skittering out
of the way, when she braced herself against the wall at the

last moment—with her injured hand. She cried out and the bowls dropped loudly to the floor. Mama leaned against the wall, cradled the hand and whimpered. Cheech heard Daisy whimper also.

The feline—whose bowls always got placed first—ate greedily on the other side of the room, but Cheech ignored his food. The worry over what was wrong with his pack leader pushed aside any thought of eating.

Finished with her feeding chores, Mama made her way to the couch and flopped down heavily. He followed closely behind. Her energy gave off a heavy mixture of fear, anxiety and pain. And her smell was sickly sweet, especially around the hand that she had injured. Cheech jumped onto the couch, settled into a comfortable spot beside her and received a weak scratch behind his ears. His senses never left Mama until she slipped into sleep. Once she nodded off, he tucked himself into the snug crook between her body and her arm. The couch shifted as Daisy jumped up to join them. With his left ear, Cheech listened to the smaller dog settle into her usual place between their pack leader's feet. The comforting beat of Mama's heart and the uncomfortable grate of her ragged breathing filled his right ear. He sighed and tried to find a peaceful position, but the sickly smell emanating from the injured hand kept him awake for some time.

He was sleeping fitfully, still snuggled tightly against her body, when the changes to her body woke him. His previous concern over her well-being quickly amplified as the ever-comforting *thumpthump-thumpthump-thumpthump* of Mama's heart grew weaker. His ears informed him the moment when him her lungs stopped drawing breath while

his nose informed him that the smell oozing from her injury
had grown much worse. He whined when the weakening
beat finally paused… stuttered… stopped. The finality in
that absence of sound was deafening. He pushed himself up
and sent a single, frightened bark toward her face. But he
realized the uselessness in the act. Mama was gone. In that
moment, he knew the sadness that death leaves in those still
living.

He stayed where he was until the heat left the body;
then he jumped down from the couch and made his way to
the bedroom that the small pack—suddenly reduced by
one—shared. His bed rested on the floor next to Daisy's.
Her shivering form was already huddled under her blanket,
and he quietly curled up onto his own.

Unable to shake a growing sense of fear and
uncertainty, he couldn't hold back a small, anxious whine. He
trembled, lowered his nose to the blanket, and pulled in the
lingering scent of Mama it still held. He stared into the
darkness until—at last—he slept.

Cheech was startled awake some time later by a
piercing shriek.

"Raaawwr—"

The frightful wail ended in mid-squeal, and Cheech
barely recognized it as coming from the feline. A blur of
motion passed him as Daisy bolted for the dark space under
Mama's bed. He fought the urge to follow the younger dog.
Instead of giving in to his fear, though, he crept quietly to the
doorway. His eyes, ears and nose searched for signals as to
what was happening.

His nose easily detected the stench of Mama's injury.
The stink had grown. The almost-unbearable smell was

joined by an undercurrent of fresh blood. He was unfamiliar with the feline's blood scent, but the scream indicated that something very painful and frightening had happened to the animal. His ears stood erect and honed in on a series of sounds. Wetness. Grunting. Tearing. He recognized the sounds individually but could not tie them together. The urge to hide was great, but his curiosity was greater. With nose and ears on alert, Cheech crept out of the room. Daisy, he noted, stayed firmly hidden.

He stayed next to the wall as he approached the kitchen area that separated the bedroom from the main room. He recalled that Mama was still out there. Dead. Lying on the couch. He pushed away the anxiousness that flared into being at the thought and pushed on. He reached the end of the hallway, lowered his head, and looked around the corner toward where the strange sounds originated. The sight that greeted him froze him in place.

Mama grunted as she held the feline up to her face and… ripped into its belly. The wet, tearing sounds suddenly made sense. But that's where Cheech's understanding ended and where the terror began. Mama had died. And because she had died, Mama couldn't walk. And—most importantly—even if she could walk, Mama would never eat the feline.

An involuntary *woof* of confusion escaped Cheech's chest.

Alerted by the sound, Mama lifted her face from the feline's innards, moaned, and turned her dead eyes toward the dog. She dropped the carcass and shifted her body slowly, awkwardly toward him. That was the moment when Cheech knew without doubt that the stench-covered abomination across the room was no longer Mama.

Cheech released another weak bark.

Mama's blood-covered maw groaned excitedly.

Then she charged.

Cheech scrambled backward, his claws rattling on the wooden floor as they sought purchase. The instinct to escape was immediate and overpowering. Finally gaining traction, he turned and ran. The overpowering stink grew as the pounding of the heavy feet followed close behind. He turned to the left just inside the bedroom door and made for the safety under the bed. In his fear-induced panic, he didn't duck and rapped his head soundly on the bottom rail of the bed as he entered. The pain of the collision, combined with the panic of the chase, blinded him as he sought refuge against the far wall.

With a final effort, he bumped against the shivering shape of Daisy as the thing-that-used-to-be-Mama slammed into the bed from above. The two dogs huddled together against the violence of the large form as it tried to claw its way through to them.

After several minutes, the vicious pounding began to peter out. Either the rank creature forgot what had caused its frenzy, or it realized the uselessness of its efforts.

Then Daisy barked and the attack began anew.

The cycle repeated itself twice more before Cheech acted against his female companion with a harsh grip of teeth to her throat. The message was simple. *Stop barking or I will hurt you.* Daisy stopped. An hour later, the two bare feet that represented the only visual cue of their tormenter—not Mama—turned and left the room.

Chapter 2

At any other time, the room that lay beyond the narrow gap would have represented a haven for Cheech—a place of contentment, security and comfort. It was where the pack slept, after all.

But not now.

Now, it offered rank helpings of stench, terror and death.

The gap between the bottom of Mama's bed and the thickly carpeted floor didn't allow much clearance, so the small dog kept his head low. His crown throbbed from a combination of terror-induced bangs against the bed frame overhead and a growing need for water. The bruises he could live with. It was the incessant, aching desire for a drink that worried him, and had him scanning the room beyond the darkened hiding spot.

Dehydration was threatening to kill them.

Then again, so was the monster that waited somewhere *out there*, beyond the safety of the space under the bed.

He was pressed into making a choice. Stay hidden and endure what was certain—a slow, agonizing death. Or leave the security of the hideout and risk a quick, but decidedly more horrific death. His instinct for *fight* compelled him forward toward the water dish that waited in the next room. His instinct for *flight* kept him rooted in place, unwilling to face the terror that waited.

But there was no real choice. The dog's primary instinct was to survive. And only one of the options offered that possibility. He inched closer to the opening, and seeing no immediate danger, snatched a quick glance over his left shoulder at his pack mate.

Daisy tagged close, as usual. Her nose twitched wildly and her eyes flitted nervously from side to side as she scanned the now-empty room. The younger dog vibrated and those who didn't know her might have thought she was cold. But the shivering was a product of the fear that controlled her body. Cheech was prepared to nip at her again, but she remained silent—which was no small accomplishment for her—so he withheld the bite. She was learning. Making noise was *not* good. He tolerated the incessant trembling. It was her nature to shake, and didn't put them in danger. It was also her nature to bark, but he'd already put her on notice that he wouldn't tolerate any more of *that* nonsense.

Barking brought Mama.

But it wasn't really Mama any more. The Mama that they had known—the human who had loved them, fed them, and been their pack leader—had died three days ago. The rank, bloated shell that had arisen from the couch where Mama had laid down to nurse an injured hand was something… *else*. It was clumsy, angry and devoid of anything resembling their former companion.

And it was hungry.

For the past three days, they remained hidden in place, afraid to leave their darkened corner. They slept. They awoke. Feeding time passed, and they swallowed their hunger. They shivered with fear and uncertainty.

Occasionally, the two feet returned to the room; their approach preceded by a slow, plodding gait that seemed aimless and somehow lost. It was obvious to Cheech that he and Daisy had been forgotten. That allowed him to relax— for a while.

But now, on the morning of their fourth day, thirst was driving him to action. The need for water had ultimately overruled the need for safety. Daisy trailed close behind as he edged forward to the opening. He sensed her disquiet and heard her heartbeat quicken with concern. She didn't move to prevent his inspection, though, which was the same as granting approval. She too was driven by the need to live; the need to survive.

Cheech poked his nose out first, testing the air. The room was filled with stink and rot—the stench seemed to get worse with each passing hour. There was little chance he would be able to smell Mama's approach. There was too much scent in the air. Instead, he kept his eyes on the door and his ears on high alert. He did not detect the sound of footsteps, which meant she was on the far side of their den, or not moving at all.

He crawled out slowly and took his first, tentative steps into the room. Standing for the first time in days, however, brought on a sudden cramping of muscles that forced him into a slow, painful stretch. The normal process of stretching was languid and pleasantly soothing, but the danger of the present situation turned the movement into a frightful exercise of necessity. He kept his eyes and ears pointed toward the door to the hallway as the knots of tired muscle loosened and allowed him to move with a measure of relatively painless fluidity.

The dog finally stood tall, and focused his full attention on the open doorway ahead. A sudden, quick touch of nose to his right flank alerted him to Daisy's position, and let him know she was ready. He moved forward slowly, and upon reaching the doorway, took a slow, cautious look.

The hallway was almost empty. At the far end, he recognized the tattered, bloody carcass of what had once been the feline. There were tracks of the animal's blood leading both ways, made by the two feet that haunted them—hunted them. But there was no sign of Mama.

Cheech didn't hesitate.

He moved forward quickly, careful that his nails didn't make a sound on the hard floor. He reached the kitchen and peered into the room. To his left, the dried trail of blood led into the main room of the pack's den. To the right sat two bowls of food—one empty, the other full—and one gloriously full bowl of water.

His thirst drove him toward the water. A blur passed him as Daisy raced to reach the dish first. Cheech heard her nails beating against the hard, tile floor. The sound of her nails set off alarms in his head, but the overpowering need for a drink, combined with its proximity, drove him forward.

His nose joined Daisy's in the bowl and he lapped greedily. He managed three swallows of the precious liquid before he heard the moan and recognized the sound of Mama's plodding footsteps. Only the footsteps weren't plodding, they were running.

Cheech turned around just as Mama-monster entered the other side of the kitchen. She didn't slow down when she saw the two dogs. If anything, she picked up the pace and—arms outstretched, as if wanting a hug—rushed to close the short distance that separated them. The moaning sound that poured from her mouth filled Cheech's mind with visions of insistent, needy hunger. It was a hunger that easily outmatched his thirst—a thirst that was now completely forgotten as the Mama-monster bore down on him.

Daisy's nails drummed the tile as she shot to the right and, quicker than Cheech would have thought possible, flew past Mama. Mama barely registered the younger dog's passing as she reached down for the dog directly to her front. Cheech, however, was spurred to action by his partner's decisiveness. He felt the fingers of death brush his fur briefly, but managed to escape the groping hands by darting for the gap between the monster's legs. He heard the enraged moan behind him as he leaped over the feline carcass, and sprinted down the hallway to safety.

Once again, he cracked his head on the wooden frame as he ducked under the bed and scrambled for the safety of the far corner. He felt the bed sag above with the weight of the moaning demon at the same instant that Daisy's frantic barking joined the fray.

He wanted to nip her into silence again, but the pain and darkness swallowed him before he could follow through.

Chapter 3

"On the right. On the right!"

"Got it," Cody answered as he jerked the wheel to the right.

He heard the awful "whump" as they struck another of the undead creatures. Cody winced as the body pirouetted away from the contact. He barely had time to register the gore-splattered uniform as belonging to a U.S. postal worker before they moved past. That mailman had seen his last delivery.

Since entering Boise, the number of hostile contacts had jumped dramatically. The five hundred miles of road between Joint Base Lewis-McCord—the combined Army-Air Force garrison that most Army folks still knew as Fort Lewis—and their current location had been largely deserted of the dead. What creepers they *had* spotted were centered around the Seattle area where I-5 met with I-90, and they had been too busy chasing down hordes of stranded motorists to worry about a single, still-moving vehicle. The stalled traffic caused by the rush of so many vehicles—all intent on escaping the growing swarm of dead—had proved to be the end of most.

Staff Sergeant Cody Wilkins, formerly of the U.S. Army's 2nd Battalion, 75th Ranger Regiment, was remembering the carnage they had left behind when another of the undead suddenly rushed the vehicle from the left.

Thump-thump.

"Dammit!" Specialist Fourth Class James Swanson, also formerly of the Rangers, yelled from the passenger seat. "This is gonna be another Seattle, Sarge."

Cody merely grunted and patted the steering wheel in admiration. The Army up-armored M1114, weighing in at nearly three tons, maintained its steady pace of 25 mph along the center, turn lane of the deserted street.

Except for the need to feed the hungry beast a never-ending diet of diesel, the armored High Mobility Multipurpose Wheeled Vehicle—better known as a Humvee—made the perfect vehicle for their current situation. The spacious, air conditioned interior offered its passengers a sufficiently comfortable ride. The fully armored sides and bullet-resistant glass offered protection from hostiles, living or dead; and the turbocharged engine and strengthened suspension system allowed them to traverse terrain that would stop a normal car or truck. As far as Cody was concerned, it was the ride you wanted when you found yourself in the middle of the zombie apocalypse.

"Keep your eyes peeled. We're getting close."

"About damn time, Sarge. I don't like riding out the end of the world without a weapon."

"I hear ya, Jimbo," Cody agreed. It had been a running topic of conversation between the two since leaving Fort Lewis. When the shit hit the fan, and their departure from the base became necessary for their personal survival, they hadn't been able to get their hands on weapons or ammunition. While it might sound counter-intuitive to civilians, it was a well understood fact among military personnel that U.S. bases have some of the tightest restrictions on weapons you will find anywhere. Unless you

were in a combat zone or on an active exercise, everything
that went *boom* was locked down tight. Vehicles, on the other
hand, were kept under a lot less security. As a result, they
were able to easily "liberate" the Humvee.

Cody slowed the vehicle and rolled to a stop at the
next intersection: Overland and Cloverdale. There were a few
cars abandoned in the street, but no sign of anyone about.
He spied a dark handprint on the window of one of the cars.
A large, dark splotch painted the pavement next to the
driver's open door. Dried blood. No body. *Just great.* He or
she was no doubt stumbling through a nearby neighborhood
right about now, just another dead walker on the prowl for
the next meal. The hair stood up on the back of his neck and
Cody did a quick three-sixty, resolved not to be on *that*
particular menu. Nothing moved except for the wind-blown
leaves in the trees that lined the road. He twisted his neck
and rolled his shoulders in an attempt to release some
tension. Satisfied that nothing was creeping up on them, he
finished his review of their surroundings.

These were his old stomping grounds, and he took in
the familiar sights. Little had changed since his last visit, a
year before, and he briefly recalled the funeral that had called
him back home. He felt a sharp, stab of guilt.

*There's nothing like the end of the world to make you realize
what a bad son you've been,* he thought. *She deserved better.*

"You okay, man?"

"Yeah. Just peachy." Cody sighed and wondered
what he'd find when he reached his mother's place. He
hoped she was waiting for him. Even more, he hoped she
could forgive him for not being there when she needed him.
Neglect is an act of passivity, exhibited more through

procrastination and thoughtlessness than by any deed or action. Unfortunately, its effect on the neglected isn't any less hurtful or wounding.

He lifted his left hand and massaged his eyes, anxious to release the burn of heartache and exhaustion. It was a useless gesture. The irritation refused to release its angry hold. It had been more than a week since he or Jimbo had slept for longer than four hours at a stretch. Hopefully that would change when he reached his boyhood home.

Before he slept, though, he would apologize.

Cody pointed the vehicle north onto Cloverdale and accelerated.

*   *   *

Daisy shivered and pushed her rump into the farthest corner of their hiding spot. The security of the position was minimally better than any other location under the bed, but the increased darkness helped her cope. She couldn't bark. Cheech had made it clear that he wouldn't tolerate it any longer, and she had to admit, it didn't help at keeping the *thing* away from them.

Barking did, however, make her feel better. Expelling the sounds from her body kept her mind off of the fear, her growing hunger, and thirst. Except for the few precious laps of water the day before, they hadn't eaten or had water for three days. Sooner or later, she knew they'd have to chance facing the giant monster that used to be her human. Food and water waited in the next room.

The worst part of the situation—even worse than the ever-present fear and the growing thirst—was the *smell*. The overpowering stench of disease and rot that surrounded the monster was an affront to Daisy's entire being. Her sensitive nose—always a source of pride for the young canine, and the one area where Cheech accepted her superiority—absolutely *ached* under the relentless assault. She pushed it as far down into the carpeted floor as possible and, for the first time in her four years of existence, wished she had a weaker nose. A small, painful whine escaped her dry throat, and she cast an expectant glance toward Cheech. But no rebuke was forthcoming. He was too weak; too filled with his own pain and suffering to send a nip her way for the small noise.

Daisy lay her head down, just as Cheech lifted his. The set of his ears alerted her that the other dog had heard something. His body language indicated it might be important. She focused her own, weaker antenna in the direction he indicated.

Cheech stood up—as well as he could stand in the cramped space—and edged to the opening. That's when Daisy heard the muted rumble of the garage door opening. Her response was automatic and uncontrollable.

She began barking wildly.

*   *   *

There was a brief moment of anxiety as Cody struggled to recall the code. His finger hovered in front of the garage door keypad before remembering it was keyed to his parent's anniversary date. June 28. He quickly punched in

0-6-2-8, then turned his back to the house and scanned the neighborhood for unwanted visitors.

The garage door rumbled noisily upward.

Jimbo stood at the end of the driveway; his head swiveling left and right. The baseball bat he had snagged during a brief stop at a sporting goods store in Baker City, Oregon was held loosely in his right hand. Cody held his own bat, a white Easton XL1 (price tag, $299.99) in a two-handed, ready-to-hit-shit grip. The Easton was an aluminum beauty, but as a defensive weapon for surviving the zombie apocalypse, it was far from perfect. Unfortunately, the guns they had hoped to find had already been taken by previous looters.

The Humvee sat between them; backed into the driveway for a quick escape should it be needed. Although the front was splattered with the blood and gore, the vehicle showed no sign of real damage from the impacts it had taken. The same couldn't be said for any of the already-dead runners who had tried to catch it.

The door reached the top and silence fell over the small neighborhood of single family homes. It was too quiet. A shredded body strewn across the lawn two doors down proved that the violence that had visited the rest of the northwest—and the world, if the last television news reports that aired more than a week ago were to be believed—had not bypassed his hometown. Jim and Cody had been on the lookout for other survivors since arriving at the outskirts of Boise. There were signs that other survivors were around. Curtains moved as the Humvee passed. Shadows appeared in windows. Once they spied a pickup truck, but it turned away when it spotted them and sped quickly away. Others lived here, but they seemed unwilling to show themselves to a single vehicle, obviously frightened of the horrors that waited for them to show themselves.

Cody understood the emotions driving most of the survivors. Americans had become conditioned to keeping their heads down. Unlike when the country was young, and most folks had only themselves, or perhaps their neighbors, to rely on, the tendency ingrained in the current American psyche seemed to lean toward *not* taking any real or immediate action. Hunkering down and waiting for rescue had become a natural response for many. When something bad happened these days—earthquake, flood, hurricane, you-name-the-disaster—few of his countrymen seemed able or willing to take care of themselves or their families. FEMA, insurance companies, The Red Cross and other agencies always stepped in within days or hours. Movie stars and popular singing sensations lined up to put on "relief efforts" so that no one hurt or suffered more than necessary. And while relief agencies and relief efforts were all good things— things that really, *truly* helped—they had an unfortunate downside that few—Cody included—had understood until now. They conditioned humanity to rely on others for their survival. Few Americans ever had to take full responsibility for their own lives when faced with calamity. Not really. They didn't have to warm themselves, or find their own water, or hunt their own food. Those items were provided for them from a local shelter or off the back of a truck. But not now. Now that everyone was *equally* affected, help wouldn't come from the outside.

It was a new world and Cody understood the reality of the situation. Within a span of less than two weeks, the

world of the living had given way to a world where the dead
no longer stayed dead. Instead, the dead hunted the living.
The fortunate ones were consumed, and the less fortunate
were turned into fellow hunters. No one was coming to the
rescue this time. Survival depended solely upon an
individual's actions and the actions of those he chose to
surround himself with.

"You ready, Jimbo?"

"Oh, hell yeah," the younger man replied nervously,
pointing to the right. Two creepers—an older woman
wearing a blood-stained summer dress, the other a teenaged
boy wearing nothing but a stained pair of loose tightey-
whiteys—had appeared from between the house directly
across the street and the next one to the right. At the sound
of Jimbo's voice, they turned toward the two soldiers and
began that determined, trotting shuffle that Cody had come
to recognize and despise in the undead.

A loud crash to their left revealed another excited
creeper heading their way. The contents of the garbage can it
had pushed over spilled into the street. Cody recognized this
one. It was the neighborhood a-hole, Mr. Douglas. "Mr. D"
was well known for his obsessive compulsive, anal retentive
behavior that encompassed everything within the
development. The exacting attention he paid to every bush,
tree and blade of grass in his yard was strange enough. But
his attentions never stopped there. You were quick to hear
about an uncut lawn, a broken fence slat, or a trash can that
had been left too long at the curb. His all-time worst pet
peeve, though, was litter. He walked the sidewalks picking up
stray candy wrappers and cigarette butts, and if he thought
the trash originated with any single house or person, they

were certain to hear about it promptly. Cody had been the recipient of more than one "litterbug talks" when he was in high school.

"Who's the litterbug now," Cody yelled to the now-dead neighbor.

Jim double timed it up the driveway and into the garage, giving Cody a 'what the hell are you talking about' look as he passed. Cody took two steps backward. He now stood just inside the garage door. With an anxious nod of his head, he pointed to the garage door button on the far wall.

"Hit it, quick!"

The creepers were almost to the end of the driveway. The squealing rumble seemed even louder than before as the door began its slow, laborious descent. The three undead seemed to sense that their window of opportunity was closing and their graceless trots turned into awkward runs. The zombies weren't fast, but they weren't the slow, shuffling undead that Cody recalled from television either. He gripped the Easton tighter and drew it back, ready to take a swing. Jim joined him, his bat also ready.

The door dropped lower, covering the top third of the opening, and Cody backed up another step to keep the creepers in view. The aluminum door was half closed when the first of the three undead—Tightey Whitey—slammed into it. The impact rattled the door and knocked the former teen backwards onto the ground. He was struggling to turn himself over when Mr. D ran face-first into the door and bounced away. Neither had tried to duck under the lowering door, which reinforced for Cody that the monsters they were facing weren't all that bright.

The door was two-thirds closed, when Summer Dress's feet—one bare, the other still wearing a tan sandal—heralded her own thunderous collision and subsequent recoil. Cody was just beginning to giggle at the idiocy of his adversaries when Tightey Whitey stretched a grayish, blood-stained hand under the door.

"Oh, shit," the former Army Ranger muttered as the door closed on the appendage, causing the safety sensor—the one that prevented the door from accidentally closing on anyone caught in its path—to engage and automatically reverse the door's path.

"Hit the button! Hit the button!" But it was too late. Tightey Whitey crawled under the rapidly ascending door and grabbed Jim's foot. A quick glance revealed Mr. D's legs as he pressed against the rising door. In another few moments, he would be inside and on them as well.

Cody stared in horror as Jim tried to pull away from the creeper's grasp. He hopped backwards on one foot, then—as if in slow motion—fell backwards, away from the insistent, hungry hands that reached for him.

"Dammit." Cody reared back and let loose with the Easton just as the creature's mouth closed over Jim's boot-covered foot. The swing caught Tightey in the forehead, slamming the zombie's head back and away. The resulting dent was proof that the thick bone had crumbled under the blow, and the thing slumped to the ground.

A second swing hit Mr. D in the chest and drove him backward several feet as the garage door opened fully. It wasn't a killing blow, but it gave Cody a moment to re-load and aim a home run swing at Summer Dress, who was approaching from the right with hands groping and mouth chomping. The sweet spot of the bat connected with the right side of her head, causing the thick skull to collapse in a sickening crunch that forced a mixture of gray, black and red gore from her nose, mouth and eyes. Cody turned his face away from the mess and yanked the bat from the woman's head. She collapsed noisily to the concrete driveway.

Jim was struggling to his feet as Cody cocked the bat for another go at his former neighbor. Before he could swing though, he noted movement beyond Mr. D and spied several more figures headed their way. They were several houses away, but getting closer by the second.

"You gotta close that door, Jim," he shouted as he swung for the fences. The blow connected perfectly and the former nuisance of the neighborhood toppled backward like a felled oak. His body slapped the hard surface, bounced an inch or so, then lay still beside Summer Dress.

Cody heard the door begin another, infuriatingly slow descent. A scan of the creepers outside showed they were still far enough away that they would be okay...for now.

He was almost ready to breathe a sigh of relief when he realized that Tightey Whitey was lying across the threshold. With an exasperated groan, he reached down, grabbed the single handful of cotton that presented itself and yanked the dead teen inside the garage.

Several seconds after the door finally settled into place, the first of the undead slammed into it. It was then that Cody recognized his mother's car behind them. On the driver's door, he could make out a smear of something dark on the white paint.

An involuntary groan escaped as he recognized the stain for what it represented.

Chapter 4

"You want me to go first, Sarge?" Jimbo asked.

"Stop calling me 'Sarge', Jimbo. We're not in the Army any longer. Hell, there is no more Army."

They had to shout to be heard over the repeated, loud hammerings of the undead as they pounded at the garage door. The door was a newer model, replaced by his father only a few years back. As such, it was sturdy, and apart from the incessant banging, showed no sign of distress.

"Sorry," Jim acknowledged. "Just an old habit, ya know?"

"Yeah, I know." Cody wished he was anywhere except where he was: standing in front of the door to his mother's house. He offered a silent prayer that she was okay; that the bloodstain on her car door was something... else. But he was a realist and the smear was about as ominous a warning as you could get. He hoped for the best with all his heart, but with his mind, he prepared for the worst. Whatever waited on the other side of the door—redemption for ignoring her for the past year, or a lifetime of hell because he never got to let her know how deeply sorry he was—he couldn't put it off any longer. And he couldn't let another take the lead. She was *his* mother; she was *his* was responsibility.

Please. Just let her be okay.

"Stay close, but not too close," he warned the twenty year-old, former corporal. "The last thing I want to do is clock you by mistake."

"No problem. What's the layout of the house?"

It was a good question, and Cody should have thought to explain it to Jim without being asked. Again, he felt an overwhelming sense of fatigue, and as he had done just fifteen minutes earlier, he rolled his head and flexed his shoulders. He realized that the simple action had recently become a seemingly necessary habit that relieved tension like a pressure relief valve on a steam engine. For the briefest of moments, he thought maybe Jimbo *should* take the lead. He wasn't thinking with the clarity of mind needed for this situation. Then again, he had never faced a situation that might require him to kill his already dead (*undead*) mother. The unwelcome thought passed quickly, though, (*she's fine*) and he steeled himself.

"On the other side of this door is a small laundry room and pantry. There's a door that separates that room from the kitchen. That door may or may not be open," he explained. "From the kitchen, you can go left to a hallway that leads to the master bedroom, or right to the living room and other bedrooms."

"We going right or left when we hit the kitchen?"

"We have to play it safe," Cody replied, thinking through a plan on the spot. "If she's not in the kitchen, I'll take up a position leading to the master bedroom on the left; you guard the right."

"And then?"

"Then I sweep her into my arms and give her the biggest hug you ever saw, while she cries and tells me how much she's missed me."

Jimbo nodded and Cody saw the unspoken question. What if she's *not* okay?

"If she hasn't spotted us by then, we make some noise and bring her to us," Cody answered with a sigh.

Jim nodded again. "You sure you don't want me to go in alone? Check things out first?"

Cody knew what he was being offered. He silently thanked his friend, but would have no part of it. His mother, his responsibility. He shook his head and grasped the door knob.

"Ready?"

Cody received a single, curt nod in response. Cody nodded back and, without further pause, he turned the knob and pushed through the door.

*   *   *

Through the enraged melee that Mama was creating above their heads, Cheech heard the door open and felt the air pressure inside the den change. Someone had just entered the house. Despite his recent admonition to Daisy against barking, he let out two sharp yaps of warning. He wanted to alert the newcomer of two things: their location, and the danger that was present.

Mama was either oblivious to the intrusion or didn't care, because she redoubled her efforts against the bed. Daisy buried her nose in the hair on his rump and whined.

Cheech offered another, single yelp, then ducked back down. He had done all he was willing to do to warn whoever had just walked into the house.

*   *   *

Cody passed swiftly through the laundry room and into the kitchen. His entrance into the room was met by the unexpected sound of barking, and he felt a sliver of hope that all was well inside the house. Quickly on the heels of the bark, however, came the god-awful snarls that could only be associated with the enraged undead. Walking into a brick wall couldn't have stopped his forward momentum any quicker.

Without thinking, his body turned slightly into a defensive position; his feet shoulder-width apart, his attention focused fully on the hallway entrance, the aluminum bat cocked and ready. The movement took less than a second, but it was long enough for his mind to process the sight of blood tracks on the floor.

"Dammit."

His oh-so-slim hope that his mother was safe had been ripped away and replaced by the ugly truth: She was a creeper. He swallowed the heave of bile rising from his gut, and blinked away the unexpected blurriness that threatened his vision. *What a piss poor son you are*, he thought before forcing down the emotions that struggled to bubble forth.

He regained his focus and began a silent count as he waited for his undead mother to come running.

One...two...three...

At "ten", Cody knew she wasn't on her way. The snarling hadn't abated, but it also hadn't gotten any closer. The monster had its attention focused elsewhere, and the initial barking, though silent now, hinted at who that might be. Cheech or Daisy. The blood on the floor was a strong indication one of them had already been killed.

Cody looked back to Jim and silently motioned for him to stay put. He then moved further into the kitchen and ventured a cautious look down the hallway. From the vantage point he had, Cody couldn't see anything inside his mother's bedroom. He did, however, spot the blood splatter and tufts of white fur that marked the death of some animal. The sight induced a recollection of his mother telling him (on one of the rare times he had called over the past twelve months) that she had gotten another pet, a white cat she had named "Toodles." The thought that "Noodles" might have been a more appropriate name—considering how the cat died—flashed unexpectedly in his head.

Toodles ended up as Noodles.

He suppressed an unwelcome giggle at the macabre notion. A more rational portion of his consciousness wondered if he was beginning to crack. An even more rational segment of his mind told him he needed to end this situation post-haste, before he or Jim ended up on the wrong side of the teeth that had done in the damn cat.

Eschewing further thought, Cody smacked the end of the bat angrily against the kitchen floor. The crisp metallic "clang" of the contact cracked one of the tiles and had the immediate effect of silencing the monster in the other room—the one that had once been his mother.

"Mom, I'm home!" The former soldier called out, interrupting the brief silence.

A confused symphony of barking, snarling, and undead footsteps pounding rapidly along the hallway, followed the announcement.

*   *   *

Cheech recognized the voice that called out. It was The Boy. Unexpected, but pleasant recollections of The Boy passed through his mind as what-once-was-Mama fell silent. Long buried memories of walks around the neighborhood, chasing balls, and unexpected but tasty treats filled Cheech's head.

The Boy—absent from the pack for so, so long—had returned.

He offered a single bark, one full of excitement and welcome. Daisy understood the emotion contained in his single yelp because she lifted her head and excitedly resumed her normal cadence of *bark, bark, bark!*

Then Cheech heard what-once-was-Mama turn away from its attack on the bed and race toward the kitchen. He recognized the danger to The Boy as the rancid feet slapped heavily on the floor and the thing picked up speed.

His yaps immediately joined Daisy's in sending out a warning.

*   *   *

The presence of so much dried blood succeeded in further corrupting the ghastly image Cody expected to encounter as his undead mother rounded the corner. The flaky gore matted the already-dark hair to the right side of her face and liberally coated the front of the nursing scrubs she wore. Who knew a freaking cat held so much of the crimson liquid? Then again, she could have met other unfortunate victims besides the cat since turning.

Her hands were outstretched talons and her mouth gaped in a hideous opening and closing motion that suggested an anxious expectation of her next meal. Topping the horror charts for Cody though, was the awful clamor that spat forth from the monstrosity's oral cavity. The snarling, snapping moan sounded like death itself. In the brief second he had to consider the noise before swinging the bat, he supposed it was as suitable a precursor to life's final act as any. But not *his* life's final act. Not today, at least.

Since his first year in Little League, he had been a power hitter, batting cleanup for whatever team he played for. He had learned early on that batting power was generated through a well-timed combination of body movement, bat swing and weight transfer. Today he couldn't help but add generous rations of anger, shame, and atonement to the recipe. Anger at the situation; shame and atonement for his actions (or non-actions) over the past year. A simple base hit wouldn't suffice. Not today. Today, he was swinging for the fences. He owed her that much.

The movement started in the hips and continued forward as he stepped into the swing. The energy generated by the forward motion was transferred to his shoulders, then into his arms, then into the already blood-stained Easton

XL1. Finally, it was transferred to the front of his approaching un-mother's head. The resulting explosion of bone, brain and gore propelled the damaged body backward into the hallway, where it collapsed onto the bloodstained tufts that once belonged to Toodles.

With one blow—a blow filled with all the power and hurt in his soul—the undead, ravenous monstrosity ceased to exist. In its place, lay the body of his dead, neglected mother.

The bat clattered to the ground and Cody slumped to his knees.

Chapter 5

Jim looked on in amazed horror as the scene unfolded before him. He felt for the man he had come to know so well over the past week. The need to make amends to the woman who now lay before them would never be fulfilled, and the agony of that realization was written on the other man's haggard, tightly drawn face. Jim hesitated a moment, then laid a hand on his friend's shoulder and offered a light squeeze.

"I'm sorry, Sarge," he mumbled quietly. Cody forced himself to his feet using the bat as a crutch, and Jim stepped back to give the man room.

Despite seeing the obvious anguish Cody was struggling with, Jim acknowledged that Sergeant Wilkins was one bad-ass mofo. It wasn't news, really. The guy had proven his mettle daily since Jim joined the Rangers sixth months earlier. As one of the youngest Platoon Sergeants in the battalion, Wilkins was known as a take charge, lead-by-example NCO, who never asked any of his subordinates to do anything he wouldn't do.

Like this thing with his mother. He probably never considered taking a step back and letting someone else handle the situation.

Jim doubted he would have been able to stand up to the task if their roles had been reversed. Nope. He would have stepped back, and let the Sarge do what was necessary. Not that Jim had a mother, but still.

He thought back to that moment a week earlier when the shit had finally reached critical mass at the base. Jimbo had just put down two of his former platoon members—one with a snap of his neck, the other with a well-time swing of a cinderblock—and was weighing his chances against another half-dozen honing in on him, when he heard a squeal of tires on the road behind him. He turned to see the Sarge leaning out the window of his beat up pickup and waving him over in a casual manner. Jim hadn't hesitated. He raced to the passenger side, leaped into the vehicle and yelled, "Let's roll!" The feeling of comfort as the steel cab surrounded him was immediate but passed quickly as he viewed the mayhem and death that surrounded them through the windshield. Jim had never been so relieved as when the rusty Ford F-150 pulled away from the building that had previously been their unit HQ, but was now a fiery, body-strewn death pit.

"How was your vacation?" The word "vacation" exited his mouth as an embarrassing squeak when one of their undead brothers-in-arms slammed into the door he had just entered. The hungry moaner fell away as the truck picked up speed, and Sergeant Wilkins tugged the wheel slightly to the right. The truck lurched violently, and Jim knew the body must have fallen beneath the truck. He didn't see who the attacker was and didn't want to know. Instead, he kept his eyes focused on the side of his platoon sergeant's stubbled countenance and silently urged the old truck to *hurry the fuck up and move it.*

"Not bad, apparently," his NCO replied, eyes glancing to the rear view mirror to examine the damage left in their wake. "The shit's bad in Oregon, but nothing like this… at least not yet."

"Hell, Sarge. It wasn't like this until today," Jim panted. He thought he might need to change his underwear soon. He took a deep breath and waved at the apocalyptic scene outside the truck. "It started small...like everywhere else, I guess. Then, *wham!* This morning, the shit seemed to hit the fan all at once. I woke up to my roommate getting his throat torn out and have been fighting for my life ever since. If you hadn't come along when you did..."

He didn't have to say anything else. The crashed vehicles they had to dodge, the burning buildings they passed, and the growing crowd of the undead—all of whom seemed to be honing in on the truck as it moved through them—told the story far better than he ever could.

Jim saw Sergeant Wilkins glance right a second before the truck bucked over the curb and left the road. He allowed his eyes to track their new path and saw what drew the sergeant's attention. Sitting in the middle of a nearly empty parking lot was a solitary military passenger bus. Atop the bus, two soldiers wielded what looked like metal pipes. A dozen or more angry creepers surrounded the bus. Although their reach was too short to grasp the living food above them, they had the men trapped. It was just a matter of time.

"Slight detour, Jimbo," Sergeant Wilkins announced as they closed in on a zombie who had spied the meal and was making its way toward the bus. The truck, traveling at nearly thirty miles an hour, hit the undead walker from behind and bounced wildly as the body was churned over by the under carriage. "Hold on!"

Jim was already moving and managed to secure his seat belt just seconds before the front of the Ford plowed through the crowd surrounding the bus. The jarring of multiple contacts managed to rattle the truck, his nerves and his teeth.

To its credit, the old F-150 waited until its right side ground noisily against the passenger side of the bus before it quit.

"Jump in the back!" Sarge shouted through a two-inch gap in his window as he turned the key and pumped the gas pedal. He received little in return for his efforts. The truck's engine merely added its own pitiful groan to those of the hungry undead. The men, whose shocked faces Jim could see through the windshield, gawked down at the truck but refused to move. He couldn't blame them. Leaving the relative safety of the bus's rooftop for the open bed of a dead pickup truck was a fool's errand. But then again, so was staying in place.

The scattered undead were beginning to regroup when those closest to the pickup suddenly noticed the two tender flesh-morsels inside. As a unit, their groaning increased in volume as their anxious hands began hammering an angry beat on the exterior of the cab. Jim was weighing his personal survival options—stay in the truck or move to the top of the bus—when the engine finally roared to life.

"Now or never!" Sergeant Wilkins shouted at the men on the bus as he shifted into first gear. He tossed Jim a smile that somehow alleviated the tormented pounding that threatened to explode from his chest.

Jim looked up in time to see the two men share a look and a nod. The truck rocked forward against the bodies in front. Would the old truck make it? The two on the bus were betting that it would, Jim noticed as they hung their legs over the side of the bus. The sounds of their feet slapping the metal bed rang out and the old truck dipped slightly under their added weight. The weight must have helped somehow because the truck found purchase and plowed over the half dozen undead to its front.

One of the men behind yelled and Jim looked back to see him pull his arm from the bloody maw of one of the zombies. The second man smashed the biter with his metal rod and the body fell away. He could tell it was too late for the other man, though. Anyone who knows anything about zombies knows what happens to the bitten.

Seconds later, they dropped over the cement curb and back onto the street. They still had chasers, but they were quickly left behind. Jim considered what they had just been through and felt it was time to interject some sanity into the situation.

"Sarge, can you do us a favor and head for the motor pool?" Sergeant Wilkins raised his eyebrows in confusion. "Um...no offense to your truck, but if we're gonna survive the zombie apocalypse we need better wheels."

Thirty minutes later, they were hauling ass away from the military base in the hardened Humvee. The two men they had rescued—brothers, as it turned out—had elected to stay behind. Both knew it was a matter of time before Brad, the bitten sibling, turned. Jason, the uninfected one, refused to leave Brad's side despite the combined urging of the other three. Sarge finally conceded the fight and wished the two well before pulling away.

When Jim asked him why he hadn't forced Jason to go with them, he was met with a shake of the head and a rigid stare.

"It was his decision and he was entitled to make it," the sergeant stated simply. "You should never force another man to accept your choices when he's capable of making his own."

"Sarge, the Army might disagree with you on that point," Jim countered. He was thinking of all the orders he had been forced to follow since enlisting two years earlier—many of them issued by the man behind the wheel.

"Jimbo, there isn't any more Army." Sergeant Wilkins waved at the chaos outside the protected shell of the Humvee. "Or haven't you noticed?"

Jim paused to consider the statement. If the rest of the country was experiencing a similar wave of the rising dead, it was entirely possible that the US Army *had* ceased to exist as a viable unit. It had certainly ceased to be an effective force within the confines of Lewis-McCord, home of one of the most respected and highly efficient combat units in the world. The implications staggered the corporal like a blow to the face. No Army. No Marines. No Air Force. It was possible—even probable—that the Navy had ships in operation that were unaffected by the plague, but what could they do to help restore order? How could they help save humanity against the onslaught that was coming—the onslaught that was already here.

Jim was a self-proclaimed zombie-phile. He had gotten hooked on the genre after seeing George Romero's *Night of the Living Dead* as a pre-teen, and had proceeded to consume everything zombie-related that he could get his hands on. Movies, books, video games—if it had to do with zombies, he ate it up like a nine year-old trick-or-treater eating Smarties on Halloween. He had taken a lot of shit, most of it good-natured, from his friends in high school. The ribbing had continued in the barracks once his fellow troops discovered his fascination with undead flesh-eaters. Shrugging off the razzing was easy, he just cracked open the latest zombie book and lost himself in the story.

He suddenly realized that he was getting the last laugh over all of those who teased him, as non-humorous as that laugh was. He was using (in fact, had already used) his knowledge of the undead to keep himself alive. Dodging the growing masses of the zombies, ducking into Sarge's car, suggesting they take one of the armored Humvees—all had been instinctive, a result of his knowledge. The untold hours of self-study had given him some very valuable tools.

"Sarge, where are we headed?" Not that it really mattered. He was an only child and his parents had died in an automobile accident when he was seventeen. He just wanted to be prepared for whatever they might be facing.

"I thought we might head to Boise," his former platoon sergeant rasped. "And stop calling me 'Sarge.' The name is Cody."

Jim grinned at the thought of calling his platoon sergeant by his first name. "Whatever you say, Sarge."

Chapter 6

Cody shook out the blue and orange Boise State
Broncos blanket he retrieved from the sofa and laid it out
next to his mother's body. They had to move her out of the
house and into the back yard, but he didn't want to look at
her while they did it.

"Take her feet and roll her onto the blanket," he
instructed. The young soldier moved at once to do his part.
He had been awfully silent since they entered the house and
Cody couldn't blame him. His first visit to his former
sergeant's childhood home wasn't a pleasant experience. In
fact, it had to be the most awkward homecoming that either
of them could have imagined.

They moved the body onto the blanket and folded the
sides up and over, creating an informal shroud. That task
accomplished, Cody moved to the sliding door that led from
the dining room to the back patio. He moved the curtain
aside just enough to allow a visual inspection of the patio and
the small yard. He didn't expect any unwanted visitors; all of
the houses in the neighborhood were fully fenced. And while
the five-foot high barriers of cedar and redwood weren't
impenetrable—they served to define property lines and
provide privacy, more than anything else—the creepers didn't
seem mentally or physically capable of scaling them. At least,
not without a fresh meal on the other side to encourage
them. Even then, it didn't seem likely that one or two could
topple a well-built fence. More than one or two might be a
problem.

As expected, the back yard was clear. Over the fencing, Cody surveyed the surrounding yards and houses. From his vantage point, he could see the backs of three houses: the one that shared their property and fence line and the ones to each side of it. In typical suburban style, those houses faced a different street, one that was parallel to the street he lived on. He didn't see any deadheads walking about in any of those yards.

Satisfied that the coast was clear, he was turning away from the view when he spotted movement from the two-story house on the left. The curtain in a second floor window had been inched open and a face was peering out. He couldn't tell if it was a man or woman, adult or child. But whoever it was, they were *not* one of the undead.

Cody considered stepping outside and waving, but the face disappeared and the curtain fell back into place before he could act.

"We have neighbors at ten o'clock, Jimbo," he announced. "Live ones."

"Nice," the younger man replied. "But it's what's in here that I'm concerned about right now."

"What do you mean?" Cody released the curtain and turned. He spied Jimbo creeping toward the hallway leading to the master bedroom. His bat was raised over his right shoulder.

"I seem to recall barking when we entered. We need to check it out."

"Take it easy. My mom had dogs." Cody mentally kicked himself for not thinking to check on them before now. He had known both Cheech and Daisy since they were pups. Cheech was the first dog his mother ever owned. He was a sweet, lovable Chihuahua that went against most of the stereotypes for the breed. He wasn't an excited barker, didn't shiver twenty-four-seven and loved all strangers, even little kids. Daisy, on the other hand... well she was adorable, even when she shivered and barked.

"Yeah, well, they could be zombie dogs."

"Um... seriously? Zombie dogs?"

Jimbo halted his movement and turned toward Cody. The look on his face showed a mix of impatience and fear. The reason for the fear was understandable. The look of impatience was no doubt a result of Cody's obvious lack of knowledge about zombies—apparently, dogs could become zombies. *Who knew?*

"Shit." The last thing he wanted right now was to kill his family's dogs, but it didn't look like he had a choice. He felt like curling up in grief at the thought but gave a resolved shrug and moved toward the hallway. If they had turned, he would do what needed to be done. "Fine. We'll do this just like before."

*   *   *

Cheech was torn between checking out what was happening outside of the room and staying hidden. All of his senses—but mainly his ears—were tuned in; anxiously gathering what little data was available.

The hungry growling that signified the monster's presence had ceased. The metallic clang and subsequent thump that announced the sudden silence were followed by whispers between The Boy and another, unknown human.

This suggested that Mama was no longer a threat. But still…
he and Daisy hadn't survived the past few days by taking
chances.

Although his body thrummed with the need to know,
he settled down at the edge of the bed to wait. If it was safe
to approach, The Boy would let him know.

As soon as the decision to wait was made, he heard
his name. He lifted his head and cocked it to the right,
searching for the perfect angle to hear The Boy and to
determine his intent. The beckon hadn't sounded right.

"Cheech. Daisy!"

The call came again, and Cheech sensed a problem.
Fear. Nervousness. Fatigue. The Boy's voice announced all of
these things. There was very little of the excitement,
affection and anticipation that he had been conditioned to
expect. Cheech inched closer, half of his body now clear of
the bed. Daisy settled down on his right rear, still fully
hidden. He could tell that she was anxious to greet The Boy,
but would wait for him to initiate any movement. The past
few days had trained her to obey his will, accept his decisions.
He had kept her alive.

"Come on Cheech," The Boy called again. *Fatigue.*
Fear. Hope. A better combination, but still the dog hesitated,
holding his position.

"Are you there, boy? Daisy-girl? You can come out
now." Cheech moved forward, stood up. The soreness in his
body nearly caused him to lie back down, but he fought
through it. His muscles cried out for a good stretch.

The Boy whistled. *Hope. Sadness. Affection.*

Cheech moved toward the door.

*   *   *

Cheech was the first to show himself. The small black and tan Chihuahua poked his lowered head slowly around the doorframe. His ears were perked forward, his nose twitched, and the large, dark eyes looked out nervously. But it was clear to Cody that the dog was just a dog. Not a freaking zombie dog.

His shoulders, locked into frozen balls of tension until that moment, sagged with relief and he fumbled the Easton onto the tiled floor of the kitchen. It bounced along the tile with a series of resounding *clangs!* The sudden clatter caused Cheech to retreat quickly backwards and scamper out of sight. A surge of emotion filled Cody. Despite the fright he had just given to the little dog, the grief of his mom's passing suddenly seemed less heavy. He fought back the sudden wetness that threatened to fill his vision.

He retrieved the errant bat and held it out to Jimbo. "Hang onto this. I need to see to my dogs."

Chapter 7

Daisy finished eating and lifted her head from the bowl.

Her belly was full and the thirst had been beaten back. Those were good things. She was safe, but she wasn't happy. The lingering stench left by the Mama-monster made her head throb, and the knowledge that her master was gone kept her positive energy firmly in check.

Cheech sat beside her, already finished with his meal. He was calmly observing the two male humans working across the room. The confusing presence of the two humans kept her tail planted firmly between her legs. Cheech seemed pleased with their presence, though, so she took some comfort in that.

An unexpected rumbling in her stomach forewarned of an impending need to *go-potty-outside*. She considered using the now-open door on the other side of the room, but the two humans were dragging Mama's body through that opening. Instead, she headed for the doggie door that had been tempting her for days. The absence of an enraged, hungry monster trolling the house between the bed and the small, flapped opening now made its use possible. She trotted to it, then nosed the flap up and away. She passed into the back yard and—

—was met with the taste of fresh air.

Good!Good!Good!

The stench she had been breathing for the past few days was still present, but greatly subdued. The sudden lack of rot-particles filling the air caused her to sneeze violently, and the action helped clear her nasal passages of the dirty residue that had built up.

Her tail lifted along with her mood and her nose dropped to the grass as she searched for a spot to *go-potty-outside*. The need was urgent, so the search was short. Ten feet from the house she turned a quick, perfunctory circle and squatted.

She was finishing her business when the light wind— which had been coming from the South—suddenly shifted, and blew in from the West. Instinct took over and her nose tested the air for whatever it carried.

Daisy whined and headed back into the house. Her tail was once again tucked.

The scent carried on the wind was the stink of death.

*   *   *

Cody gently lowered his end of the blanket-covered body to the earth, and was pleased to see Jimbo do the same. His mother couldn't care how her remains were handled, but Cody had a debt to pay, and burying her with some semblance of dignity was an easy place to start.

"There should be a shovel in the garage. Can you grab it?"

"Sure, Sarge," Jimbo agreed, then set off for the house. Cody sighed and wiped a hand across his brow. He might have to surrender the notion of being called by his real name. He had obviously become "Sarge" to the younger man. It was less formal than "Sergeant Wilkins," so he counted that as a step in the right direction.

Cody spotted Daisy taking a dump on the far side of the yard, and shook his head in wonder. It was hard to believe that she and Cheech had somehow survived being locked in for who-knows-how-long with his undead mother. It had taken several minutes of coaxing to get the tiny dogs out from under his mother's bed. They were crowded into the far corner and appeared half dead with dehydration and hunger. A bowl of water had been the deciding factor that finally got Cheech to move. Only after the older dog began greedily lapping at the bowl did Daisy slink forward. Once they slaked their thirst, the tiny canines crowded around his feet and he stooped over to accept their anxious tongues and affections. Cody had then picked them up, carried them to the kitchen, and filled their food bowls. He didn't know how they had survived the last few days, but now they were safe and he took comfort in their presence.

Daisy lifted her nose, sniffed the air, then scurried through the doggie door and back into the house. It was obvious she was still upset by everything that had happened.

"I found two, Sarge," Jimbo announced as he exited the house. He held up a standard, round-headed shovel and a long, thin-headed shovel that Cody recognized from when he helped his dad dig post holes for the fence. It would be almost worthless for this task.

"Great. We'll use the one with the round head to dig."

"You know what else I found, Sarge?"

"No idea."

"I found no sign of the creepers that chased us into the garage." Jimbo looked at him and continued. "You know what that means?"

"That they went away?"

"Well, yeah," Jimbo agreed. "That's true. But what it really *means* is that these zombies may not be your everyday, keep-at-it-zombies. You know, the kind that catch a scent or a sight of prey and then pursue it relentlessly until a competing scent catches their attention."

Cody didn't know, but he understood the importance of what the other man was saying.

"You're saying these are the get-bored-and-go-away-easily zombies?"

"Ha," Jimbo chortled. "Yeah, something like that. More like the out-of-sight, out-of-mind type. If we're lucky, anyway. Whatever kind they are, I have no doubt that if they knew we were here, they'd still be trying to get at us. I'm just glad the coast out front is relatively clear."

"True enough," Cody had to agree. He pointed to a spot of grass under the oak tree in the middle of the yard. "I thought that would be a good spot."

They took turns. One dug while the other kept watch. Their bats were inside, so the person on guard held tightly to the thin-head shovel. Even with the protection the fences around them offered, neither wanted to take a chance at being surprised. Two hours later, they had a hole large enough for his mother's body. Twenty minutes later, the job was done. The two former soldiers leaned heavily on their shovels, their bodies drenched with sweat. The shade of the oak screened them from the worst of the July sun, but they could not fully escape its scorching heat. Daisy and Cheech sat close by, and Cody wondered what they were thinking; what they felt.

"You gonna say some words, Sarge?"

Cody looked at the raised mound of dirt that marked his mother's final resting place. The words to express what he was feeling were stuck inside his head and his soul. The last year, since his father had died, had been rough. He was close to his father and had been too wrapped up in his own emotions, too absorbed in his own pain, to consider what his mother might be going through. Instead of comforting her after the loss, he had run away. He kept to himself, left her calls unreturned and ignored the requests—which had soon turned to pleas—to visit. He kept putting her off though, always thinking he would have time later, when the hurt wasn't so bad. He had failed at being a son and, as a result, his mother had been forced to grieve alone. Now it was too late, and he'd never be able to right the wrongs that he had heaped upon her shoulders.

"I'm sorry, Mom."

$$* \qquad * \qquad *$$

Cheech sat in the shade and watched The Boy and The Other One lower what used to be Mama into the ground. His future was in jeopardy. Mama was the leader of their little pack, but she was more than that. She provided for them. She fed them; gave them water. She protected them from the dangers of the world beyond the walls of their den. Cheech was smart enough to know that neither he nor Daisy had the ability—the skills—to survive on their own.

The Chihuahua lifted his nose and tasted the air; found it still rank. The stench of death, danger and disease surrounded them, and he knew that whatever had killed Mama had infected many more humans. The smell was growing, becoming more prevalent; drowning out the other, natural scents that usually fought for dominance. And it wasn't just the smells that had changed. The sounds he associated with humans going about their daily lives had gone quiet. The hum of machines in the distance, the chatter of human voices, the calls of fellow canines from surrounding yards—all had gone silent. All had been seemingly absorbed by the stench, and the distant moans of the *bad things* that surrounded them.

The Boy finished pushing the dirt over Mama's body and stepped back from the work. Cheech recognized the clench of jaw, the tightness in the shoulders and the slumped posture as signs of distress. The intense, sour-like tang that radiated from the human's pores and entered his nose confirmed the pain the male felt. His silent suffering was somehow comforting because it matched Cheech's own feelings. This human had loved Mama. That recognition of shared emotion joined with the pleasant memories of The Boy from long ago and triggered an instinctive connection in the canine's mind. The decision wasn't a conscious one, but that didn't make it any less real. The Boy and The Other— through association—were now members of the pack.

The humans spoke to each other, then turned away from their work and went inside.

Cheech waited a few moments, then stood up and trotted over to Mama. He couldn't see her, but the unnatural reek of her body wafted up from the mounded dirt. Doing the only thing he knew to do, he lifted his leg and urinated. It couldn't begin to mask the malodorous disease that had taken her life, but it was the only gift he had to offer.

Giving Mama his scent was a small tribute, but he knew she would be pleased.

Chapter 8

"Damn, Sarge, your dad was a prepper, huh?"

Cody had to chuckle as he gazed down at the array of weapons and ammunition they had pulled from the gun safe in his mother's walk-in closet. The assortment now lay stacked neatly on her bed.

"He believed in being prepared, yeah," he agreed as he lifted the tactical Mossberg 500 from the pile and checked to see if it was loaded. It was. He tested the folding stock and found it to be in good, working condition. The mini flashlight mounted to the front rail still cast a strong beam. "He kept a year's worth of food, water and other supplies in the crawl space under the house. I'm guessing it's still there just waiting for us."

Cody propped the shotgun against the bed and picked up the Berretta 9mm; checked to ensure the magazine was full. The gun was locked and loaded, with a round in the chamber and the safety off. He was thinking of his mother's body resting under the tree in the back yard.

"So, this is why you wanted to come to Boise?"

"One reason, anyway."

Something in his tone must have alerted Jimbo that he had touched a nerve. "Um. Sorry, Sarge. I know it wasn't the only reason."

"S'alright, Jimbo. I didn't expect she'd still be alive. Hoping. But not expecting." He strapped the 9mm to this belt using the Safariland holster and leg harness that his dad had bought. The weight of the loaded weapon felt good resting against his thigh. "I'm taking the Mossberg and the Berretta. What strikes your fancy?"

Jimbo rubbed his hands together and grinned. "I was getting to like that baseball bat, but it's past time for an upgrade." As Cody knew he would, he went straight for the North Idaho Tech-15, a variant of the Colt AR15. His dad had added a single point sling and a 4x20 scope to the weapon. The quad rail held an aftermarket front grip and a small, but expensive flashlight. Jimbo ran the weapon through a quick check and found rounds in both the magazine and the chamber. "Damn, your dad didn't believe in messing around. He kept all his weapons locked and loaded?"

"No kids in the house and everything locked in the safe. Why not?" Suddenly remembering his dad's tendencies, Cody moved to the head of the bed and inspected the space between the headboard and the wall. Sure enough, the small gun safe was still tucked into the gap—a protective measure against midnight intruders. Cody swiped his fingers over the biometric reader and smiled when then the light blinked green and the safe popped open. The last time he saw his father alive, the old man had insisted on entering Cody's fingers into the system. He blinked away the painful memory and withdrew a Ruger LC9. He held the small pistol up for Jimbo to see. "Bingo. My dad's concealed carry weapon. I haven't seen this in years."

"Nice, Sarge," Jimbo nodded. He swung the AR15 over his shoulder and picked up a Browning 9mm handgun nestled in a leather leg rig. It apparently suited the young soldier because he promptly strapped it on. "I'm feeling

better about this zombie situation, thanks to your old man.
Did he believe in the zompocalypse?"

"The zom-what?"

"The zompocalypse, Sarge. You know, the zombie
apocalypse?"

"Ha! No, my dad laughed at guys like you, to be
honest. He thought the notion of undead zombies walking
around, trying to eat people's brains, was a bit crazy."

"Hmm." Jimbo frowned. He seemed disappointed
that the old man hadn't been a believer; probably thought he
had found a kindred soul because of the armament his dad
had collected. The disappointment was replaced by a slow
grin. "Guess guys like me got the last laugh, though. Huh,
Sarge?"

Cody had to smile.

"Yeah, I guess you did, Jimbo," he acknowledged.
"Why don't you do an ammo inventory while I check out the
supplies in the crawl space?

"Sure thing, Sarge.

Cody left the other man to his task and moved back
to the walk-in closet.

Cheech trailed along six feet behind him, and he
realized the dog hadn't left his presence since they had
finished burying his mother. Though the little guy stayed
close, he never seemed to get under foot or in the way. Being
so small had probably taught him some tough lessons, one of
which undoubtedly included how to keep from getting
trampled or kicked by the humans he came into contact with.

The dog didn't follow him into the closet; instead, he
sat down just outside the entrance and watched as Cody went
to work. The crawl space accessed through a carpet-covered

access panel set into the closet floor. He kicked several pairs of his mother's shoes to the side then dropped to his knees. He pried the panel up to get his fingers under the lip. Once he had a firm grasp, he lifted the covering off and moved it to his right, where he leaned it against a clothes hamper.

The overhead fixture cast just enough light into the hole to reveal a flashlight affixed to one of the 2x6 framing studs that formed the mouth of the crawl space. Another of his father's preparations, no doubt. He grabbed the light and flicked the switch to see if it worked. He was rewarded with a bright, steady beam. Satisfied with his light source, he sat on his butt and dropped his legs into the hole. Using his arms to control his descent, he lowered his body slowly until his feet touched the ground. His head still stuck out of the hole by more than a foot. He nodded at Cheech who had moved closer to inspect the situation, then ducked down beneath the house. Once his head cleared the floor, he directed the beam into the darkness.

Illuminated brightly in the cool space were rows of boxes and plastic containers. To the right, Cody counted no less than twenty five-gallon water containers, with potentially more stacked behind those. To the left, food and medical supplies were neatly stacked in marked and unmarked boxes. He counted two dozen boxes of Meals-Ready-to-Eat, several boxes labeled "canned fruit", and still more marked simply "freeze dried supplies." The last time Cody had been invited by his dad to check out their underground stores had been about five years earlier. At that time, there had been less than half of what he now spied. His dad hadn't stopped preparing for the worst.

"Jackpot."

He received a yip in response and looked up from his crouched position. Cheech's head was clearly framed in the lighted opening above. From the side-to-side movement, it was apparent that the dog's tail was wagging with excitement. The little guy was enjoying the adventure.

"Aren't you a nosey one."

Cheech offered another small "whuff" which Cody took to mean, "Hell yeah."

"Well don't get too excited. I'm not gonna be down here long."

Cody resumed his assessment of the supply cache and figured his dad had managed to store away enough food for two people to last well over a year—maybe two. The water wouldn't last that long, but it was good to know it was here if they needed it. He was getting ready to extract himself from the crawlspace when the light illuminated a large, black duffel bag at his feet. Six inches to the right and he would have tripped over it. There were no external markings on the bag, so he grabbed it and—with a warning to Cheech to move out of the way—he hefted the heavy canvas bag up and out of the hole. It landed with a solid "thump."

Standing with his head in the closet once again, he turned off the light and put it back in its clamp. He levered himself out of the hole and returned the access panel to its place, effectively hiding the supplies below. He then grabbed the duffel and rejoined Jimbo in the bedroom.

"Well, Jimbo," he said, tossing the bag on the floor next to the bed. "We're not going to starve any time soon, that's for sure."

"Your old man came through, I assume?"

"Yep. We've got enough food down there to last a year. Water to last about six months, if needed."

"Sweet, Sarge." Jimbo nodded to the ammo arranged on the bed. "We aren't as well off for ammo, I'm afraid. Not bad, but not enough to last if we get into a real shit storm with these creepers."

"What's the count?"

"Three hundred rounds of twelve-gauge for the Mossy. Most of it is number-one shot, but some double-aught. Makes sense if your dad was preparing for home defense scenarios, but they should work just as well for our purposes.

"We have just under five-hundred rounds of 9mm, and several spare magazines for each of the handguns. Again, not a whole lot, but it should last until we can find more. The good news is we have almost a thousand rounds for the AR," Jimbo continued as he patted the rifle slung over his shoulder. "For the most part, it's a good stock of rounds for the primary weapons, and all of the handguns use 9mm, so that's a plus. Did your dad ever collect bladed weapons?"

Cody thought back, shook his head. "Not that I recall, why?"

"Well, in a zompocalypse, it's generally preferable to have a heavy blade or a crossbow as a primary weapon and only use guns in an emergency."

"Oh yeah, and why is that?"

"Sarge... duh. Noise attracts zombies; everyone knows that."

"Of course." Common sense, really, but it was good to have a true zombie-phile to keep him on his toes.

"So, what's in the bag?"

Cody had almost forgotten. Looking down at it now, the black canvas reminded him of the equipment bags his baseball teams always used to transport their bats and other gear. It was almost that heavy, but not quite.

"Dunno. Let's find out." He squatted down and turned the bag around so he could reach the zipper. He noticed Cheech creep in to give it a good sniff as he did. The dog's tail gave a few wags, so whatever it was obviously had the canine seal of approval. Maybe he picked up a lingering scent of the old man on the canvas. That was a pleasant thought.

He tugged on the zipper and spread open the sides of the bag so they could see inside. His first thought was "catcher's gear." Unfortunately, he didn't have time to clarify or revise that assessment because Jimbo moved him aside and dove elbows deep into the bag.

"Sarge! Do you know what this is?" The excited soldier didn't wait for a reply. Instead, he shoved a sheet of paper into Cody's hands. "This is freaking awesome!"

Cody stepped back from the eager beaver pawing the gear in the bag and held up the paper he had been given. He read it silently.

FX-1 FlexForce™ Modular Hard-Shell Crowd Control System. The FX-1 System is the ultimate high-threat-level riot control, domestic disturbance and cell extraction suit. The FlexForce™ design provides substantial protection from blunt-force trauma without sacrificing fit or comfort.

"Okay, so what is it, Jimbo?"

"Sarge, technically it's lightweight riot control gear."
Jimbo ceased his examination of the equipment long enough
to face Cody as he explained. "But anyone who knows
anything about zombies knows that this is—simply put—the
best zombie-fighting suit on the market!"

"No shit? Huh," Cody replied matter-of-factly. He
didn't share in the other man's obvious excitement, but he
could acknowledge how riot control gear might come in
handy when facing down a horde of the undead.

"Absolutely no shit, Sarge." He wasn't sure it was
possible but the grin splashed across Jimbo's excited mug
seemed to get wider than it already was. "And do you know
what this means?"

"Um... no."

"Sarge!" Jimbo stood up, grabbed his former
sergeant by the shoulders, and shook him with excitement.
"It means your dad *totally* believed in zombies!"

*   *   *

The sun still lit up the farthest corner of the yard, and
Daisy basked quietly in the last few minutes of the day's
direct light. Her thin, tan coat sucked up the rays like a
sponge and passed the warmth through her skin to her tired
muscles and internal organs. Most animals would have been
uncomfortable, but the tiny dog came from a long line of sun
worshippers. Her body was made for warm climates and the
heat provided her wounded spirit with a small degree of
comfort.

Mama was dead. The world—already a strange, dangerous place for one so small—had become even stranger and more dangerous. The ever-present danger had evolved into acts of outright hostility by the one that had always kept her safe. The resulting fear and anxiety that coursed through her mind threatened to consume her entire being.

Despite the warmth of the sunshine on her coat, Daisy shivered.

She briefly considered joining Cheech inside the house. Now that Mama was gone, she would have to select one of the two humans as her own, and the quicker she acted, the better her chance of attaching herself to the human of her preference. But her nose throbbed from sensory overload, and the stink of Mama's body still filled the house. The decay that surrounded them was less intense out here in the open and that settled the issue for her.

Let Cheech select the human he wanted; she would take the other. At least they wouldn't have to compete for attention like they had with Mama.

*   *   *

Cheech danced carefully between the feet of the two men and nosed the bag eagerly, searching for the largest remnants of *Papa's* smell. The scent covered the fabric and brought back memories—good memories that had been forgotten or been dulled by time. The Other seemed equally excited by their good fortune, and his regard for the second human increased a notch. He might make a good pack mate.

If so, they would be four, which was infinitely better than three.

* * *

"Check it out, Sarge. Even the little guy is excited about the suit!" Jimbo nodded at the black and tan Chihuahua. Cheech had his nose buried in the opening of the canvas bag. He was rooting through the interior; his tail wagging back and forth in quick, even strokes.

"He probably smells something in there he likes." Cody squatted down beside the dog and pulled the sides of the bag apart to inspect the inside. He didn't see anything of note; stood back up and shrugged. "So, Jimbo. We're armed. We've got a ride and one zombie-fighting suit. What next? Hightail it to the middle of the wilderness and wait out the rest of the apocalypse?"

"Hmm. I guess that's one way to go." Jim ran his fingers slowly along the edge of the helmet he had found with the rest of the zombie-suit. Cody could tell the other man had something else in mind. For some reason, he was reluctant to share it.

"You're the zombie expert, man. If you've got an idea, spit it out."

Jimbo smiled.

"Well, Sarge. What I was thinking was…"

Chapter 9

"So you're suggesting we build a compound?" Cody envisioned a wooden stockade from a western movie. But instead of the cavalry holed up inside against a tide of angry Indians, they would be holed up against a horde of the undead. It held little appeal.

"No, Sarge," Jimbo explained as he strapped on the riot gear Cody had allowed him to claim. "I'm suggesting we use what's already around us—with some modifications. Every house in this neighborhood is surrounded by a five foot high fence—"

"*Cedar* fence," Cody interrupted. "A five foot fence made of very thin *cedar*."

"Granted, it's not ideal. We'd have to reinforce it. Probably even repair it in places, but we can use the fencing between the houses to build up the perimeter. And if I'm not mistaken, isn't the entire neighborhood surrounded by a bigger fence?"

"Yeah." Cody nodded as he considered the idea. With few exceptions, every backyard in the area was fully enclosed by a cedar privacy fence. Those fences would probably be fine against one or two creepers. He wouldn't want to be on the other side against a half a dozen of them, though. On the other hand, Jimbo had a point. The entire subdivision was surrounded by a seven foot high, concrete barrier covered with stucco. As a teen, he had occasionally found it necessary to scale that wall. It was a solid, substantial barrier, and would prohibit all but the tallest of the undead from seeing over. "But this is a huge neighborhood. That's a lot of perimeter to guard."

"We start small, Sarge. How many entrances are there through the outer wall?"

"Three."

"And how many entrances to the street out front?"

"Two," Cody replied. Like many neighborhoods around Boise, this one had very few main entrances. Once inside those entrances, though, there were dozens of streets that meandered through the property, carving it up into smaller pieces. These smaller pieces formed mini-neighborhoods—Cody thought of them as *sub*-subdivisions. The sub-subdivision that was formed by the street out front was bordered on the south and west by the tall concrete perimeter fence. The houses that made up the east and north boundary—Cody's mother's house was on the eastern side— were protected only by the cedar fences.

"Okay, we start by blocking the main entrances. That will keep out stray creepers," Jimbo explained. "Then we block the two entrances of this street while we clear it out— house by house. Once we clear this street, we move our inner perimeter out to the next street and begin clearing it."

Cody grasped the concept; thought it was sound. He recalled the movement he had spied in the house behind theirs. "There are people still hiding out here. We need to find them as well as kill any creepers inside the wall."

"I'm counting on that, Sarge. You and I can secure the entrances, but there's no way the two of us can do the rest of this on our own. We're gonna need help."

"First things first, though. We need to block off the main entrances. I'd suggest finding some semi's and parking them across the road."

"Ah, Sarge," Jimbo clapped him on the back and grinned. "You're on the right track, but I've got a much better idea."

*   *   *

An hour later, the two men were armed and ready to face the zombie world once more. Jimbo looked extremely formidable in the black riot gear and Cody briefly envied the extra protection. The weight of the Mossberg 12 gauge hanging from a detachable single point sling helped alleviate the feeling. The Easton bat was gripped in his right hand, ready to use. It would be his primary weapon when possible. Stealth and silence were his friends against the foes that waited outside. The shotgun and the 9mm strapped to his right thigh were contingency weapons, only to be used when absolutely necessary.

"I don't see any hostiles."

"Me either, Sarge." Cody peered through the narrow window on the right side of the front door. Jimbo was inspecting the front of the house from the window on the left side. The front *looked* clear, but both men knew there were creepers about. They might have wandered away in search of easier prey or forgotten about the two men who had escaped into the garage hours earlier. Or they might be just around the corner of the garage, which neither could see.

Regardless, the pathway to the Humvee seemed clear. "Whenever you're ready."

Cody dropped the curtain and stepped away from his window. His heart pumped furiously as the adrenalin kicked in; he could feel his pulse pounding strongly through his body. His mind raced as he visualized potential scenarios and his possible reactions to each. He felt alive in a way that only came from facing death. It was a condition he had come to recognize during his time in the Army.

He took a deep breath, nodded to Jimbo that he was ready, and put his hand on the door knob.

"We'll be back soon," he called to Cheech and Daisy. The two Chihuahuas watched them intently from six feet away. Cheech's tail was wagging. Daisy's was tucked firmly between her legs. He had put out large helpings of water and dry food in case they were gone longer than they planned— or worse. It was the best he could do. They certainly couldn't go with them, which was undoubtedly what Cheech hoped for if that damned tail wag was any indication. "Stay outta trouble."

Cody gave a final nod to Jimbo and turned the knob.

He exited the door and moved quickly down the front steps with Jimbo close on his heels. He scanned the front of the house as he went. No creepers. He slowed his pace as he approached the corner of the garage, and taking a wide path around the blind corner, readied the Easton.

Mr. Douglas and Summer Dress were still lying behind the Humvee where they had collapsed. On the other side of them, at the far end of the garage, an undead postal worker was turning toward Cody. Past the postal worker, he saw several others gathered on the next lawn over. All were turning toward the sounds the two men were making.

"Get in and start it up, Sarge. I've got this!" Jimbo rushed past and stepped over Summer Dress's prone form.

The creeper was on the far side of the vehicle so it made sense for Jimbo to take it out on his way to the passenger compartment. Cody didn't argue, but waited until the other man's bat rang out with a perfect swing before turning toward the driver's door of the Humvee.

Cody closed his door and started the engine. A second later, the passenger door released and he saw Jimbo's back fill the opening. He did not get in immediately though. Cody opened his mouth to yell at his partner when the AR15 barked, cutting him off.

So much for stealth and silence, he thought. Four more shots cracked out in rapid succession before Jimbo settled into the passenger seat and slammed his door. He obviously noted the "what the hell was that for" look on his sergeant's face.

"*Never* leave a zombie alive if you can kill it safely, Sarge," Jimbo explained. Cody realized he was getting another lesson in Zombie Survival 101. "In the movies, it's always the ones you don't kill, when you have the chance, that end up gnawing on your ass later on."

"Duly noted."

The armored Humvee pulled out of the driveway and moved quickly along the street. Neither man noticed the undead as they converged on the location where the rifle had spat out its violent clatter.

They also didn't notice the two small dogs trailing in their wake.

Chapter 10

The door swung closed but didn't latch. That was all the invitation Cheech needed. He hadn't been on a walk in over a week, and he wasn't about to be left behind. It took a few moments for him to nose the door open, but his persistence was rewarded and he stepped out the front door. He offered a small yap of invitation to Daisy and felt her nose bump his right flank, letting him know she was there.

Together, the two Chihuahuas trotted down the steps and made their way cautiously around the corner of the garage where they spotted The Boy getting into the *car*. Caution was quickly abandoned and they raced for the open door. Cheech skidded to a stop and crouched, preparing his body for the jump. The distance was much higher than it was for Mama's car and he had to pause to calculate the amount of power needed from his rear legs to launch him safely through the opening. He was about to leap when The Boy pulled his foot inside and slammed the door.

The shock of being refused entry was immediately pushed aside when he heard the door on the far side of the car open. He dipped his head and spied the feet of The Other, still firmly planted on the ground. Cheech considered his options. He could go around the car, which would be safer, or he could go under the car, which would be quicker. Quicker won. The height of the car from the ground made it an easy decision, and he bolted under. He noted, with some distant degree of satisfaction, that there was more clearance here than under Mama's bed, but he still kept his head low.

"Craaaack!"

A white-hot bolt of pain tore through his already sore head as the unexpected explosion battered his sensitive eardrums. Instinctively, he ducked down and tucked his tail. The initial boom was followed by several more. His ears were now tucked, so the pain was minimal, but each blast was still a physical blow. He heard Daisy whining to his right.

The blasts ceased but they were followed by two sounds that were just as fearful. The door banged shut, and the mechanical growl at the front of the car grew.

Cheech didn't have time to react as the car moved above them. Panic kept him pressed firmly to the ground, unable to budge. From his right, he watched as the large, rear tire advanced. It was going to crush him, he saw. Still, he couldn't move.

He could not look away as certain death loomed. Suddenly, and almost outside of the poor dog's facility to comprehend, the front of the car swung to the right and the giant wheel of death obediently swerved to follow. The instinct for survival finally kicked in and compelled him to pull his nose back just enough to avoid the violent rubber monstrosity that passed an inch in front of his face.

Cheech suddenly found himself and Daisy lying in the open as the giant car moved into the street. The recognition that The Boy was leaving them behind at last managed to prod his body into motion. He boosted his stiff form off the hard cement and gave chase. A quick peek over his shoulder showed Daisy on the right, her nose even with his tail—exactly where she should be. Good girl.

Ahead, the car holding The Boy turned left, and the two dogs shadowed the movement seconds later. It was a lost cause though. The car was now well ahead, moving much faster than the dogs' tiny legs could match. It was pulling farther and farther ahead by the second. Cheech issued a bark, hoping to catch the humans' attention, but it was no use. The vehicle took a right turn in the distance and disappeared.

The dog slowed to a trot; then to a walk. Finally, he stopped and sat down in the middle of the street. Daisy stood beside him. Both dogs panted from the unfamiliar exertion. They were house dogs, unused to running. Exercise was limited to the occasional walk, and they hadn't had one of those in over a week.

Cheech considered their options and decided they should return to the house. The door was open and they could wait for The Boy there. Having decided on a plan, he rose and turned back the way that had come.

That's when he noticed the creatures moving in their direction.

*   *   *

Daisy was reluctant to leave the house. Her nose recognized the danger waiting outside. The smell was overpowering and spilled into the house as soon as the door opened. Unfortunately, there was no way to communicate the threat to the two men or to Cheech, and when her pack leader called her forward and bolted through the doorway, she was compelled to follow.

They had been on the run since.

First, they ran after the car. Then they ran from the monsters.

Now she lay huddled beneath a car on a street she didn't recognize. She was exhausted, terrified, and she hurt all over—from the tip of her still-tucked tail to the end of her sensitive nose. The pads of her feet, softened by the years of contact with the soft, pliant floors of their den, now thrummed with the violent bruising caused by running at top speed along hard pavement.

Her aches were forgotten for now, though. She had other things to consider. Like the creatures that had seemingly risen up from the ground to fill the world over the past week. They were closing in on them. Again.

A whine escaped Daisy's throat at the sight of the numerous feet shuffling and lurching quickly towards them. The feet brought the groans and the smell. Apart from the knowledge that she was now considered prey—a shocking turn of events for the previously sheltered dog—the overpowering smell was the worst thing she could imagine. There were so many of the rancid monsters around them, the air was painted by their stench.

The first of them reached the car, and a crash of loud banging immediately joined the malodorous groans as hands slammed against the car over and over. As more of the pursuers reached the car, the monstrous discord of horrible sights, smells and sounds grew until Daisy collapsed fully onto the hard ground. She felt the will to go on departing her body like a dying breath and looked to Cheech in desperation.

The other dog was crouched next to her, his eyes scanning the crowd of feet encircling them. Like her, his mouth was open and his tongue lolled. He panted in rapid, shallow breaths in an attempt to feed his body's need for oxygen. Although it was a useless act, he had also stopped taking in scents. They both knew there was only one smell that mattered and it surrounded them.

Just as Daisy was prepared to give up fully, Cheech rose up, looked her way, and moved toward the far side of the car. There was a gap in the crowd, and before she had time to fully understand what he was doing, he was moving.

Without a second's pause, she was up and after him.

The will to fight on—nearly extinguished just moments before—was back and stronger than ever.

*   *   *

Cheech dashed past the feet that circled the car and quickly left most of the pack of monsters behind. Another minute or two under the car and they would have been fully encircled and trapped in place with no options for escape. He found himself on grass and immediately turned to the right and crossed the yard. He vaguely remembered this yard from his walks with Mama, but couldn't remember which direction led him back to their own den. So, after checking to be sure Daisy was still with him, he kept running.

He had to dodge a few stragglers as he made his way back to the sidewalk, and they promptly turned to give chase.

The dog was quickly learning that the monsters weren't smart or fast, but they were extremely persistent. He had been leading Daisy on a series of mad dashes through the streets—each one no more successful at shaking their chasers than the last. He was getting to the end of his endurance and knew that Daisy couldn't be far behind. They needed somewhere that offered long term protection, and fast. Hiding under cars wasn't going to save them. At best, they offered a temporary respite. Even though the monsters didn't seem capable of dropping to ground to grab them, the sheer number of them would eventually trap them in place. Their one attempt at trying to dash between two houses had ended badly, with their nearly being trapped against a fence by half a dozen of the repulsive creatures. Cheech would hide out under a car again if needed, but he refused to make *that* particular mistake again. They needed something new, something that offered long term safety.

He spied a house ahead that was surrounded by a long row of large bushes. Though not ideal, it was a new tact and the low-hanging branches might offer enough concealment to hide them, so he headed that way. Before he reached the hedge row, though, he noted something that looked even more promising. The garage door to the home was open just enough that he and Daisy should be able to squeeze under. Better yet, the gap wasn't large enough to allow anything the size of one of their pursuers to enter, even if they were able to crawl on the ground.

They reached the opening and Cheech halted briefly before committing himself the darkened space beyond the door. The last thing they wanted was to run into one of the things that chased them. For the first time in a while, he used his nose to test the air. Finding the garage empty of potential attackers, he crawled inside as quickly as his battered body

would allow and moved to the back of the space. Daisy
followed close behind.

They collapsed to the cool floor with their attention
focused on the tiny opening they had just entered and waited.

It wasn't long before the first of their chasers showed
up and started banging. As before, the crowd and the noise
grew rapidly until—after all of their efforts—they were
finally trapped in place, with no opportunity for further
escape.

Resigned to the fact that he had done all he could,
Cheech lowered his head to the ground and tried to ignore
the horror gnawing his stomach.

Chapter 11

The Feeling.

Again.

Pain-Anxious-Tingle-Joy-Hard-Yessss!

It entered his being as it always did: completely and instantly. At once, he surrendered his physical-self to the experience and his upper body shivered as a wicked cocktail of ecstasy, fear and anticipation sluiced through his body. His mental-self merely observed. Noted. Waited. The journey that would eventually culminate with another entry into his historical record was just beginning, and he didn't want to miss a single moment. It was well-trodden path that—

—suddenly veered as the epiphany landed upon his mind like a leather strap across a lover's thighs. There was an immediate sense of understanding and awareness.

This wasn't the same Hell that existed a month ago. No, this was a new Hell. The old rules no longer applied; the fear and guile that once held him in check were no longer needed. This new existence was a playground; one that encouraged the Feeling like a wet sneeze facilitates the spread of sickness.

Finding yourself in Hell was a thoroughly liberating experience. In this new Hell, there were no legal or societal constraints on his primeval actions or instinctual urges. Society had ceased to exist and he could grow into himself, his actions filling the void around him like his words filled the pages of his journals. For the first time ever, he was a free man.

The moment of liberation had finally arrived. The Feeling could be released without worry; free to roam the world at will, pouring forth from the soulless prison that had held it in check for so long.

Chapter 12

"What do they want?"

"I don't know, *mijo*. But lower your voice. We don't want to let them know we're in here."

Maria Trujillo rolled her eyes at the brother's question and her father's reply. It was apparent what the zombies outside their house wanted. They wanted to *eat* them! They had already witnessed what those things would do to anyone who was dumb enough to show their faces. Mrs. Clark from next door had been foolish enough to check her mail—her *mail*, for heaven's sake—when she was attacked by, first one, then a crowd of zombies. There had to be at least a dozen of them pushing and fighting over the scraps. All that was left of the old lady was a puddle of guts and a stained wig, both still easily visible from Maria's bedroom window. Everything else had been eaten in the middle of the road where she had been dragged, or toted off piece-by-piece by the ghouls outside. She shivered violently and shoved the memory down. Again.

From the way he stood back away from the blinds—that were firmly closed, thank goodness—Maria knew her father was being careful to not give away their presence as he observed. The crowd outside was already anxious about something they had seen; there was no telling what they would do if they actually spotted a meal peering at them from inside the house.

"They're gathered in front of the garage," her father announced. "But why?"

"Maybe it was another squirrel?" Estevan offered.

If her brother was being truthful, a trio of zombies had chased a squirrel across the front yard just yesterday. Maria doubted it was true, but even if it was, she doubted the zombies had any chance of catching it. Heck, the way their food situation was deteriorating, she might toss her hat into the ring and give chase as well. Eating squirrel was better than starving, and they were on their last box of mac and cheese. Tomorrow or the next day, at the latest, they would be forced to leave the house and search out something to eat. *Mrs. Clark's house*, she thought with a sudden burst of clarity. She could jump the fence, break a window (if the door was locked), grab what she could find, then be back in her own house. Fifteen minutes tops.

"Squirrel or not, something's got those *chupacabra's* riled up."

Maria put her planning on hold and smiled at her dad's reference to the mythical beast that was the Hispanic version of the boogie man. The *chupacabra* reportedly survived by sucking the blood from goats and sheep. All in all, it wasn't a bad analogy to what roamed the streets outside their house. Whatever you called them, they existed for the sole purpose of eating meat—living meat. And human was the meat most readily available in the suburbs.

The thought that she could be their next meal drew a chill up her spine and she rubbed her arms briskly. The trip to Mrs. Clark's house would be delayed as long as possible, she conceded. They needed food, but another day or two of dieting wouldn't hurt her figure. A bite or two taken out of her backside would, though, and permanently.

Not knowing what else to do while the clamor outside wailed, Maria walked to the door leading to the garage and put her ear against it. The growling-moaning-banging seemed to be louder here than from the living room. Without giving the decision much thought, she opened the door and took a quick peek outside.

"What the heck," she gasped. She slapped at the garage door button and missed. She slapped at it again. Missed. On the third try, her hand struck the white plastic hard enough to bruise her palm and shatter the tiny light bulb that sat beneath the cover. But the action had the affect she wanted and the door—cracked open less than a foot—began to move down.

*   *   *

Cheech heard the door to the house open and jumped up, ready to fight. But just as soon as the thought of defense entered his mind, it left—giving way to the signals he received from his nose and ears. The figure outlined in the doorway wasn't a monster. This was a real person. His tail gave a tiny wag of hope. He nosed Daisy and took a step forward, ready for an invitation to enter the house.

Instead of receiving the expected invitation to enter, the figure in the doorway began banging the wall next to the door and Cheech hesitated. The sound of the garage door closing was familiar to Cheech and his tail wagged a second time.

Then, without warning, the sound of the door closing turned into the sound of the door opening. To Cheech, that was the sound of death.

He needed no further invitation and bolted for the only safe place he saw.

*   *   *

At first, Maria didn't know which scared her more: the two tiny shapes that dashed through her legs into the house or the sight of the garage door hitting the foot of a zombie and beginning a slow, steady rise upward. The indecision lasted less than a second, though. The two shapes *(Squirrels? Really?)* were obviously alive and not much of a threat when compared to what was banging on the garage door. In desperation, she slapped the garage door button again hoping the action would halt the door's course, but it was a useless gesture.

Angry at herself for being stupid, she slammed the door and locked it. *It might hold.*

"What did you do?"

The harried voice of her father reached her ears from a spot less than three feet behind her, and it spoke volumes. He already knew the danger.

"I'm sorry! I didn't know!" Warm tears spilled over the banks of her eyes and began the journey down her face. She had just killed them; brought the damn *chupacabras* into their house. She, her brother and her father would suffer the same fate as Mrs. Clark. And it was her fault. "They're coming! We're going to die! Papa, they're going to—"

"Shush, Maria!" Her father's words jarred her with
their intensity. Her father was a calm man, not given over to
outbursts, and she stopped speaking immediately. He put his
back to the door and braced his legs firmly to bolster it from
the beating they both knew would soon come. "Go into the
hall closet and bring my tool chest. Hurry!"

She moved at once toward the closet and threw open
the door. The tool box sat on the floor and she grabbed it
hurriedly. It was heavier than she expected, but she got it off
the floor and half-carried, half-drug it to where her father
waited with his back pressed against the door. On the other
side of the wooden barrier, the first of the zombies had
begun to hammer away. The lock wouldn't last long, Maria
knew.

With his shoulder pressed against the door, her father
bent down and opened the tool box. He shuffled through
the contents briefly before coming out with his hammer and
an unopened container of nails. Using his teeth, he bit into
the cardboard box and tore off one end. He then dumped
the contents into the pocket of his shirt. Less than a third of
the nails ended up in his pocket; the rest clattered to the
floor. Keeping his left shoulder against the door, he father
calmly squatted (*how can he be so calm?*), took a nail from his
pocket, and drove it through the bottom of the door at an
angle so that it entered the floor beneath the door. He then
repeated the process several more times before moving to do
the same with the side of the door.

"Here, use this!"

Maria and her father looked up to see Estevan
holding the leaf insert to their formal dining room table. It

was made of oak, strong, and perfectly suited for the task at hand.

"That's my boy!" her father shouted. "Quick, let's get it across the door!"

Estevan moved around her and levered the wooden insert across the doorway. He held it in while their father quickly and expertly nailed it into place. The banging from the other side grew louder, but the door seemed to shake less. The fix was solid for now, but she knew it wouldn't hold forever. They needed a long-term plan.

"Mrs. Clark's house!" Maria knew that was their best option. "We can climb the fence out back and go over there."

A quick nod of agreement from her father was all it took to seal the deal.

"Two minutes to grab what you need, then we move. This door should be good for at least twenty minutes, but I want to be out of here long before then."

"Can we take the dogs?"

Maria and her father gaped at Estevan with raised eyebrows.

The teen pointed to the couch. There, sitting up and looking at them with large dark eyes, were two small Chihuahuas. One was black with brown and white markings. It offered a quick tail-wag at the sudden inspection. The other was a blonde with a white patch on its chest. It was quite obviously inspecting the air for smells. The rapid twitching of its nose soon gave way to another tail wag. Apparently, the house had passed inspection.

Maria now knew what had dashed past her from the garage. "Well, at least they aren't squirrels."

Chapter 13

The journey to Dick's Sporting Goods went much like every other trip they had taken recently. The streets were filled with hungry creepers who thought trying to catch a rolling Humvee was a good idea.

When Cody and Jimbo finally arrived, the parking lot was littered with half a dozen creepers. In the distance, they spotted more than a score of others that had been alerted to their arrival and who began the slow, steady inbound trek to their location. Cody ran down four of the undead before pulling the vehicle onto the wide sidewalk that fronted the building and parking within a few feet of the store's automatic doors.

At Cody's direction, Jimbo entered the front of the store and stopped just inside. He left the door to the vehicle open to facilitate a hasty retreat. Cody opened his own door, stepped outside and waited for the two remaining creepers to reach his position. It didn't take long. Two quick swings of the bat took care of the threat. With no other targets in the immediate vicinity, he closed the driver door and trotted around the Humvee. The automatic sliding doors swooshed open easily, and he briefly considered the danger inherent in the damn things. Then again, perhaps the doors' sensors were heat activated and wouldn't open for a creeper who had already reached room temperature. He didn't want to find out, so made a mental note to keep an eye on the doors. They didn't have time to explore a way to lock them down. In the next five or six minutes, the distant undead wouldn't be very distant.

"Anything?" he asked, pulling up next to Jimbo.

The younger man pointed to the skeletal remains of what appeared to have once been a male employee of the store. A mess of bones and a Dick's name tag that said "Nick" were surrounded by a wide pool of heavily congealed, blackened goo. Cody had no doubt the goo had been crimson red several days before.

"Okay, we've gotta move quick. We've got hostiles inbound, five minutes out at best." Cody checked his watch quickly to note the time.

"No problem, Sarge. These stores are usually laid out the same." Jimbo smiled, then pointed at the large, bold signs scattered around the building. They easily identified the locations of the store's contents. He pointed to the left rear of the store. A large sign pinpointed the Hunting and Shooting section. "Plus, we've got directions."

Cody grunted acknowledgment, quick-stepped a wide path around what was left of Nick, and made haste for the far corner. Within seconds of arriving at the gun counter, disappointment set in. While the store still held numerous rifles, it had already been picked clean of handguns and ammunition. He considered looking for reloading equipment and supplies but knew they didn't have time. *Maybe on the next trip.*

While Cody fussed over the lack of rounds for their weapons, Jimbo was busy scouring the archery section and, apparently finding something worthwhile, let loose with a subdued *whoop* of glee. He reappeared toting two large, professional-looking crossbows.

"TenPoint XLT's, Sarge! Effing *sub-weeet!*" A flash of teeth and the bright gleam from his over-wide eyes provoked a similar smile to appear on Cody's face. Despite the dire circumstances in which the world found itself, at least one person was having a blast. Jimbo handed the crossbows to Cody before grabbing a nearby cart. He then loaded up as many bolts as he could fit into the cart.

Other than the crossbows, their only other find was protective gear for Cody, who initially nixed the suggestion as taking too much time. Jimbo just laughed and made a beeline for the team sports section which, luckily, they had to pass on their way out of the store. Cody watched in amazement as the young soldier went straight for specific items. It was obvious that he knew exactly what he wanted and where to find it. From the hockey section, he snagged a neck protector, lightweight shoulder/chest pads and elbow pads. He then made a quick detour into the baseball aisle for shin guards.

Five minutes after entering the store, they were dumping their haul into the Humvee. The nearest creeper—a thirty-ish blond woman, wearing a stained tank top, yellow capris and a single wedge-type shoe—was still twenty yards away when they started the engine. The missing shoe gave her a staggered, skip-hop gait that was almost funny. Almost. He imagined the woman had kids before turning; perhaps she was president of the school PTA or a devoted soccer mom. Not that it mattered now. Now she was the enemy. The dark, wet stains on her chin and shirt were proof that she had eaten recently. The outstretched, clawing hands—the left one

missing three fingers—were a good indication that she was
anxious to eat again.

The anger was sudden and ferocious, landing heavily
upon his shoulders like an anvil. He wasn't angry at this
woman, or at the others like her. No, he was enraged at what
the world had become and what he was being forced to do.
Cody strangled the steering wheel with a twisting, steel-like
grip. His jaw was a vice that caused his teeth to throb in time
with the pounding of his heart. He stomped the pedal and
the engine delivered a burst of speed to the vehicle despite its
massive weight.

An incensed groan began in his chest, passed through
his dry throat, and spewed forth between clenched teeth as
the front of the vehicle hit the soccer mom head on. A sour
burn twisted his stomach as he watched her body tossed to
the side like a discarded piece of trash. Her remaining shoe
separated from her foot, glanced off the hood and struck the
windshield before flying off to the left. Cody kept his eyes to
the front, unable to look in the rear view mirror—afraid to
see where the woman or the shoe landed.

He pounded the wheel with his right hand. With his
left, he aimed the blemished front grill at the shambling figure
just ahead.

*   *   *

Five miles, twenty minutes and twenty-some creeper
collisions later, Cody passed through the open gates of
Camping World. He stopped just inside the entrance and
looked at his partner.

"See if you can close those gates, Jimbo," he said. They were the first words he had uttered since leaving Dick's. Jimbo, to his credit, had also kept it zipped, obviously aware of the tension his sergeant had been feeling.

"Sure thing, Sarge," he answered at once, exiting the vehicle.

Cody felt and heard the *pop-snap-pop* of his neck as he rolled his head trying to release some tension. The knotted coils of stiffness that were his shoulders reminded him that he hadn't stretched or exercised in more than a week. He'd need to remedy that soon so his body didn't go soft. He needed quick reflexes and limber muscles more than ever in this new world.

He scanned the large campus ahead, searching for signs of either life or un-life. He saw neither. What he did see were rows and rows of RVs. Of particular interest were the massive Class A motor homes that they had come to find. He wasn't disappointed. From where he sat, he spied more than a dozen of the largest and most expensive vehicles on the lot. *Perfect.*

Jimbo opened the door and climbed into the cab.

"It won't keep out the living, but—unless these clowns have more intelligence than we've seen so far—it should keep out the dead. At least for a while."

"Good deal." Cody dipped his head toward the rows of motor homes on display ahead of them. "This should do it, don't you think?"

Jimbo grinned at the vehicles and nodded. "Perfect."

"That's exactly what I was thinking." Cody noted the location of the sun and checked his watch. "Gonna be dark soon. Let's find us some keys and bed down in one of these fine campers, shall we?"

"Sounds like a plan to me, Sarge. Will the dogs be okay without us for the evening?"

Cody winced inwardly, aware that he hadn't thought about Cheech or Daisy since they'd left the house. They were his responsibility now and he felt guilty. He wouldn't abandon them like he had his mother.

He checked the time again. It would be dark in about thirty minutes. He worried over the decision to bed down here or try to make it back to the house after dark.

"They should be fine," he finally decided, though he didn't like it. "We fed them and gave them water before we left."

Chapter 14

The forced exodus from their home was an odd, emotion-filled journey that left Maria feeling like a week-old turkey leg being fought over by angry Rotweillers. The clamor of clawing, banging and groaning that filled their home urged her toward flight, while the memories and possessions of their lives fought to keep her feet rooted in place. Never had she been so torn.

The internal debate over what to take with her when they abandoned their home to a crowd of freaking zombies was short-lived but intense. The desire to grab her laptop was strong. They still had power, but she doubted that could last—who would maintain the grid? Besides, there was no more Facebook, email or Skype. She hadn't been able to reach any of her friends for days. In the end, she compromised by leaving the computer and grabbing her iPhone. In the few minutes her dad had given them, she also filled a small backpack with a random choice of clothes, grabbed her journal (you didn't need the grid for that) and snagged her favorite photo—the one that had their mother in it. It wasn't much, but enough.

She sprinted down the stairs to find her dad and Estevan waiting by the sliding doors that led to the back yard. Her brother had a backpack tossed over his left shoulder. Each of his hands was filled with a shivering Chihuahua. She was about to ask him if he was crazy but caught a slight shake of head from their father. The issue of whether the dogs were going with them had apparently already been decided.

"Fine," she conceded. She grabbed the last remaining cartons of food from the counter, pushed her way past her brother and exited the house. Passing through the doors for what she knew was the last time ever felt like an act of betrayal. This was her plan though, and she intended to put it into action without complaint.

Maria surveyed the homes to the back and right before jogging toward the fence line on the left—the one that separated their back yard from Mrs. Clark's. She grabbed a patio chair as she passed, quickly placed the back of it against the fence, then tossed her backpack over. Slowly, she stood up on the chair and looked into the yard that was their goal. As expected, it was empty of zombies. Carefully using the chair-back as a step, she swung her right leg up and over. A quick drop and a five-inch scratch on her left thigh later, left her standing in Mrs. Clark's rose bed.

"Take the dogs," Estevan commanded from the top of the fence. Maria looked up to find him holding the little blond female out to her. She grabbed the dog, dropped it gently to the ground, then reached up for the black and tan male. The pair immediately headed off across the yard, their little noses exploring their new surroundings. The male cocked his right leg and anointed the leg of a wooden gardening table that was six feet to the left next to the fence.

"Move the chair over about six feet. It'll be easier to cross," she instructed her brother. He peeked over, spotted the table, and his head disappeared while he moved the chair.

Three minutes later, the Trujillo family and two small dogs entered Mrs. Clark's house through the unlocked back door.

*   *   *

Surviving as the smallest being in the room, or at the park, or on the street, was tough enough before the world went crazy. It was a never-ending cycle of dodging human feet, skittering away from people sitting down on top of you, or—the worst—staying ahead of the insistent, grabbing paws of young, human pups. Humans were clumsy animals at best. At worst, they were clumsy animals who insisted on rubbing your head, scratching your ears or picking you up. And most of the time, they never even bothered to sniff. They just went straight for the grab, grope and rub. Rude.

Now, she had the monsters to deal with. Daisy understood how close she and Cheech had come to being caught and eaten. Her sore feet and aching legs were persistent reminders. That's why she was allowing these unknown humans to pick her up and toss her around without much argument or teeth. She had nearly nipped the female when the younger male handed her across the fence but had withheld at the last moment. She was tired and irritable, but she needed these humans to survive. Besides, Cheech seemed to think they were trustworthy.

A short, crisp whistle from the older male redirected her attention from inspecting the yard where the female had dropped her, and she limp-trotted after Cheech and the beckoning human into an unfamiliar den. Her nose immediately tested the air for danger-food-strangers-death while her ears searched out the same. The inside of the new place seemed safe. She could still hear and smell the monsters outside, but it was a muted kind of recognition—

one that she could live with after what they had just been through.

The relative quiet and the lack of the ever-present "dead" smell landed upon Daisy like a warm blanket. After a quick but thorough inspection of the small house, she joined Cheech in a safe area where they wouldn't be stepped on, nursed her sore paws briefly, and fell asleep.

*   *   *

"*Mija*, check the kitchen," her father directed. "See what you can find for food. Make sure the water still works, too."

Maria dropped her backpack onto the table and moved woodenly toward Mrs. Clark's pantry and cabinets. The life she had known was over. Zombies were running amok, she hadn't heard from any of her friends in days, and she was stuck in a strange home with her father and her brother—and two small mutts. She was supposed to be the first of her family to attend college, but there was little chance that she or anyone else would be starting at Boise State *this* fall. The university, known primarily for its blue football field, had probably graduated its last class—ever. With a shudder of regret, she realized the same could probably be said for the other schools where she had been accepted: Harvard, UCLA and Stanford. As she did at least a dozen times a day since deciding to stay in Boise, she wondered what it might have been like to leave her family and think only about herself for a change. Now, she'd never find out. The way things looked, she'd die beneath a mob of hungry flesh-eaters, her brother and father right by her side, in the not-too-distant future. *Some freakin' future.*

Her macabre, woe-is-me thoughts disappeared when she opened the pantry.

"Wow."

"What'd you find, *Mija?*"

Maria stepped back and waved a hand at the stacks of boxes, cans and bottled water that filled the larger, walk-in pantry. From the amount of food stored there, Mrs. Clark had obviously been preparing for *something*. Too bad her preparations hadn't considered the dangers of checking her mail during a zombie outbreak.

Her dad stepped to the small room and checked out the contents; gave a low, appreciative whistle.

"Looks like Mrs. Clark was a good Mormon," he remarked. "There's at least a year's worth of food in here for one person."

The light suddenly went on for Maria. She knew Mrs. Clark was a member of the Church of Latter Day Saints—known to most as Mormons—but hadn't given the fact much thought when she considered how much food their neighbor might have in the house. The LDS church recommended that its members keep at least a year's worth of emergency food and other supplies on hand. Viewed in that context, the bountiful display before them made sense. There had to be thousands of homes out there like Mrs. Clark's. Many which might be occupied by families waiting out the end of the world—families who were perhaps counting on receiving help that might never arrive. For the first time, she considered that survival would be up to them—they couldn't count on help from a government that might no longer exist.

It was an odd feeling, but for the first time in her life, Maria felt fully responsible for her own well-being and that of her family.

The knowledge that their survival—or their eventual death—was completely in *their* hands delivered mixed feelings to the teenager. There was an achingly powerful sense of responsibility that settled in her gut like a heavy, lead weight. But it was counter-balanced by a buoyant sense of freedom that was exhilarating. Her mind churned with a rapid infusion of thoughts, ideas and possibilities.

There's a lot to do, she thought.

Chapter 15

Another creeper latched onto the rear strap of his shoulder pads and pulled Cody in for a bite. The cold, slimy feel of the attacker's lips brushing against his right ear caused his head to tremble violently with an involuntary, quaking shudder of disgust and repulsion. The reflex saved his life as the zombie's teeth missed his ear and gnashed against the plastic neck protector that Jimbo had insisted he wear.

The near-miss caused a moment of panic for the Army Ranger, who had been too occupied fighting off the attacker hanging from his chest to notice the approach from his rear. Panic was a killer, the soldier knew, so he took half a second to assess the situation before making another move. Time seemed to slow as Cody's training kicked in.

He was now engaged on two sides, with more of the foul-smelling creatures entering the storefront. Jimbo wasn't faring much better. He was hand-to-hand with his own creeper—a burley biker chick with half a face—just steps away. The zombie at Cody's front was using a handful of his protective gear to give itself leverage as its blackened teeth gnawed against the thick padding that covered his chest. The one at his back, probably because it sensed the futility of the action, had relinquished its attack against the covering that protected the neck of its meal. It was no doubt trying to determine where to direct its attention next.

Without pausing to second guess his actions, Cody dropped the Easton and reached for the 9mm strapped to his right thigh. To an observer, the sound would have been a near-simultaneous *clang-BLAM*. But to Cody, the sounds were separate and distinct, as the bat hit the floor (*clang*) and was followed some time later by the sound of the round exploding from the gun's chamber (*BLAM*). The wet splatter of bone, brain and gore that slapped against the wall six feet behind the creeper offered a silent but viscerally pleasing encore to the gun's explosive aftermath.

Having made the decision to abandon stealth-mode in favor of survival-mode, Cody placed the muzzle of the pistol against the attacker—who continued to gnaw aggressively but ineffectively at the chest pad—and pulled the trigger. He noted with a casual sense of *oh well*, that the resulting slop liberally drenched his shoes and lower legs. He then turned the weapon toward the creeper wrestling with Jimbo but the other man was already pulling the trigger of his own pistol.

The two warriors shared a grim look, turned to faced the small crowd lurching inexorably their way, and began selecting targets.

"You take the right, Jimbo. I've got the left."

*   *   *

"That was a bit hairy for a second there, Sarge," Jimbo stated as they peered out the front of the Harley Davidson store. Neither man saw any more creepers headed their way. "When that fat Z jumped you from behind, I thought you were a goner for sure."

Cody had thought the same but didn't say so. Instead, he grinned, tried to lighten the mood. "Saw that did you? Hell, I thought you were too busy dancing with your girlfriend to notice what I was up to."

"Hell," Jimbo retorted without missing a beat. "I tried dancing with her, but she couldn't two-step to save her ass."

"Ha! Is that why you shot her?"

"You know me, Sarge. Love 'em and leave 'em!"

The banter was cut short as another creeper, this one a grandmotherly type dragging a cane in her right fist, turned the far corner of the building. Cody re-loaded a full magazine before sliding his pistol back into his thigh holster. He retreated back into the store and grabbed the Easton, pausing briefly to wipe the gore-covered surface on a nearby rack of t-shirts.

"I'll take care of this one. Then let's grab our gear and go before more show up." Both men knew it was a matter of time before the store was swarming with the undead, all drawn to the location by the gunfire.

They had stopped by the store to grab Cody a helmet, but the creepers' ability to grab onto the straps of their protective gear convinced the men that leather jackets were a necessary addition. Their pads were valuable, but only if they didn't offer their enemy an advantage that could be used against them.

Jimbo stayed with the all-black motif of the Damascus riot gear he wore and selected a jacket two sizes larger than normal to accommodate the pads underneath.

Cody, feeling a touch ghoulish after their recent fight with the undead, went with a more grisly ensemble. He chose an armored leather jacket that displayed a series of three flaming skulls stitched across the front, and a single, large skull stitched artfully on the back. The full-face helmet he picked up was similarly adorned in screaming skulls. The outfit was perfected by the addition of leather jeans and a set of gauntlet gloves with polycarbonate knuckles. The only modification Cody made to his new equipment was to cut the fingers off of the gauntlet gloves. He made a mental note to keep his digits away from the hungry mouths of the creepers. Despite the loss of protection, he couldn't envision trying to shoot or reload wearing full gloves.

He stripped off the gore-splattered jeans he had been wearing and re-suited quickly while his partner stood watch. When he pulled the jacket on over the lightweight hockey pads, the uniform felt *right*. He took a quick peek in one of the nearby mirrors and was pleased to note the uniform looked as good as it felt—it was an outfit a person *should* be wearing while fighting the undead.

"You look like a real-life zombie hunter, Sarge."

"Good." He picked up the Easton from where it leaned against the checkout counter and perching it on his shoulder. "Cause that's the look I was going for."

Three minutes later, they were re-seated and back on the road to his mother's house. Cody was at the wheel of the Humvee. Jimbo drove the Itasca Class A motor home they had slept in the night before.

Nothing's changed, Cody thought as they turned into the subdivision and navigated the streets toward their destination. There were creepers about and all turned to follow the small convoy. They still moved slow, so most were left behind, but he knew they would catch up. Plus, there were bound to be more ahead.

He picked up the Cobra 2-way radio they had nabbed from the RV place and keyed the mike. There was a sudden moment of awkwardness and he released the button. It was strange to be talking over an unsecured, open radio. Radio communications had always been encrypted in the Army and very strict protocols for back and forth discussions were required. He was torn between sticking with those and going full-civvy. He opted for a happy medium and re-keyed the radio.

"You there, Jimbo? Over."

"Here, Sarge, over."

"You see we've got slow-moving enemy closing in on our six. No doubt there will be more when we reach our destination. Don't dally when we get there—just park the darn thing where we discussed and jump in the Humvee. Over."

"Roger. Out."

Cody turned right onto their street and stopped. He could see his mother's house just ahead. Between his position and the house were three creepers, all turning his way. He looked at Jimbo's progress parking the RV and assessed the likelihood of making his way to the Humvee ahead of the three advancing toward them. It didn't look good. Plus, they'd still have to consider them afterwards.

His decision made, he opened his door, grabbed the Easton, and trotted the thirty feet to the closest zombie, a short, balding gentleman wearing a blackened tank top and cargo shorts. The man reached out anxiously as Cody made his approach with the bat cocked and ready. The solid *tang* of the aluminum weapon bashing the man's head in was followed by an intensification of moaning sounds coming from the two follow-on creepers. The haunting *nuhn-nuhn-nuhn* sounds coming from the chomping, undead mouths were freaky. He didn't know if the amplification of their moaning/groaning was a result of what he had just done to their partner or if it was because they were getting closer to their next meal. Either way, Cody didn't care. He re-cocked the bat over his right shoulder and took a quick hop-step across the still body of bald-guy.

The former teen goth with black hair, black lipstick and black fingernails was two steps closer than the aging man with the scraggly beard and hobo-like clothes. The Easton lashed out and connected with the black mop of greasy hair and the bone beneath.

CLANG!

Cody's swing followed through and without slowing his pace, he stepped nimbly to the right of the still-collapsing body of goth-girl. He took another step forward and reversed his swing to the left.

Clang!

Never much of a switch hitter, the left-handed blow to Hobo's head carried less force than his previous swing. As a result, the creeper was knocked sideways and to the right toward the middle of the street. He was now facing away from Cody, but didn't go down.

Strike one.

Cody lined up for a second swing—this time from his right—and let the bat fly. Unfortunately, Hobo was in the motion of turning around and staggered backwards just as the Easton collided.

Ting! The errant swing, though not fatal, still did damage. Hobo fell backward to the street; his lower jaw was now attached to the rest of his face by little more than a grisly strip of muscle. Cody stared in horror as the creature rolled slowly to his left. The loosened jaw flapped with the movement like a loose shutter set in motion by a sudden gust of wind.

Strike two.

"Let's go, Sarge!" The call pulled Cody back to the reality of where he was and what they were doing. He looked to the Humvee and saw Jimbo standing next to the vehicle, his door open and ready. The RV was parked with its nose flush up against the garage door of the house on the left. It blocked more than a third of the open space between that house and the one across the road to Cody's right. Two more RVs and that gap would be closed tight—the first of their barriers to be completed.

But now, it was just an RV blocking part of the road and that was evidenced by the creeper—now two—that was rounding the rear of the large vehicle. It was time to go. He hightailed it to his side of the Humvee, jumped inside and revved the engine.

Hobo hadn't yet regained his feet. He was sitting up now, though and staring their way. His arms were reaching out toward them, but the hug they offered wasn't any type of hug that Cody wanted. Jimbo closed his door and slapped the dash.

"Let's move!"

Cody obliged at once. The vehicle lurched forward, toward their destination and away from the growing crowd of creepers coming around the RV. The act of aiming for the undead was old hat now and the front of the heavy armored vehicle struck Hobo squarely with a *whump*. A satisfied feeling of *finally* being done with *that* particular creeper flushed through Cody's body.

The satisfaction was short-lived, however. A movement in the side mirror showed Hobo's arm reaching for the vehicle as it pulled away.

"Dammit," Cody cursed. In response to the questioning look he received from Jimbo, all he could say was, "Strike three."

Parking the RV had taken longer than either man had hoped. As a result, the crowd entering the street behind them was larger than it should have been. At least twenty creepers were making their way around the RV and headed their way, with more no doubt just behind. The odds were not in their favor, so Cody made a snap decision to keep driving past his mother's house. The road made a large loop of the neighborhood and, if he went slow, he could draw the followers away from his mother's house before circling back behind the crowd.

It took five minutes of slow driving to reach the end of the road. The undead crowd still managed a slow, steady pursuit and he paused at the stop sign for the crowd to catch up. Turning left would take them back out of the subdivision. A right turn would re-trace their previous path. When the first half dozen chasers reached them and began their monotonous moaning and banging, he turned right and sped away, leaving the crowd quickly behind. A quarter-mile further, he took the right onto their street once more, the loop completed. They passed the RV—still parked with its nose flush against the first house to the right—and made their way quickly to their house, three doors ahead, on the left.

The only creeper in sight was Hobo. He had managed to drag his damaged body along the street so that he now rested directly in front of Cody's mother's house. Cody just shook his head, pulled past the driveway and backed the Humvee into the driveway. Their first trip had taken less than a day to complete, but it seemed like weeks had passed since they left the house and his mother dogs. He exited the vehicle and jogged to the street, bat in hand. A quick, slap of the aluminum ended Hobo's journey at last and Cody surveyed the street for more creepers. None were visible. Apparently, they had successfully led the hungry crowd away.

"Um, Sarge?"

Cody turned and saw Jimbo standing on the front porch, peering cautiously into the interior of the house. "Yeah?"

"I think we may have a problem."

Chapter 16

Maria awoke with a start, confused by her surroundings. Neither the flowered wallpaper surrounding her, nor the abundant scent of potpourri filling the room, helped her gain mental footing. A wisp of the nightmare that had chased her willingly from a bothered sleep still lingered. She lurched up to a sitting position and looked about, anxious for a clue as to where she was or how she came to be there.

A pert lift of ears and a wag of tail did the trick. The small black and tan Chihuahua was lying prone at the foot of the bed, his attention focused fully on her. She was in Mrs. Clark's guest bedroom. Her father and brother were in the master. And zombies were roaming the streets.

She plopped back down and groaned with the weight of reality. She had awoken from a bad dream only to find herself firmly planted in a real-life nightmare. Maria turned onto her stomach, buried her head in an over-soft pillow, and tried to will the reality of their situation away. How had the world come to this? She considered the question for a moment, before realizing that she would probably never find out. So what? A plague, biological warfare, God's wrath, an infection delivered by aliens… the how or the why didn't really matter, did it? The only thing that mattered was what she was going to do in response to the situation. She could curl up and wait to die. That would be the easiest thing, wouldn't it? She could just lie low and wait for the food to run out or the water to stop flowing. Eventually, one or the other—or both—would happen.

Alternatively, she could put on her big girl panties and fight like hell to survive. It was the harder choice, of course. Fighting for yourself is always harder than giving up on yourself.

For some reason, she didn't think there was much room for middle ground. Wait to die. Or fight to live.

In the end, there was no real choice. Her dad and brother depended on her. In the three years since her mom had been stolen away by breast cancer, she had become the glue that held their family together. Her father worked 16-hour days as a chef for two local restaurants just to pay the bills and put food in the fridge. She was the one who filled the gaps left by her mom's death. She cleaned the house, made the meals, and washed their clothes. It was her constant checking and nagging that ensured Estevan's homework was done and that he passed his classes. On top of all that, she had managed to stay ahead of her own workload and earn invitations to some of the nation's top colleges. Most of those invitations she ultimately had to decline, and for the same reason that she couldn't just give up now—her family needed her.

She pounded the mattress and expelled a bellow of frustration into the muffling softness of the down pillow before giving herself over to the idea of another hour of sleep. Fighting could wait at least that long.

*   *   *

Cheech wasn't having it. He was hungry and it was time for the female to get up. She was sad and angry, but food would make her feel better. A good meal made everything better.

He slunk slowly up the bed and nosed a bare shoulder. A tongue to the ear would have been more effective, but her head was buried under her pillow. He waited for a response and, getting none, pushed his nose under the pillow, daintily nudged her neck, and sat back on his haunches. He was trying to be polite.

He received an irritated grunt and a shrug in reply.

No problem. He was patient and he knew the tricks and triggers needed from his mornings with Mama. Mama loved to sleep and, on those mornings when she didn't leave their den, she would try to sleep long after it was time for breakfast. Usually he let her rest for as long as she wanted, but when he or Daisy was especially hungry, he sometimes had to prod her into movement. It was an entertaining process that pitted his tenacity and doggedness against her ability to ignore his efforts. Apparently, all humans were the same because this female wasn't getting the message.

He offered a low *woof!* and sat back to observe the results. Not even an irritated grunt. She was trying the ignore-him-and-he'll-go-away ploy.

Cheech jumped to his feet, enjoying the game.

The small dog stepped his front paws onto the female's back and, applying a gentle downward push, released another excited *woof!*

"Go away!"

The reply was muted by the pillow tugged tightly around her head, but fully expected. Now that he had her attention, it was time to press the advantage. He selected a naked patch of neck—necks were always good—pressed is nose to it and exhaled a small blast of warm, moist breath against the skin. He immediately followed that up with a long lick before backing off and tendering another *woof!* The message was clear—*get up!*

The girl grunted, clearly exasperated. She released her grip on the pillow and wiped her neck with her left hand. It was the movement Cheech was waiting for, and he wasted no time in burrowing his nose into the gap that presented itself. The ear was unprotected and he flicked a tip of tongue into the opening before artfully skirting backwards. Ears were good targets, but usually resulted in retaliatory measures. This time was no different, but he easily dodged the hand that tried to shoo him away.

Knowing the ante had been raised, he leaped onto— then immediately off of—the girl's back. It turned out to be a winning move. The girl withdrew her head from the pillow and turned to face him.

"What, *dog*?" Cheech didn't understand the words, but he recognized the groan of surrender that they carried. He turned a tight circle, issued a victorious *woof,* and jumped off the bed. He trotted across the floor to the door and turned around to make sure the female understood what was expected.

"Arrgh!" The dog watched her slap the bed in resignation, throw off the covers, and swing her feet to the floor.

Cheech spun around in another circle—a canine victory lap—and led the way to the kitchen.

*   *   *

Maria trudged after the little shit. Another hour of sleep was apparently too much to ask when a dog needed to take a leak. She was just glad the hound was house trained.

She crossed the kitchen to the sliding glass doors that led to the backyard and grabbed the handle. Her thoughts caught up to her actions just before yanking the door, and she mentally kicked herself for the almost-mistake. A deep breath later and she parted the vertical blinds just enough to scan the yard beyond the door. She paid special attention to the right where her own back yard was but spotted not a single zombie. The coast seemed clear and she edged the door to the left as silently as possible, stopped when she had a six-inch gap, then turned to the dog—correction, dogs. The little blond female had joined them. She stepped aside and nodded to them to get moving. She wanted to tell them to be quiet, but knew they wouldn't understand. Hopefully, they remembered and had learned from the close call they had with the zombies the day before.

Her concerns were unwarranted. The male stepped forward, eased his head outside the door and carefully scanned the yard beyond. Both noses twitched rapidly, taking in the smells that waited outside. Apparently satisfied that there was no danger, the male, followed closely by the female, stepped outside and moved to a grassy spot less than ten feet away. Maria watched as the dogs did their business quickly and silently. The female squatted first while the male observed their surroundings. When she finished, the male nosed her aside and lifted his leg. He promptly covered her piss with his as she watched for danger. Their needs taken care of, they immediately turned toward the door and scooted inside.

"Good dogs," she commended as she closed and locked the door. Apparently, the little mutts understood there was danger about and were smart enough to act accordingly.

"Now, let's find something for you guys. Who's ready to eat." The comment was rewarded with dual spins from the Chihuahuas. The female spun a circle clockwise, while the male spun counter-clockwise.

Maria raised an eyebrow at the unexpected display, intrigued at what other surprises the little shits might have up their sleeves—not that they wore sleeves. She also wondered where the dogs had come from and what had happened to their owners. Most likely, they had belonged to one of the growing number of the undead, or worse, had become a victim a la Mrs. Clark. How they could have escaped being eaten for this long was certainly a mystery, and she wished they could tell their story. No doubt, they were able to shimmy through a gap in a fence or squeeze out of an open door somewhere. Then again, their owner could still be alive, and if so, he or she was undoubtedly missing them. Unfortunately, it was unlikely that anyone would be posting 'Lost Dog' signs around the neighborhood. Still, she'd keep her eyes open for the possibility. Better yet, she suddenly decided to go on the offensive and put up her own 'Dog Found' sign.

A can of potted meat served as breakfast for the turds. She found a fork in the sink and divided the smelly mess in half. Maria noted that it couldn't be much different than canned cat food and lumped each half onto separate plates. She plopped the plates onto the floor in front of the dishwasher and stood back to watch. The dogs approached the piles of mush without preamble, sniffed it briefly and set to gobbling it down. The blond finished first, swallowing her half in what looked to be two large inhalations. The black and tan finished his in a more relaxed manner. Both licked their plates clean. Potted meat was a winner.

Maria shook her head, grabbed a bowl from the cupboard and filled it with water from the tap. As the water filled the dish, she wondered how long the system that delivered the liquid would last. She didn't have any idea how the process worked but doubted that it could go on indefinitely without regular human intervention. Same with the electricity; when would that go out? Her guess was it would be sooner rather than later, and she made a mental note to speak with her dad about steps they should be taking. She wouldn't wait for the water to stop running or the lights to go before thinking about a solution. That was the same as giving up and she had already decided to fight. No, her survival depended on thinking ahead, considering the problems that they might face, then taking action to address those problems.

As the dogs began lapping up the water in the dish, Maria recognized that she now had two more lives depending on her. She hadn't asked for the additional burden, but she would shoulder it until their owner claimed them. The thought propelled her into action, and she headed to Mrs. Clarks's spare bedroom in search of a white sheet.

She had work to do.

Chapter 17

It took them another day to retrieve six more Class A motor homes. The going was slow, but the two men finally managed to secure the access points to their street. The large vehicles were parked end-to-end between the houses that fronted the two entrances. They made surprisingly effective barriers. The center vehicle in each line could be moved as needed to allow the Humvee to enter and exit. The foot of clearance beneath each motor home was guarded by a line of railroad ties that had been pulled from a well-manicured home and lodged into place. Cody didn't think the homeowners would mind the loss of the handy landscaping timber. The front door of the residence had gaped open, exposing a dim, threatening interior. A quick peek inside had revealed a mess of gory bits and pieces scattered liberally across the foyer. They hadn't bothered to investigate further.

The day's goal accomplished, the two men stood back from their handiwork and looked around. There was no visible movement—living or otherwise—on this side of the barrier. They had put down the last of the undead in their immediate vicinity, but Cody knew that wouldn't last. A lesson they'd already learned was that if you stood in the same place long enough, you'd eventually be spotted, and mayhem would promptly ensue. That's why setting up a safe zone was so important to their continued survival. Without a base to operate from where they could make long-term plans, they'd never be more than nomads, living off the leftovers of a crumbling society and fighting to stay a step ahead of the monsters that chased them. That wasn't an existence that Cody wanted. His nature was to grow and move forward—always had been. It was what made him such a success in the Army where ability and motivation were respected, recognized and rewarded.

He understood—without ever having been told—that progress took one of three forms: decline, stagnation or advancement. For years, Cody had viewed the world as being in a period of stagnation, with relatively little progress being made in any socially meaningful area. Medicine, technology, ecology, social-economic reform—all had remained relatively unchanged, despite billions of dollars of investments in research, and an intensely passionate focus at the grass roots level. The slogan "Think Globally, Act Locally" had been a banner under which millions of well-intentioned people from all walks of life had joined together, Cody included. Unfortunately, that slogan and the former period of stagnation were just two more creepers, casualties of the new zombie world order.

Over the past several weeks, the world had moved from a period of stagnation into a period of grave decline. And while there was nothing he could do locally that would halt the inevitable, global slide, he refused to stand by helplessly. Instead, he was forced to revise his outlook. He had to focus on the here and now, just like his ancestors had been forced to do when fighting to take care of their own hides. The slogan he now operated under was more akin to "Think Locally, Act Locally." Or, perhaps even more appropriate: "Think Locally, Act as Needed to Protect Your Ass."

For Cody, thinking locally started with cleaning out the creepers in the immediate area. Moving forward is impossible when distractions consume all of your time. To reach your goals, you have to eliminate the interruptions and diversions that sap your energy. For Cody, the enemy they faced was a distraction—a deadly distraction, certainly—that needed to be removed so they could begin to move forward.

One benefit of making successive runs back and forth to the RV lot was that the creepers in the neighborhood were thinning out—at least the ones that were still able to walk. Unfortunately, the road and sidewalks were littered with the broken bodies of the kamikaze creepers who couldn't resist the urge to step in front of a rolling, two ton meal. Cleaning up the mess was high on their list of things to accomplish, and it needed to happen soon to prevent the spread of disease and, hopefully, cut down on the smell of the rotting corpses. Neither man looked forward to that task.

First, though, they needed to check the homes behind their rolling wall. There were people in the houses around them, and probably more than a few of the undead. With luck, they would find survivors willing to pitch in and help.

"You boys with the Gov'mint or did ya steal that there Hummer?" The piercing voice startled Cody and, from the way Jimbo spun around, he was caught by surprise as well. Its owner—an octogenarian if he was a day—and the large double barreled shotgun he had aimed in their direction, filled the front door of the home to their immediate right. The man wore khaki shorts, a dingy gray tank top, and black socks pulled up to his knobby knees. The thin wisps of hair that topped his head in a weak comb-over matched the fish-belly white of his spindly legs.

"Army Rangers, sir." Cody raised his left hand in greeting as he spoke. His right fell to his side toward his 9mm. "Formerly stationed at Ft. Lewis, Washington."

"You boys ain't dressed like the Army. Look like damn fools in that leather and those helmets," the old man pointed out. The large, dark barrels aimed loosely in their direction danced nervously about with each word. "Shit, it's got to be eighty degrees outside and you're layered up like it's the middle of winter!"

"Um," Jimbo took a step forward. "It's protection against a bite. There's like... a million zombies running around in case you hadn't noticed."

Although still held in a loose, waist high fashion, the shotgun stopped dancing and moved an inch to the right, now fully aimed at Jim.

"Boy, I might be old but I ain't stupid. Nor *senile*." The old man pronounced the word as 'see-nile' and spit a dark wad—Cody guessed tobacco—to his left. "A'course there's damn zombies running around. I got eyes and I watch the television from time to time. But there ain't no million of 'em. Least not around here. Shit, Boise's only got a quarter-million folks in the city limits. Just over six hunnerd thousand if you include the greater metropolitan area."

He offered a wink and a sly grin. "Thass accordin' to the last census, anyhow."

Cody had already worked out the particulars. If the shotgun held birdshot, a blast wouldn't be lethal, especially with the padding and helmets that they wore. If it held buckshot, their chances of survival dropped a bit, but he still

felt they'd be okay. Odds were that the old gent's weapon
held one of these types of rounds as they were the most
common. Either would hurt like a bitch. Cody looked over
his shoulder and scanned the area behind them. He knew
there weren't any creepers, but he used the move to mask his
right hand. The pistol grip was a warm, welcome handshake.

"I'm packin' slugs in this old pig-killer, son." Cody
turned back to the old man who had taken two steps in his
direction. The shotgun was now tucked firmly into the bony
nook between his shoulder and chest. "If'n I was you, I'd
take my hand off the pistol."

Cody shrugged and raised his hand away from the
gun. The guy was old, but he was sharp. That much was *very*
clear. A slug from this distance would do a lot more than
hurt.

"The name's Kotter, boy. Jackson Kotter." The
announcement was accompanied by a wide grin of
satisfaction, and Cody thought the man might break out into
a little, skinny-kneed jig. It was apparent he enjoyed having
the upper hand on the two younger men. "Saw you and that
Hummer show up three days ago and been watching you go
in and out of the street ever since. Good job with that there
wall, too, I gotta say."

"Uh. Thanks. I guess," Jimbo replied. He had his
hands held up at shoulder level also.

"You boys have a plan?"

"Yes sir," Cody answered. "We do."

Kotter lowered the shotgun from its ready position
and propelled another glob of dark spit off the small porch
where he stood. He nodded to the open doorway behind

him. "A'aight. Ya'll come on in the house. We can eat these beans I got cooking on the stove and talk about it some."

The old man turned and walked into the house. He stopped inside the doorway and propped the shotgun against the wall before moving out of sight.

"Sarge?" The question didn't need to be spoken.

"Why not? We don't have anything better to do right now."

Jimbo merely shrugged, dropped his hand to his sides and followed Cody into the house. The smell of burnt beans greeted them as they crossed the threshold.

*   *   *

"So, if you boys are Army, why the black leather get ups?" Kotter mumbled around a mouth full of darkened navy beans. Cody and Jimbo had declined to partake of the meal, citing full stomachs—a tiny white lie. Both were hungry, but they had plenty food at the house and didn't want to use supplies from the old codger's dwindling stocks. The probability was high that the little tan and black orbs tasted exactly like the rancid tang of char that filled the house. That smell alone had easily quieted the hunger chewing at Cody's stomach. Kotter, though, was unperturbed, and it was probably for the best. Food would become harder and harder to come by as time passed.

Another thing to add to the honey-do list, Cody thought.

"We just added the leather yesterday," Jimbo explained. Both he and Cody had already stripped off their leather jackets. They were hung over the chair backs in the kitchen where they sat. "It's hot but it keeps the creepers from grabbing onto the padding underneath. Now *that* was a scary learning experience."

"And there's no more Army, Mr. Kotter," Cody added, remembering their forced escape from Lewis-McCord. "Air Force, either. At least not that we've seen. Our installation was overrun weeks ago."

"Don't call me 'mister,' son. Plain ol' Kotter will do fine." A stray bean jumped off the spoon as it was lifted to Kotter's mouth and rolled down the front of the man's gray wife beater. It left a thin trail of juice to mark its path. "Don't want no one getting' me confused for that television teacher from the 70's!"

"Huh?" Jimbo looked to Cody, who had to shrug in reply. Kotter spotted the exchange and slapped his spoon on the table.

"Really? You boys are young, but you mean to tell me you never heard of the television show *Welcome Back, Kotter*?" He was met by blank stares and dual shakes of the head.

"C'mon! Horshack, Epstein, the Sweathogs? Up your nose with a rubber hose? Any of this ringing a bell?"

"Afraid not," Jimbo apologized with a shrug.

"Jeezus H!" Kotter pounded the table with his right hand while his left waved in the air like a runaway air hose. "You heard of John Travolta before, right?"

"Sure, sure," Jimbo replied. Both soldiers were visibly relieved to have finally found some common ground with the old man. "He was in *Pulp Fiction*, right?"

"Yeah, yeah. Pulp Fiction," Kotter conceded with a dismissive wave.

"Love that movie," Jimbo added with an enthusiastic nod. "It's a classic!"

"Really, son?" Kotter pushed away from the table and sat back in the chair. He stared at Jimbo with disbelief. "You never heard o' *Welcome Back Kotter,* but you think that trashy movie, with it's drugs, and sex, and killin' is a classic?"

Cody kept his mouth firmly shut. *Pulp Fiction* was up there with *Cool Hand Luke* and *The Wizard of Oz* as his favorite movies of all time. He doubted that *now* would be a good time to disclose that little nugget of information. Instead, he leaned back and watched as the old man got wound up and vented at Jimbo. There was a tiny tickle of humor in the situation that almost had him feeling guilty. Almost.

"*Welcome Back Kotter* was a classic! Me and Annie—"

The elderly man turned to Cody and offered an aside, "That's my missus, she passed along eight year ago."

He then turned back to Jimbo, who sat straight up in his seat, apparently frozen in place. Cody hid a grin at the thought of the young Ranger—who had spent a good portion of the past two weeks killing malevolent creatures from hell—being tamed by an eighty-plus year old man in a stained wife beater.

"—used to watch it every week, rain or shine. Funny shit, that show was. Only problem was, they used the name 'Kotter' for the damned ol' teacher. Don't know why they couldn't have picked 'Cooper' or 'Smith' or—hell anything else, I guess. No, they had to go and use my last name! You shoulda heard the crap I used to get at work: 'How are the Sweathogs, today, Mr. Kotter?' 'Gotta a rubber hose up your nose today, Mr. Kotter?' On and on and on with that kinda crap. It was a funny show, and we loved it, Annie and me, but after years of that nonsense, I was glad to see it go. That television teacher can go screw hisself with his *Mister* Kotter. Now I'm retired and *nobody* calls me *Mister* Kotter, cuz I don't allow it. Now it's just Kotter."

The spark went out as quickly as it had flared and— his rant either over or on hiatus—Kotter (not *Mister* Kotter) leaned forward and put his elbows on the table. Quiet settled awkwardly over the trio. Jimbo looked like a schoolboy who just got paddled by the principal.

"So, um, Kotter," Cody interrupted the silence after another minute. As much fun as it had been watching his partner-in-creepers get the wrong end of the older man's attention, it was time to change the topic of conversation to something a bit less touchy. "What kind of work did you do?"

Kotter jerked upright in his chair and sent a hot scowl across the table. The emotion that had dissipated only minutes before, reignited with a new intensity. And this time it was fixated on Cody.

"I was a high school English teacher."

Cody recognized the unspoken dare evident in the man's declaration and stare, but there was zero chance of him pointing out the irony of *that* particular coincidence. Instead, he just smiled and nodded.

Jimbo's boot connected soundly with Cody's shin under the table. Above the table, a tiny smirk appeared on the younger Ranger's face.

*   *   *

"You boys ready?" Kotter asked as they stepped off
of his front porch. He pulled a wad of tobacco from a
pouch he had tucked inside one of his cargo pockets. His
shotgun was cradled in his arms with the barrel pointed at the
ground. Cody watched with interest as the dark wad was
crammed to the far corner of the older man's maw and
tucked firmly behind his teeth. Kotter noted the interest
from the young Ranger. "Problem, son?"

"None that come to mind."

"Good. Cuz iffen you was gonna start in with all that
'tobaccy's gonna kill ya' crap, I'd just as soon you shut the hell
up before you start."

"No sir," Cody grinned and shook his head. He was
thinking it, but—as someone who enjoyed a fine cigar from
time to time—thought it might be tad hypocritical.

"I'm eighty-four gosh damned years-old," Kotter
winked and smiled. "I figure I can gnaw a chaw of chew
every now and then without having to worry that it'll
prematurely hasten my demise."

"You do have a point."

There were two hours of daylight left, and at the old
man's urging, they had decided to begin their door-to-door
visits immediately instead of waiting another day. Of course,
the former teacher insisted on joining them. His argument
was that he knew most of the folks on this end of the street
and had spied movement in a couple of the houses nearby.
Seeing no reason *not* to allow him to join them, Cody had
given him the okay.

The trio made an odd pair. Cody and Jimbo were young, fit and decked out in full anti-creeper apparel. Kotter wore the same outfit as earlier, but had added a pair of white Reeboks over the knee-high black socks that covered his pasty calves. The only modification to Cody's previous attire was he had left the skull jacket and helmet with the Humvee. Kotter pointed out that folks might be somewhat hesitant to open their door for a man wearing skulls while toting a dented, bloody baseball bat and a couple of guns, and Cody had to agree. He had urged Jimbo to go without his helmet also.

The plan was a simple one. Armed with several cans of white spray paint that Kotter had stored in his garage, the group would walk door-to-door and ring doorbells. If someone answered, they would introduce themselves briefly, ask how they were doing, then offer up an invitation to a group meeting to be held the following morning next to the RV wall. The intent of the group meeting would be to make more detailed introductions, explain what they were trying to accomplish, and solicit volunteers.

On the other hand, if ringing a bell was met with banging, moaning and grunting from inside, they would assume the worst and paint a large white "X" on the front door. They had no intention of allowing any creepers to exist within their safety zone. The painted symbol signified a home that needed a follow up visit by an armed crew within the next couple of days. If their visit was met with total silence that didn't reveal a survivor or a creeper, a large question mark would be painted on the door. They would need to enter and investigate each one of these residences using a fully armed team, but the priority for doing so was lower than for an X-marked home.

"I'm just along for the ride, fellas, but iffen it's all the same to you, I thought we might start across the street at the Johnson's house." Kotter pointed the barrel of his double barrel at the single story ranch-style home across the road. "I remember seein' Missus Johnson and her two little uns playing out front just afore most of this nonsense started. Haven't seen 'em since."

"Sounds like a good a place to start as any," Cody agreed. "We'll move down the line, hose-by-house until we reach the far end. Then we can cross over and work our way back on this side." He nodded to Jimbo to take the lead and the Ranger moved out at once.

Two hours later, just as it was getting dark, they had checked all forty-six houses in their closed off portion of the subdivision. Only twelve of those had revealed survivors. They were moving quickly—trying to beat the dark—so hadn't had taken time to do more than make sure those they found were safe and had food to last at least another night. They then requested that the survivors meet them the following morning. After getting a similar "no freaking way" response from the first two households, Cody had begun offering to collect the individual groups the following morning and escort them to the meeting. That had gone over a bit easier, though a couple of folks had remained reluctant, despite the fact that he and Jimbo were reasonably well armed and informed them of the RV walls they had erected. Cody understood the reluctance to leave the relative safety of their homes. They were scared. But it still frustrated him that seemingly rational people would decide to remain in place, willing to die slowly, instead of taking action to save themselves.

Although they hadn't taken a formal headcount, Cody estimated between twenty and thirty survivors lived in the twelve homes they had identified. There might be more still hiding in the thirteen homes that had been painted with a question mark but, even so, it was fewer than Cody had hoped for.

Twenty-one of the forty-six doors they had visited were now marked with a large, bright "X".

Chapter 18

The sun was peeking out over the mountains in the distance, which meant it was finally time to go. Her father and brother had always been late sleepers, and that hadn't changed with the end of the world. Neither would miss her for at least a couple of hours. Their proclivity for rising late had always bugged her in an internal, unspoken kind of way. The morning was the best part of the day, the time when she felt most alive and mentally alert. It made perfect sense that she would venture out into the world now. On the other hand, their inclination toward sleeping in suddenly made an ironic kind of sense in the new order of things. The more time you could spend with your head under the covers, meant the less time you had to be bored while waiting for the zombies to break down your door or for the food to run out. As long as you could evade the nightmares that came along with it, sleep made for an awfully good diversion.

Maria took a calming breath, tucked the bundle she was carrying under her arm, and quietly inched the sliding glass door open. She stepped onto the back patio and shivered as a flood of adrenalin washed through her body. It was one thing to leave the comfort and protection of solid walls when being chased by the dregs of hell. It was another thing entirely to step outside those walls willingly.

This is crazy.

Crazy? Perhaps. But it was also necessary—not just for her for her short-term mental health, but for the long-term survival of her family and her neighbors. She couldn't spend another day trapped like a rat in a cage, especially knowing it was nothing but a prolonged death sentence. She had once read somewhere that pro-action beats reaction when your life is in danger, and the idea made a lot of sense to her at the present.

She scanned the tops of the surrounding wooden fencing surrounding the back yard, paying special attention to the fence line that separated this house from their previous home. There were no bobbing heads to be seen; no moans to be heard. A tiny sigh of relief escaped her throat and she moved to the left, circling behind the house toward the gate on the far side. Her eyes searched her surroundings as she crept towards the far corner. Upon reaching it, she held her breath and inched her head around, prepared to turn and run back toward safety if she spied anything or—heaven forbid— if anything spied her.

The six-foot wide alley between the side of the house and the fence on that side was empty. Twenty feet ahead, the fencing ended at the gate that led to the front. So far, so good and she released the air trapped in her lungs.

"Gloria al Padre, al Hijo y al Espíritu Santo," she whispered.

The unbidden phrase surprised her, reminded her of her mother. A devout Catholic, her mother had prayed regularly while gently urging her children to follow her lead. For some reason, belief had never taken root with Maria—at least not until now. Surrounded by death and dying; gripped by the fear of what waited outside the fence, Maria suddenly felt embraced by her mother's presence; caressed by a touch of love and warmth. Some might say she had just received a calling, others might say she was merely struck by a delusional fantasy brought on by elevated levels of stress. Either way, she gripped her newfound belief tightly, draped it across her shoulders, and gave herself over willfully to the wave of warm, overwhelming emotion that suddenly flooded her being. Just like that, she had become a believer and the knowledge threatened to drive her to her knees while also giving her comfort, strength and courage. She put a hand against the side of the house, seeking to balance herself and waited for her senses to return.

The first thing she noticed when her facilities returned was a shovel. Someone—Mrs. Clark, she presumed—had leaned it against the house next to the gate. She moved toward it with a renewed sense of confidence and direction.

*   *   *

It was common sense. If you left the door open, you wanted to be followed. Any dog could tell you that, if they could speak. At least, that's the way Cheech's mind worked, and this instance was no different. The female left the door cracked open, so he and Daisy followed close behind.

It was dangerous to leave the house, but neither of the canine noses detected monsters in the immediate vicinity. If anything, the stench that indicated their presence had steadily declined as they hid inside the house. Unsafe or not, however, it was up to them to watch over the girl. Human noses and ears were far inferior, Cheech knew.

Despite their superior ability for detecting potential threats, they took their cue from the human as they passed through the yard. When she paused, they paused. When she moved forward, they did the same.

Cheech felt a moment of temporary concern when the girl reached the corner of the house and began to wobble unsteadily. He was going in for a lick to her ankle when she recovered and quickly pressed forward.

When she picked up the long stick with the metal end, he was pleased. One thing dogs couldn't do was pick things up, and he knew a weapon when he saw one. Teeth and claws were fine against small prey like a bird or a squirrel, but virtually useless against anything as large as the monsters that wanted to catch and eat them. A large stick in the hands of a capable human would be much more effective. His assessment of the human's ability to survive the monsters that hunted them increased a bit.

The female pushed on the wooden doorway and Cheech cringed at the sound that reverberated noisily off the buildings to either side. The urge to bark at the girl for the offense was strong, but he held back, knowing it would only add to the din. Didn't she know the monsters were attracted to noise as well as sight? He tested the scent beyond the opening and pointed his ears forward. Daisy shivered beside him, but her senses were on full alert as well. He was pleased to learn that she also didn't detect any immediate threat.

The human conducted her own surveillance and, apparently satisfied that the going was clear, stepped slowly through the opening. Cheech and Daisy were right behind. Cheech had to dodge quickly to the left to avoid being stepped on as the girl turned to push the gate closed.

"What the—"

*   *   *

"—hell?" Maria screeched as she tripped over the little black dog. Already on pins and needles, the unexpected presence of the dogs nearly caused her to pee her pants. She winced inwardly at the outburst, acutely aware of the need to keep her voice down. Her anger spilled forward over the fact that the two dogs had followed her unbidden from the house. Whoever owned the little shits hadn't trained them very well.

"Get your little asses back in the yard," she whispered anxiously. Her command was punctuated with a series of short, shooing motions designed to drive the canines back inside the gate. The tiny interlopers were either oblivious to her urgings or deliberately ignored them. Instead they passed her and moved toward the front of the yard as a pair, sniffing the ground and the air as they went.

"Dogs," she whispered urgently, wishing they wore tags so she could call them by their names. Who in their right mind doesn't put name tags on their dogs these days? Wasn't that a law? She desperately wished they would just listen and get back inside the protection of the fence, but neither seemed inclined to do anything so sensible. Instead, they seemed focused on scanning the yard and the neighborhood beyond. The pair stopped ten feet ahead and the little black male looked back at her as if to say, "You coming?" Neither had made so much as a sound.

Maria debated. She could head back inside and *hope* the dogs followed, but there was no guarantee that they would. Or she could press on. If she pressed on, the dogs would either head off on their own or they would stay with her. She didn't know what they were thinking or what they would do, but she knew she didn't want to go backwards. It had taken too much for her to get this far. If she turned back now she might not get up the courage to venture out again for several hours—or even days.

She gave an irritated grunt of resignation and decided to press on. Hopefully, the dogs would stay with her. If not, well, that wouldn't be her fault, would it? They had chosen to come without being invited and they weren't her responsibility. That's what she told herself. Deep down, though, she knew it was an empty rationalization. The reason she was out here was for their benefit. If they found themselves in trouble, she'd have to protect them.

Resigned to a plan of action, she moved forward. Ten minutes later, she had the large white sheet rolled out on the lawn. It's edges were held down securely with several large rocks she had liberated from Mrs. Clark's landscaping. Printed on the sheet in large black letters was a sign that read:

FOUND:
TWO CHIHUAHUAS
SAFE INSIDE

It was simple and direct. Mrs. Clark's front lawn was on a sloping grade so anyone passing by in a car, or stuck inside a nearby home would be able to read it. Even if the dogs' owners couldn't retrieve the animals right away, Maria hoped they would be relieved to know that they were safe and being cared for. It wasn't much, but it was all she could think of doing. She certainly couldn't go door-to-door in the current situation. She just hoped that the dogs would still be "safe inside" after this morning.

She had kept a close watch on the Chihuahuas while she worked and had been impressed. Neither had ventured off while she was gathering stones or rolling out the sheet. Instead, they stayed close, with the black male appearing to patrol the left side of the yard, while the little blond female patrolled the right side. Their noses never stopped twitching, their ears never relaxed, and their eyes constantly surveyed the distance. As a result of their obvious vigilance, Maria's sense of safety grew. The little shits wouldn't make very good guard dogs, but they seemed to perform very well as watch dogs.

Once the sheet-sign was rolled out, Maria moved to the sidewalk and studied the neighborhood. For weeks, there had been a constant stream of the walking dead moving freely among the lawns that surrounded them and along the street. Now there wasn't a single zombie in sight. She paid particular attention to the house next door—their former home. Although they had lived there for years, the structure seemed like a foreign country, a place she couldn't imagine going back to now. In her head, she could picture the destruction left behind; she could smell the overt corruption left oozing from the walls, carpet and furniture. Two days ago, dozens of zombies had chased them from the structure, and now it seemed as empty and abandoned as the rest of the street. Where had the undead army gone?

She lifted her shovel and clicked her tongue against the roof of her mouth. The noise got the dogs' attention and they moved to her side.

"Let's go for a short walk," she told the dogs, then moved to the center of the road to keep the free space around them as wide as possible. "Stay close."

The black male wagged his tale and settled into position immediately to her right and a step behind. The female moved into a position to his right rear. Apparently, the marching order of their tiny group had been established.

Chapter 19

Cody looked out over the assembled faces of the men, women and children that were left of the neighborhood. Thirty-six people in all. Several of them were from houses that had received a white question mark—their occupants too nervous to answer the door the day before.

Of the group, twenty-six seemed able bodied enough to help them move forward with their plan. Hopefully, they would all be willing. Nine of the remaining ten were too young to perform the arduous tasks ahead of them, and one—a blue-haired sprite of eighty-four, named Mary Fitzgerald—was too old. Mary had poo-poo'ed Cody's suggestion that she forgo the meeting and doggedly made her way to the barrier with the help of a walker. Fortunately, she lived in a nearby home so they wouldn't have to wait too much longer to begin.

Three dogs were part of the assembled families—an overweight Beagle, a German Shepherd pup, and a little white fluffy thing that reminded him of a mop head. Their unexpected presence was a harsh reminder that his own dogs were either dead or lost. The knowledge that it had been his failure that caused their disappearance gave another twist to the tight ball of anguish that filled his stomach. First his dad, then his mother. Now, the only remaining members of his extended family—all gone. He twisted his neck in a tight circle and flexed his knotted shoulders. The popping of strained vertebrae and slight release of tension that accompanied the motion helped him momentarily shelve the mistakes of his not-too-distant past and refocus on the actions required of the here and now.

The Ranger was pleased to note that more than half of the adults, and many of the teens present, were armed with an assortment of rifles and handguns. One teen boy, who seemed to be alone, was heavily outfitted with an AR-15, a large compound bow, and dual handguns concealed in closed holsters on each hip. Cody shouldn't have been surprised—they were in Idaho, after all—but he made a mental note to pull the youngster aside and find out his story.

The persistent groans and banging of the undead supplied a continuous soundtrack of background noise as they pushed against the RVs assembled at this end of the street. Throughout the night, he and Jimbo had taken turns patrolling the barriers—first killing off the creepers that had gathered around one, then driving to the other to clear it— while the other man grabbed a few hours of sleep. It was a tedious process that left both men exhausted, but they didn't want to risk letting the numbers grow too large. Despite their best efforts to keep the barriers cleared of creepers, so far, more always appeared.

Mrs. Fitzgerald's arrival was met by Kotter, who had dragged a chair from his kitchen table onto his lawn for her to sit in. Although they were basically the same age, Kotter seemed years younger. Cody wrote it off to the man's cantankerous manner and seemingly boundless energy. The fact that he had managed to get the drop on him and Jimbo the day before probably entered into the equation as well. Whatever the reason, he was undoubtedly someone who could help them accomplish what needed to be done.

With Mary seated and the rest of the crowd appearing anxious at the noises drifting over from the far side of the barrier, Cody began.

"Good morning," he started. "My name is Cody Wilkins and I grew up in this neighborhood. I've been gone for a few years but my mother's house is on the far end of the street, 704 W. Johnston. Maybe some of you knew her?"

A couple of hands went up. He didn't recognize the owners but met their looks and nodded.

"Unfortunately, like a lot of other good folks, she's no longer with us." Not wanting to dwell on the topic or make a deal of his own suffering, he quickly pushed on. "Until recently, I was a Staff Sergeant in the U.S. Army, stationed at Fort Lewis, Washington. Jim Swanson, the man to my left, was a soldier in my unit. We escaped over a week ago when the base was overrun, and we came here. Before anyone asks, we don't have any intel on how this thing started or whether our government is still functional. From what we've seen and what we've experienced, I can tell you that the military—at least the part that was stationed in this part of the U.S.—has ceased to exist as an organized fighting force. That means in all likelihood that we can't expect help from the outside."

"What do you mean 'we can't expect help?'" The shout came from a thirty-something man who was standing with a woman and two children, a boy of about six and a girl around ten or so. He and his family were one of the few without guns, although he sported a wooden softball bat thrown over one shoulder. "I've got kids to look after and protect. Are you saying there's no more military? What about the National Guard? Hell, where are the Red Cross and FEMA? Shouldn't they be doing something?"

Cody took a deep breath before replying. This was
exactly the kind of thinking that could get them all killed.
They couldn't rely on help arriving from the outside world.
In all probability, the government no longer existed, so it
wouldn't be able to save them. Survival was up to them. The
question was: how did he get that across without sounding
like an arrogant jerk.

"I'm sorry, I didn't get your name," Cody asked.

"Mel Thompson. Call me Mel. This is my wife, Judy,
and our two kids, Janelle and Barry." Mel's chest puffed out
as he spoke and the attention turned in his direction. His
wife carefully studied the ground around her feet, but shyly
lifted a hand when her name was mentioned. Cody got the
impression she'd have preferred remaining one of the
unnamed crowd.

"Thanks, Mel," Cody replied. His initial reaction was
to inform the man that everyone who was formerly in one of
those organizations was probably doing one of two things:
they were either trying desperately to gnaw on their
neighbor's ass, or they were desperately trying to keep their
ass from being gnawed on by their neighbor. Instead, he
strove to set a tone of patience and candor. "I haven't been
in communication with the State or Federal governments.
For all I know, they may still exist somewhere, in some form.
On the other hand, it's been weeks since we've received a new
statement or communication from *any* type of organized
group—including the media. The radio and television
continue to loop the same recorded announcements, saying
to stay indoors and wait for further word. Same for the
internet. Ever since the government took it off line to
prevent the spread of panic, it's been a dead end for

information. I can't speak for the rest of you, but to me, all of those things point to one *very* clear conclusion. We're on our own."

"So what are you suggesting?" Mel dropped the bat from his shoulder, took a step forward and raised his hands in a shrug. "We should just lay down and die because the government won't save us?"

"No, Mel. I'm suggesting the exact opposite. I'm suggesting that we take responsibility for our own survival. We can't afford to stay holed up in our houses while we wait for the cavalry to arrive. I know most of you are running low on food. It can't be too much longer before the electricity and water go out. What happens then? Winter's only six months away. What happens then?"

Cody scanned the crowd, tried to make eye contact with each person. He could see that his statements were hitting home with most. Not all, but most. He could tell that a few, like Mel Thompson, still held firmly to the notion that some government entity was out there on the horizon, ready to swoop into town and rescue them. It was a nice notion, but one that they couldn't afford to hang onto.

"Just tell 'em what you need 'em to do, son," Kotter interjected. It was apparent that he had no patience for the undecided or the fence-sitters. He had made that known during dinner the evening before.

Cody drew a long breath then began.

"There's a lot to be done, and we need to start right away. First, we need to clean the dead from our street. I don't need to point out the obvious. You probably saw the problem from your windows, and if you didn't, you certainly couldn't miss it when you left your homes and walked here this morning. The sooner we get the bodies moved out of here, the better. Doing so will cut down on the chance of disease. And I don't mean just the creeper disease. Rotting corpses bring all types of bad mojo, and we can't allow any of those to gain a foothold. For that reason, body removal is priority number one.

"Second, we start here, on this street, by clearing out the bodies and eliminating any creepers that still remain behind our barriers. Some of you may have noticed the white X's painted on some of your neighbors' doors. Those are the homes where active undead have been positively identified. We need to kill those creepers and get rid of their bodies as well.

"But we can't stop there. We need to secure the entire neighborhood, not just our portion of it. The outer wall that surrounds this subdivision is a solid barrier and should offer effective protection. The privacy fences that separate the houses within the subdivision do not. A large group of the infected could easily topple the best built privacy fence within minutes. Two or three could probably knock down the weakest fence. Therefore, the barriers at each end of our street are just temporary. Once we've secured this street, we plan to move the barriers further out and clear the next street. After that one's clear, we move the barrier further out and clear the next. It's going to be tough, ugly work, but our numbers will grow as we expand our perimeter so there will be more hands to help.

"We think it will take a week to ten days to get our barriers moved out to the main entrances that feed the entire neighborhood. Once that's done, we won't have to rely on privacy fences for protection. The outer wall should provide decent security around the entire perimeter. Once that's done, we'll have a solid base from which to operate."

"Questions so far?" Cody paused and looked across the faces in front of him. He settled on Mel Thompson, expecting the man to speak up. He wasn't disappointed.

"Okay, let's say we execute this 'plan' of yours." The man made quote marks in the air when he said 'plan.' "What then?"

"Mister Thompson," Cody struggled to maintain his composure and swallowed a growing sense of irritation. "Then we expand out to other, nearby neighborhoods and see if we can't help them live a little bit longer. Ultimately, I'd like for us to help as many people as we can. On the other hand, if you have a better plan on how to keep everyone, including your own family, alive for longer than your food, electricity and water hold out, I'm all ears."

Mel didn't respond and Cody could tell the other man wasn't convinced. That was okay. If he didn't want to pitch in and help, he could hide his head in the sand and stay boarded up in his house. The last thing the group needed was a naysayer muddying up team efforts—especially when he couldn't offer up an alternative solution. As far as Cody could tell from the body language and the nods, just about everyone else seemed on board.

"Are there any other questions?" Cody surveyed the group and got no response. "Does anyone else have any ideas that might help us speed things up or keep the group safe? I don't profess to know it all and I'd welcome your input and your suggestions."

The teenager with the AR-15 raised his hand. Cody nodded to him.

"What's your name?"

"Um. Todd Jessup. But my friends call me Toad, so that works."

"Okay... Toad. What's on your mind?"

"I've been watching you and your partner working together to keep the number of...uh, creepers... down on the other side of the motor homes." The boy motioned to the RVs behind Cody. The din making its way over the barrier had grown noticeably in the past fifteen minutes which indicated the number of undead had likely crept back up. It was time for another sweep. "I think there's a better, safer way to thin them out than climbing to the top of the RVs and shooting them."

"I'm all ears," Cody said and looked to Jimbo. Neither of them enjoyed the process they had been following so far. It involved climbing the ladder mounted on the back of one of the RVs, walking to the farthest edge and shooting straight down. It wasn't especially dangerous as long as you watched your step and took care not to fall off into the crowd on the other side.

"We need to build a trap. Kind of like a bug zapper, except that 'zombie-zapper' is probably a better name. It would be safer than what you're doing now, plus help save ammunition."

"Hold that thought, Toad." The Ranger held up a hand. He liked what he was hearing and wanted to hear more, but first they had to get the rest of the group involved and working. "I like where you're headed. Let's discuss what you've got in mind when we're done here."

"Sure thing."

"Anyone else?" Cody was surprised when Judy Thompson raised her hand. From the way his mouth dropped open, her husband was equally surprised. "Yes. Mrs. Thompson?"

"Two things," she said, her voice barely cutting through the noise from the creepers. "First, where are we moving the bodies to? Have you thought of that?"

"We was looking to move 'em over to the playground next to the school," Kotter spoke up, relayed the plan that they had come up with earlier. "Lots of empty space and it's close by, just the other side of Cloverdale."

Judy Thompson nodded at the information, but frowned in a way that indicated she wasn't a fan of the idea. "Well… that could work. But what happens when we want to use the school again? Wouldn't it make more sense to move them to the construction site just down the hill?"

"Well—" Kotter started to speak, stopped abruptly. He scratched absently at the wiry hair on his scrawny chest as he considered the idea. Cody watched silently for the man to reach a conclusion. "Yes. It probably does make more sense, Mrs. Thompson—"

"Call me Judy."

"Sure thing, Judy," Kotter nodded and looked at Cody. "Damn good suggestion she has, son. There's a construction site a half-mile away, just down the hill at the corner of Franklin. Big building goin' up. They got the ground dug up for an underground parkin' lot, so there's a big ass hole just ripe for fillin'."

If the site was as described, it made perfect sense to Cody. They wouldn't have to dig a hole to bury the bodies if one was already there, plus Judy made a good point about being able to use the school later on. If there was a later on.

"Excellent suggestion." Cody gave the woman a thankful nod. Her husband moved a step closer to her and put a hand on her shoulder. From the way Judy flinched and crossed her arms across her chest at the contact, Cody didn't get the impression the contact was one of encouragement or gratitude. The scowl painted across the man's face didn't earn him any points, either. It was directed pointedly at Cody. Cody calmly returned the man's stare for the three seconds it took for Mel to break the contact. With a gentle nod of encouragement, he redirected his attention toward the man's wife.

"You had something else, Judy?"

"Yes," her voice seemed to gather strength as she continued. She ignored the glares Mel was now sending her way and waved at the other families around them. "We've got kids here. Not just mine. I thought it would be good to set up some type of home school or day care so more of us could help with the other work. Maybe we could rotate or something."

The suggestion got appreciative nods from several of the other parents. A few of the kids smiled and a couple actually clapped. The last few weeks couldn't have been easy for any of them. Being locked inside with no one to play with was a tough pill to swallow for any child, Cody guessed.

"That's a great idea. Can you work with the other parents to coordinate the details, Judy?" The mother offered a slim smile and a nod before she went back to staring at her feet. Cody was glad for the suggestion. Never being a parent, it wasn't something that he would have considered on his own.

"Unless there's anything else, I'd like for everyone to link up with Jim and Kotter right away. Let them know if you're willing to help and what you can offer. If you have any ideas, feel free to share them. I'd like to get started with the cleanup asap."

No one had anything else to offer. Jimbo and Kotter stepped forward to coordinate the work parties. Cody noticed Toad hanging back from the crowd and motioned him to the side. The youngster trotted over.

"We need to talk more about that trap idea. Can you hang tight for a few minutes while I thin the herd on the other side?"

"Can I join you?" the boy offered. He unslug the AR-15 from his shoulder and cradled it in a manner that indicated he was comfortable with the weapon. Cody was tempted to decline the suggestion but resisted. They were living in a new world. It was a world where boys of Toad's age would be pressed into service as soldiers and fighters to help the larger group survive.

"Sure thing." Cody unslung his own weapon and headed for the nearest RV. "Just watch your step when we get up top. I don't want to lose you to the creepers before I hear this idea of yours."

Chapter 20

The female issued a low, menacing growl from her place at the rear. Maria stopped moving forward, squatted down, and turned to find the blonde Chihuahua's nose testing the air nervously. The dog—who she had silently named Little Girl—had smelled something. And the only "something" that might elicit a growl was the one they didn't want to meet. The black and tan male—Little Boy—was standing tall with his tail erect. His eyes and ears were focused forward.

In the twenty minutes since leaving Mrs. Clark's yard, the trio had fallen into a cautious, slow rhythm of movement that seemed interconnected and somehow comforting. It was as if the teenager and the two canines had made an unspoken agreement to join their individual beings to form a single, coherent entity with a common purpose: survival from the hunters that surrounded them.

The unspoken pact was working. The only problem they had encountered thus far—other than stepping around the occasional body—had been avoided when Little Boy stepped directly into Maria's path, blocking her forward progress. The teen had been so surprised at the unexpected action that she immediately stopped moving and stared at the tiny dog. He seemed focused on something in the yard ahead so she held up and searched the landscape. After nearly a minute, she still didn't see anything out of the ordinary. Her need to determine what had caused the disappearance of the zombies from the area urged her to continue forward. Seeing no danger, she moved sideways to step around the dog. Once again the male moved to block her path. This time, though, he looked over his shoulder at her, gave a near-silent "woof," and faced forward again.

"What the—"

She didn't have to speak canine to understand. Little Boy was insistent that she not go any further. It felt like she was being chastised for even trying.

Unwilling to be deterred so easily, Maria was just about to step over the tiny mutt when movement caught her eye. A young girl, who couldn't have been more than four or five, stepped around the corner of the house ahead of them. Curiously, a toy vacuum cleaner dragged along in her wake, gripped firmly in her tiny right hand. The herky-jerky step and blank stare were the first indicators that this was no longer a little girl. The large dark splash of red that covered the front of her once-pink outfit confirmed her status as one of the undead. Maria slowly sank to one knee and tightened her grip on the shovel she carried. The last thing in the world she wanted to do was to use the weapon on this tiny creature. But she knew she would if she had to. This was a new world, and survival demanded action. Maria had always been a person of action, and killing a monster to save herself didn't seem like too difficult a task. Even when the monster was a former five-year old girl.

The zombie-girl reached the sidewalk and turned away from them. Maria released a relieved sigh, unwilling to believe their luck that they hadn't been spotted. The muted "scratch-scratch-scratch" as the toy dragged along the concrete behind her reached Maria's ears. She suddenly knew that the dragging sound had been audible to Little Boy for some time—at least since he had initially stopped her from moving forward. Her ears hadn't detected it, but his had.

"Good dog," she whispered. Little Boy's focus was still on the girl and she reached out to stroke his back. He leaped away at the unexpected contact, startled. It was then that Maria knew he was feeling as stressed as she was by their little journey. "Sorry."

They had been silently following the girl and her vacuum cleaner for the past several minutes. She was headed toward some unknown destination and Maria wondered if she was actively trailing the rest of her kind, or if something else was drawing her in this direction. From a distance of a hundred feet or so, they trailed behind, careful not to attract unwanted attention. Maria's head was on a swivel, checking every direction as they moved. She had watched enough horror flicks to know not to focus on one thing or one direction for long. Something always snuck up from behind and she was adamant that wouldn't happen to her.

The trio then tracked the girl to the entrance of the subdivision and quietly watched as she crossed Cloverdale Road and entered a housing development on the other side.

They were up and ready to follow when Little Girl's nose had apparently detected another threat.

A scan of the area around them didn't reveal any visible threats, but Maria's confidence in her companions' instincts had solidified since the previous incident. She wouldn't discount future warnings as easily as she had the first time. Content to wait for the danger to show itself, she crept to their left and pushed her way behind a row of hedges. The dogs followed and placed themselves on either side.

A minute or so later, a pair of stumbling figures appeared from across the street. Like their younger zombie counterpart had only moments before, they also shambled into the entrance across the road. Something in that subdivision was causing the undead to flock in that direction. Maria wondered what kind of pied piper scenario was drawing them in. She envisioned a gory feeding frenzy fueled by dozens of helpless humans trying to fight off a growing horde of zombies.

The sudden, unexpected bark of gunfire rang out from across the tall, concrete fence that surrounded the development. A single shot was followed by two more. The blasts were separated by two second intervals which indicated the shooting was controlled, not panicked. The shots triggered something in the two zombies across the road, though. At the sound of the first gunshot, they instantly picked up their pace. Both were nearly running when they disappeared from view. They were anxious to reach the sound, which undoubtedly signaled a potential meal to their lifeless senses.

Maria finally understood what had drawn the undead away from their neighborhood. The sound of gunfire was like a dinner bell being rung.

She settled down to wait for the dinner bell to attract its latest diners and observed another stumbler—this one an older gentleman wearing blue jean shorts and a stained Hawaiian shirt—heading toward the sound. A single shot rang out. It was followed a few moments later by two more. She envisioned the little girl, followed soon after by the pair behind her, as the recipients of those bullets. A minute later, another shot. *That could be the Hawaiian shirt guy*, she reasoned.

When ten minutes passed without another zombie sighting, she cautiously exited her hiding spot and, followed closely by her small partners, trotted quickly across the road. She looked around before entering the subdivision—Willow Hills—and made her way as quietly and quickly as she could along the road. She ducked behind a van parked on the street and observed the T-intersection ahead.

The road that turned right off of the main street was where the activity was taking place. Sitting across the road, effectively blocking access to the houses beyond, was a tightly parked row of RVs. Atop the vehicles, she spotted two figures. One was a man dressed entirely in black. The other appeared to be a younger male, about her brother's age. Both carried rifles and had them pointed loosely in her direction. A not-so-small pile of bodies lay scattered on this side of the barricade. One was the little girl, who in final death, had finally managed to release the handle of the toy vacuum. Hawaiian-shirt guy was lying ten feet away from her, his head now an exploded mush of blood, black and gray.

Maria drew a breath and prepared to announce herself, but stopped when the older man pointed. Instead, she looked in the direction he indicated and spotted a zombie trotting down the street ahead of her. It must have been drawn by the sound of the shooting, but its cloudy eyes were now fixed firmly upon her. It was three houses away, on the far side of the intersection, but getting closer.

The scared teen didn't think. Instead, she reacted instinctively.

On some level, she heard someone call out to her to stop. She also heard the sound of a single shot ring out. But neither the voice nor the gunshot was significant enough to overcome the fear. With the dogs following closely on her heels, she turned and fled.

*   *   *

Cody saw the creeper rushing along the street. Unlike the previous ones, this one seemed intent upon something other than the barricade. He watched as it passed through the intersection below and gave chase to something—a young *living* girl, he now realized—on his left. Surprisingly, she was trailed by two tiny dogs.

Chihuahuas.

Daisy and Cheech.

"Wait, stop!" He yelled for the girl, then raised the AR15 to his cheek, sighted, tracked the moving target, and gently squeezed the trigger. The creeper crashed to the road in a tangled, sliding heap.

Satisfied the threat was eliminated, the soldier turned back to the girl and the dogs. But they were gone. Just like that.

"Dammit!"

"You know her?" Toad asked.

"Nope," Cody sighed and dropped his arms to his side. They'd never get the RV moved in time to catch up with the retreating figures. He was consoled by the fact that Daisy and Cheech were alive and seemed to be fine. He was especially pleased that they had to be holed up close by. "But those are my dogs."

*   *   *

Cheech was conflicted.

The voice that had called to them as they raced away belonged to The Boy. The human male—Mama's offspring—was the pack leader. He was calling to them and it took a great deal of effort to not turn back.

But the monster was chasing them and the painful banging noise that preceded The Boy's beckoning call still echoed sharply around his head. The fear and pain combined to keep him fleeing in the opposite direction; to follow the female who had recently become a member of the pack. Her ability to adapt to the dangers around them and understand when he or Daisy issued a warning was good. Very good. He was proud to have her as a member of the pack. He was also glad that they were headed back to the safety of the den that they had shared for the past two days.

This retreat was temporary, though. Now that he knew where The Boy was, he would have to return. Soon.

Chapter 21

This time, the trip wire worked perfectly.

Cody watched calmly as the creeper run-shuffled forward, anxious to greet the three men waiting outside the door. She crossed the living room, arms outstretched, the evil moaning already issuing forth from the twisted mouth. Cody cringed inwardly at the thought of what the air being expelled from that mouth must smell like. *Gross.* She was in bad shape with large chunks of her neck and torso missing—chewed off by a family member, no doubt. A husband, a son, a daughter, perhaps.

They'd find out soon enough.

She hit the wire and went down, landing heavily on her face. The crunch of her nose as it met the concrete porch was so loud, Cody wondered briefly if the fight was over, quickly learned that it was not. The house-frau shook her head angrily and positioned her arms beneath her body to push herself upwards. Cody stopped her progress by placing a size eleven boot and a good portion of his weight onto the center of her back. The move held her firmly in place. His 9mm was pointed inside the house, alert for secondary targets.

He heard the now-familiar crunch that meant the other two men had done their work. The sound was followed immediately by the "Clear" signal. He removed his boot from the woman's back and stepped to the side.

The sound of her being dragged clear of the doorway tingled the outermost periphery of his attention. The center of his concentration was focused on the interior of the house. Someone had used the woman for a buffet before she turned, and that someone was probably still inside. From where he stood four feet outside the front door, he could see most of the living room, the bottom ten steps of a staircase on the left, and a portion of the kitchen at the end of a hallway. What he couldn't see were any creepers. *Time to make some noise.*

"Anyone home? Here, creeper, creeper, creeper," he called out. Waited. Got no response. Called out again. "Hey, dinner is served!"

The team of three—Cody and the two men, Jeremy and Don, who had volunteered to help him clear the homes in their neighborhood—had learned quickly that the sound of voices always brought the creatures running. Always.

"Looks like she was the only one," Jeremy stated. "Let's clear it and move on."

"Wait," Cody said, his attention still focused on the interior. Something wasn't right. The woman they had just put down had been gnawed on pretty well. The severity of her injuries, along with the absence of any blood trails outside the home, indicated she had been attacked and then turned while inside. The garage, front door and fence gate had been closed tight, which would indicate that whoever attacked her hadn't left the house since creepers weren't big on closing doors behind them.

"Last chance, we're coming in." Cody gave another shout, then stepped forward and rapped the doorframe with the butt of his pistol. Sixty seconds. Still nothing. "Okay, guys. Let's clear it."

Cody stepped across the wire strung at ankle height across the doorway and entered the house. He slid to the right into the living room, his weapon ready. Jeremy followed closely behind. The spike he had used to pierce the woman's head was left leaning against the front door. He now held his own pistol, a Glock 9mm, and stepped to the foot of the stairs on the left. Outside, Don stooped down and began removing the thick trip wire—designed for hanging heavy picture frames—from the door frame. They would re-use it at the next house with an "X." After two days of working, and learning what methods worked best, there were only a couple of the houses left to check.

"I'll check the upstairs," Jeremy offered.

"Not yet," Cody countered, still not feeling right about this home. "Let's clear the first level first, then we can clear the upstairs together. Don, keep your eyes on the staircase."

The soldier moved quickly across the living room, which was empty, and down the short hallway to the kitchen. He paused outside a closed door in the hallway and nodded to Jeremy to open the door. Jeremy grabbed the knob, received the "ready" signal from Cody, and yanked the door open. The small half bath was empty. They closed the door and moved on.

The hallway opened up onto a kitchen and small dining room. Both were empty. The sliding glass door at the far end of the dining room gaped open and, after a quick check of the pantry, Cody made his way to the opening. A quick scan through the glass revealed a small patio area with a table and four chairs, a back yard covered in knee-high grass, and a storage shed shaped like a small barn. From his position in the kitchen, the lock on the shed door was easy to see. No creepers hiding in there. Not seeing anything out of the ordinary, Cody stepped through the opening and quickly scanned right and left. Nothing.

He moved to the right and peeked around the corner to the narrow passageway between the fence and the house. Nothing. He retraced his steps and made his way to the left side of the house. Took a quick look around the corner. Still nothing. The downstairs area was clear.

"Aarggh—" A scream filled with fear and pain echoed down from an open window on the second floor.

"Shit," Cody cursed as he sprinted.

Jeremy was just ahead of him as he entered the kitchen and bolted for the stairway. A glance at the front door as they passed confirmed his fears. Don wasn't there. Cody pushed up the stairs and was halfway to the landing when Don staggered into view. His right hand was pressed tightly against the side of his neck, but the flow of blood couldn't be held. It pulsed angrily through his fingers and poured in a stream down his chest. The look in the man's eyes, when they latched onto Cody's, told a sad tale. He was dead and he knew it.

The man struggled to reach the top of the staircase but was attacked by a seven foot tall giant before he could reach it. The large creeper rushed out of a doorway on the left side of the upper landing and wrapped its long arms around Don's bloody body. Before Cody could react the monster lowered his mouth and clamped his blood-stained teeth onto the top of Don's skull. Like a dog shaking a chew toy, the creeper's head whipped back and forth trying to dislodge its next bite. Cody struggled to line up a shot that wouldn't hit Don, then figured that it no longer mattered. Before he could fire, a large patch of bloodied scalp was torn away and the zombie began to chew.

Don's scream filled the house and Cody fired twice. The first round took Don in the temple, silencing his scream and sparing the man from further torture. The second punched through the giant's nose, causing his head to slam backwards, and the mouthful of human skin to be released. As a trio, the creeper, Don and the torn patch of scalp dropped to the floor in a tangled, gory heap.

"Aw, shit," Jeremy muttered from behind. He collapsed to the stairs and put his face in his hands.

Cody's hand trembled as he lowered the pistol, re-holstered it at his thigh. He put his hands on his knees and drew several long, deep breaths. *This was not how I want to live my life.*

The sound of excited voices converging on the house from outside urged him back into motion.

"Jeremy, make sure Don's wife doesn't come in here," he ordered. The woman was doing body removal just down the street and would have been one of the closest to their position. He received a weak nod in reply before the other man pushed himself to his feet and slowly descended the staircase. The door closed and he heard Jeremy's muted voice calling out to someone on the other side. "Dammit."

His weapon was back in his hand as he stepped over the dead. After checking the rest of the floor and verifying that it was empty, he knelt down to inspect the dead men.

Don looked peaceful, like a soul at rest after a long ordeal. But maybe that was just Cody's wishful thinking. Either way, the man was no longer screaming and bleeding

out. The bullet he had sent the man's way was a kindness—
the man was already dead—but it didn't feel like that at the
moment. At the moment, it felt as if he had killed his
neighbor outright. He wondered briefly how Liz, Don's wife,
would view what he had done.

He turned his attention to the creeper. The man was
about thirty, bald, with bold tribal tattoos lining both of his
arms. He had earrings in each ear and another piercing above
his right eyebrow. His size was the most notable feature,
though—he was at least seven feet tall and four hundred
pounds. And those pounds were muscle. This guy would
have instilled fear in most of the population before ever
becoming a creeper.

Cody cursed again at the turn of events and was
about to stand up when he saw it. He didn't know much
about the device, but he knew that most worked on batteries
that required recharging. This guy didn't hear them calling
out because his hearing aid wasn't working. The giant was
deaf.

*   *   *

"It took us a day just to outfit the teams in protective
gear, Sarge. The last thing we needed was to put these folks
to work without the proper protection."

The younger man had a knack for organization. This
knack, paired with his obsession for all things 'zombie,' placed
him firmly in his element. If this apocalypse-by-zombie
world was tailor made for anyone, it was the former Ranger
specialist.

The two Rangers had established one of the RVs as their quarters and used it as a pseudo-command center as well. It kept them at the front of the danger zone in case they were needed while off-shift, and allowed them to assist the guards on watch duty, if needed. Strangely, neither man had problems sleeping while the tread of friendly boots passed eight feet above their heads. The occasional moan from an approaching creeper, and the following shot that silenced the moan, were a different story. Fortunately, the number of undead wandering into the line of fire had decreased markedly over the past two days. The creepers—at least those in the immediate vicinity—were being thinned out.

"Of course. So, did you get pads and leathers for everyone?"

"No, only for the people that will be outside the barriers, and we're keeping that group to a minimum," the younger man explained. "The workers doing body retrieval don't need bite protection; they need safety from biological backsplash. So, we picked up chemical coveralls, respirators, rubber gloves and face shields. The full getup provides mental security as well as physical. We didn't have a single volunteer until we showed them what they'd be wearing, and I don't blame 'em. Can you imagine cleaning up these things *without* protective gear? No freaking way!"

Cody understood the issue clearly. They had done a lot of damage to the walking dead in the neighborhood. They ran them over, belted them with baseball bats, and delivered gunshots to the heads of more than a hundred creepers by his estimate. That many bodies caused a lot of gore, splatter, and stench. The mess, combined with the fact that many of the dead were former family, friends and neighbors, required someone special, someone with a strong stomach. Body collection was the worst job a person could be asked to do in this new, unfamiliar reality—with the possible exception of performing the actual killing. That task took more than just a heavy dose of intestinal fortitude.

Just ask Don's wife.

He shrugged off the images of the man's scalp being ripped from his head and focused on the discussion at hand. There'd be time later to agonize over the events of the day; try to determine if there was something he might have done differently.

"How are we doing with body removal?"

"Well, as you know, we're taking them to the construction pit Judy Thompson told us about. That location was a God-send. Perfect for what we needed. You've probably seen the trailer the team has been using." Cody nodded. The low-bed trailer had three-feet high steel mesh sides and a ramp-gate at the rear that could be lowered. It was filled with a dozen or so of the dead. "One of our group—a guy named Barry Evans—owned a small landscape business. He donated the trailer and the Ford F-350 that he pulled it with to the cause. I guess he doesn't see the business growing any time soon."

"Yeah, I think those days may be over for a while," Cody acknowledged the lame attempt at humor.

"Anyway, he's a good man, former Navy puke. He's taken on the job of leading the unloading team at the pit. He's got his brother-in-law standing watch while the rest of the team does the lift and shift. All are armed, though. So far, they haven't run into too much problems with creepers.

They've had to put down less than a dozen total, and that's after making a half-dozen runs."

"Good deal. It's nice to have some former military on the team. It's good to have the Navy on board. Some of the best training I ever received was at the hands of the US Navy. I'm surprised we don't have more military—or do we?"

"Funny you should ask, Sarge. It seems as though our good buddy, Mel Thompson, is an ex-Marine—"

"Former Marine," Cody interrupted. The look of confusion on Jimbo's face led him to explain. "Once a Marine, always a Marine. Our brothers from the Corps detest being referred to as 'ex-Marines'. The proper term is 'former Marine'. Don't let our friend, Mel, hear you call him an ex-Marine. He would most definitely take offense."

"Um. Okay. So, Mel is a *former* Marine. He signed up for a four-year stint out of high school, but was *requested* by the Corps to leave after only doing three. He had one or more Article 15's, apparently for inability to conform to authority. "

"I'm surprised Mr. Thompson was so forthcoming. Are you two best friends now?

"Ha! Hardly," Jimbo explained. "I got the skinny from his wife. She's on board with what we're doing here, despite her husband's reluctance. Hell, she and Kotter were ready to go with their day care yesterday afternoon. They took over one of the vacant houses and set up shop. That idea has freed up several parents so they can pitch in without having to worry about their kids."

"Nice. It's good to see her fitting in. How about the former Marine? What's he doing?"

"Well...," Jimbo began. "Not so good on that front. Seems like Mel has decided to go it alone. He hasn't joined any of the work parties and refuses to take a shift on watch. Won't even let his kids attend the school that his wife has set up. Judy's embarrassed over it, but there's not much she can do. Hell, I'm surprised he's allowed her to do as much as she has."

Cody shook his head. To say he was surprised by the man's actions would be a gross understatement. He had interacted with a lot of Marines. Mel's demeanor and actions weren't in character with the good men and women he knew from the Corps. He was a puzzle that needed attention, and sooner rather than later. "I'll talk with him tomorrow. See if we can't get him aligned with our efforts. It would be nice to have his skill sets available to the community."

"Good luck."

From the younger man's tone, it was evident he had his doubts about how effective a talk with Mel would be. Not that it really mattered. Regardless of what Jimbo thought of the former Marine, they had to at least *try* to get the man involved in their efforts. With his mind settled on the next steps with Mel, Cody turned his attention back to their current situation.

"So, this street is a hundred percent free of creepers, Jimbo. Tomorrow, we move the RVs out to the next street, and start the process all over again. With what we've learned so far, we should be able to clear that one by the day after tomorrow. Then we move into position to secure the entire subdivision."

"That's great, Sarge. The folks here are running on fumes after only two days. I can't blame them, but it'll be good to get some more hands involved in the work. We're seeing signs of activity in the homes just outside the barrier. The people holed up can see what we've been doing. Heck, we even took in a family of four this morning. The father said they were out of food and wanted to come inside the barrier. We needed help with body cleanup, so it was a win-win. They were glad to hear that they'd be able to move back into their own home soon, though."

"I'm sorry most of this coordination has fallen to you, Jimbo. But you're doing a great job. One that needs to be done."

"Thanks, Sarge."

"I just wish I'd held up my end better than I did today. Somehow done a better job," Cody stated. His thoughts went back to the man he had lost today and wondered how he could have prevented that. "Hell, maybe—"

"Stop," Jimbo raised his hand before Cody could continue. "We're both doing what we should be doing for now. Let's not second guess ourselves just because we lost a man today. You know better than anyone that casualties happen in war, and even though we never thought we'd have creepers as our enemy, this is still a war."

"Agreed," Cody sighed and shook his head. "I won't mention it again."

"Good."

"So what else do we need to discuss before I tour the neighborhood and check on the guards at the far end?"

"I think that's about it except for Toad's idea."

"Ah, yes. I almost forgot. How's it coming?"

"That's what I wanted to discuss. It didn't make sense to build a trap now since we're going to be moving the barricade tomorrow, so I made a command decision to hold off for now. Once we push out to the final perimeter, we'll use the houses next to each entrance, and set up the chutes there."

"Makes sense," Cody said. "If we do it right, we can save on ammo and not have risk anyone falling off the top of an RV."

"That's the plan."

"Any word on the dogs?"

"Um. No. I've put the word out to all the teams to be on the lookout, but no one has spotted them so far."

"They're close. That young woman wouldn't chance being outside for long. They have to be in this neighborhood."

"Agreed. Which means we'll find them soon."

With nothing more to discuss, Cody exited the RV, waved to the guard up top, and began a leisurely stroll along the street where he grew up. With the bodies cleared from the streets and sidewalks, he could almost pretend life was normal. The steady slap-slap-slap of the Mossberg against his side as he walked and the sight of the white "X" that identified the house where Don was killed disallowed the pretense for long.

Reality is a bitch that can't be ignored for long.

Chapter 22

The blinds were adjusted perfectly. The sun-splashed world beyond the second story window could be viewed without risk of exposure. The darkened interior masked the watchful figure as it waited.

Waited.

Waited.

The Feeling was never wrong, but it delivered in its own fucking time.

The Montblanc weaved a rapid pattern through the fingers of the man's left hand. It was a hypnotic dance of unceasing, circular movement that might have seemed almost magical to an observer, had one been present. The writing instrument was such an integral part of his person, an extension of the hand that held it, that the wielder didn't even notice its presence. It was only recognized when it came time to document.

There.

Across the street and three doors to the right—The Bitch's house. He struggled briefly against the feelings of pleasure that arose every time he thought about her—his first. Now was not the time. There would be time for reminiscing later. He had new memories to make, and he focused on the small figure headed his way.

The creature staggered slowly through the yards lining the far side of the road and the anticipation increased as each stumbling step brought it closer. When she reached the edge of overgrown grass that delineated the lawn across the street, he knew she was the one.

He placed the Montblanc gently on his desk, aligning it perfectly in the center next to his current journal-in-progress. His mental recorder kicked into high gear as he set out to remember what might become the next chapter of his growing legacy. Intimate recall of every sight, sound, smell and act was paramount. While history is recorded through the mere act of documentation; greatness imparts itself through documentation of the details.

Early teens, sporting a short, blond bob. She wore a slightly splattered t-shirt over white shorts. Barefoot. She seemed fresh, with minimal damage.

Best of all, she was alone.

He skipped down the stairs, opened the front door and stepped boldly onto the porch. The girl didn't notice him right away so he blew a low whistle in the teen's direction.

Wheet-woot.

As expected, she slowly turned his way. Oh, yes. She was pretty. Her eyes locked onto his and her mouth opened and closed, opened and closed.

Her moaning was perfect.

He adjusted his erection, stepped back into his home, and waited for her to join him.

Chapter 23

As had become the evening ritual, a core group of survivors was gathered outside of Cody and Jimbo's RV to discuss their daily progress and to plan for the following day's work. Soon after they began cleaning up the neighborhood, Jimbo spread the word that the informal sessions were going to take place and, at Cody's insistence, made it well-known that everyone was welcome. Unfortunately, few felt inclined to attend. Kotter, Barry Evans, and Toad Jessup were regulars and, as far as Cody could recall, had never missed one of the informal sessions. Judy Thompson attended sporadically and was a welcome addition when she did. Her comments were always on point, and her suggestions and insights added a lot of value to the discussion. She was with them today, and Cody felt she would have been there every day if her husband wasn't part of the equation. Others floated in and out as the mood struck or opportunity allowed. For the most part, most of the neighborhood seemed content with having someone else handle the task of establishing goals and making plans.

A week after expanding their perimeter beyond the street where his mother's house sat, the swelling group of survivors finally pushed the RVs to the outer perimeter of the subdivision. The initial teams of workers were supplemented with fresh recruits as more houses were cleared and new families were brought into the fold. The various teams now worked in shifts, which increased morale and safety. Tired workers made mistakes. No one had been lost to the creepers since Don, and Cody was grateful for that. The refuge of safety they had carved out, insulated—however tenuously—from the ever-present undead, fostered a sense of accomplishment among the surviving families and most folks pitched in where they were needed, without complaint. For most, the relief at being given a chance for life beyond the walls of their homes easily compensated for the need to work in support of the community.

Unfortunately, there was a small but growing contingent, like Mel Thompson, who refused to get on board with what Cody and his group of survivors were trying to accomplish. The reasons for refusing to help varied wildly—distrust over a sense of perceived communism, the mourning of loved ones, a fear to leave their homes and just plain stubbornness (Cody dropped Mel into this category). Kotter was vocal in his opposition to these folks and openly called them "a bunch of damned ol' freeloaders and leeches" every time the discussion turned in their direction. Cody refused to put things in those terms, but he couldn't deny a common thread among the holdouts: although they weren't interested in contributing to the community, they still expected the community to provide for them. And while he understood the need to mourn—and knew first-hand the fear that the creepers instilled—he couldn't fathom those who held out for political reasons or just because of plain pigheadedness.

It was because of these holdouts that Jimbo suggested they open a mess hall type of arrangement to support the working teams. The food that was scavenged from the empty homes in the neighborhood went to the common kitchen, as did the food gathered on the numerous runs that Jimbo led to a nearby Albertson's Supermarket.

The volunteers who ran the kitchen set up a meal schedule that provided warm meals at breakfast and dinner. Lunch was usually a buffet of peanut butter sandwiches and canned soup. Workers, and those who were deemed unable to work, were welcome at all three meals; those who were capable of working, but chose not to, were allowed at lunch time only. The idea was simple and sent a message to the non-contributors. If you pitch in, you earn food. If you don't, we won't let you starve, but you won't get a completely free ride.

The kitchen manager, Midge Franklin, had been head cook for a local elementary school cafeteria. When the mess hall opened for business, she posted a bold, hand-written sign at the entrance and the appropriately named "Tough Love Kitchen" was born. The kitchen had been running for three days and already a third of the previous "objectors" had come to the conclusion that working wasn't such a bad thing. Cody knew that the number of holdouts would continue to decrease as individual stores of food dwindled to a point where they couldn't adequately supplement the meager lunch that was provided. Tough love—at least when combined with the threat of hunger pains—seemed to work.

Another significant accomplishment they put into action was Toad Jessup's zombie-zapper trap. It wasn't much of a zapper, as no electricity was involved, but it *was* one hell of a trap. The previous method of luring creepers to the RVs, where they were dispatched with shots to the head was effective, but created two primary hazards.

The first was the need for guards to stand atop the RVs as they fired at the approaching undead. The large vehicles didn't have hand rails and, although no one had been lost over the side yet, there had been more than one close call.

The second hazard presented itself whenever the bodies outside the RV wall had to be removed by the cleanup crews. The task entailed a complex process of moving the middle RV forward or backward to allow the crew to access the bodies beyond. In almost every instance, the RV rolled over one or more bodies in the process, which complicated removal. But the real problem was that the crews—even though wearing protective gear—were at risk of attack while they did their job. To make things worse, this laborious, time-consuming process had to be performed every time a vehicle exited or entered the perimeter.

Toad's idea was simple, but it changed the game for how the community dealt with the never-ending parade of zombies.

In each instance, when the RVs were parked nose-to-rear between the garage door of the house on the left and the garage door on the right, at least one of the houses had a front entrance that sat just outside the RV-barrier. That doorway became the opening of the trap. Previously, creepers were drawn to the barrier by the sight of guards or by the sound of gun shots. Now, they were lured to the barrier by a stereo speaker blasting an unceasing loop of music. The type of music changed with the taste of the guards working each shift, but the result was the same—creepers were drawn by sound. Once the creeper reached the barrier, the music from the RV stopped and was replaced with music that emanated from the open doorway to the right. On cue, the creepers invariably turned their attention from the RVs and made a beeline for the opening. Like cattle in a chute, they were channeled through the house by a wooden maze that had been erected using salvaged privacy fencing. The chute dumped the zombies into the back yard where the speakers were positioned. Once in the back yard, the speakers were silenced and two heavily armored guards yelled and waved at the creepers to get their attention. The creepers obediently turned in the direction of their presumed meal and entered into a second fence-lined channel. Unlike the previous chute, this one directed them up a ramp that led from the back yard toward the two guards who beckoned to them from raised platforms that were protected by more of the wooden fencing. The ramp's degree of incline served to slow the already-lumbering creepers, but the need to feed drove them relentlessly upwards toward the living meals waiting above. When the creepers reached the top of the ramp, they were within six feet of their goal—the two humans egging them on. Unfortunately for the zombies, the top of the ramp ended at the lip of a dump truck and they tumbled unceremoniously into the bed with outstretched arms and gaping mouths. Once in the bed, they were casually dispatched with head shots from the crossbows that the guards carried.

Once the cycle played itself out to the proper conclusion, the trap was re-set—the front door of the house was closed, the crossbow bolts were retrieved, and RV resumed blasting its music to the creepers. When the bed of the dump truck was sufficiently filled, the vehicle was driven to the construction site by a burial crew, and a second truck backed into position at the end of the ramp. As a result of the trap, the need for cleanup crews was reduced by more than eighty percent, nearly eliminating the need to perform

one of the worst jobs in the community. When the trap had
proven effective and the work schedules changed, Toad had
become one of the most well-liked people in the
neighborhood.

"Dude, your z-trap continues to impress." Jimbo
lightly tapped the teen on the shoulder. "We caught three
dozen of the creepers at the west entrance; I hear your team
got another dozen on the east."

"Yeah," the youngster replied, ducking his head. He
avoided eye contact with the Army Ranger. "Fifteen,
actually."

He wasn't a shy kid, but Cody knew he was still
feeling some degree of awkwardness over the number of
acknowledgments and compliments being directed his way. It
had to be a strange place for Toad. A month earlier, he had
been a freshman in high school whose biggest concern was
talking to girls, or perhaps beating the next level of Left 4
Dead on his Xbox. Now, he was a highly-valued member of
a post-apocalyptic community, making life-or-death decisions
that affected more than a hundred people. Saying it was a
drastic change seemed like the understatement of the century.

"It was a great idea, Toad," Cody added. The words
lifted the teen's head and they made eye contact. "Be sure to
speak up with any other ideas you have. We need all the help
we can get."

"I will, Sarge."

The smile remained pasted to Cody's face but he
winced inwardly. Despite repeated encouragements and
reminders to call him "Cody," Jimbo's inability to refer to him
as anything but "Sarge" seemed to hold more sway with the
folks around them. He was afraid he would be stuck with the

moniker, whether he liked it or not. He took a small slice of comfort that it could be worse; they hadn't taken to calling him 'asshole' or 'dipshit' or something equally offensive. At least, not yet, anyway.

"So," Cody continued. "We've reached a milestone. We've got a secure perimeter around the entire neighborhood and our interior has been cleared of all creepers."

The assembled group shared a brief round of back-slapping, smiles and nods. They had successfully carved out a small enclave of safety in the center of the zombie apocalypse. Who would've thought? It was an important step, and one that they all felt proud to have finally reached.

"So what's next, fellas?" Kotter asked the question that most had been thinking for days. "Do we expand or do we stay buttoned up and wait for this here crisis to end?"

Cody and Jimbo exchanged a quick glance. They had discussed next steps but hadn't reached agreement on what to do next. Cody nodded to the younger man to let the others in on their discussions.

"Okay, here's the deal," he began. "We've got a few choices, none of which are perfect."

"Well shit, son. There's a surprise," Kotter interrupted. The codger-like sarcasm wasn't unexpected, but the group had learned to ignore the outbursts for the most part. "There's no perfect choice!"

"As I was saying, we have options," Jimbo pushed on, shooting a pointed look in Kotter's direction. He received an ornery grin and a sideways spit of brown tobacco juice in return. "First, we can stay here, hunker down and protect what we have.

"Second, we can expand to other neighborhoods. Try to replicate what we've done here and save as many people as we can. Third—and the option I propose—is that we get the hell out of Boise while we can."

"What—"

"Why would we—"

"Stop!" Cody stepped forward and held up a hand, cutting off the responses. "No one has made a decision yet. That's why we're discussing this now. We certainly wouldn't leave now—after all the effort we've expended to get where we are—without presenting the idea to the entire community. But we did want to discuss this here, in a smaller setting, before we broach the subject to the larger group."

"I ain't leaving my house," Kotter asserted, his vote firmly planted against option three.

"Jim, perhaps you can tell them why you think leaving is such a good idea?" Cody suggested. "But before you do, let me state for the record—and for Mr. Kotter's benefit—that I'm not a fan of the idea."

"Don't call me *Mister* Kotter. *Sarge*." The emphasis on 'Sarge' told Cody the old man knew of his distaste for the nickname.

"Um. Sure, Sarge," Jimbo continued, oblivious to the unspoken back-and-forth. Kotter grinned again, sent a second string of brown-laced spittle to his right, and shot Cody a sly wink. "The first option, staying here, is viable as a short-term solution. We've got secure walls. Our people are protected and they're well fed. If we could maintain things as they are, we'd be fine."

"Why is staying as we are only a… a short term solution?" Judy asked.

"Lots of reasons," Jimbo explained. "We don't know how long the electricity is going to stay on. Frankly, I'm surprised it's remained on this long. But eventually, it *will* go out and when that happens, we're going to be in a world of hurt. We lose a lot more than just our lights. We'll need a steady source of alternate fuel—wood, propane, gas—just to cook our food and boil drinking water. We won't have hot water, unless we heat it over a fire. Without hot water, our ability to keep ourselves clean becomes much more difficult. It's summer right now, but what do we do when winter comes? Few of the homes here have fireplaces, and those that do will need wood to burn. Wood that we don't have unless we burn our furniture and the fences around our houses."

"There's a propane farm a coupla miles from here on Franklin," Kotter interjected. "Just this side of the Cabela's. We might wanna think about visiting that place afore too much longer."

Cody and Jimbo exchanged a look and a nod. "That's a damn good idea, Kotter," Cody said. "We'll get a team to work on it right away."

"That supply should help, but even under the most favorable conditions, we'll be in for a very rough winter," Jimbo paused to let his words sink in. It was possible that none of them had considered what life would be like soon. It wasn't a comforting future. "But the real danger lies in the lack of long-term water and food."

"Can't we just get the food we need from the local stores?" Barry, the landscaper and former Navy NCO asked. "It's been working well, so far."

"For a while, probably," Jimbo agreed. "But we aren't the only survivors around. Sure, we haven't seen many others, but they're out there—consider how many folks we've found here as we've secured the neighborhood. People have been holed up for weeks and have to be running low on supplies. They're getting low on food and will be starving soon, if they aren't already. Starvation leads to desperation. Eventually, people will have to take their chances against the creepers, whether they want to or not. Heck, it's already begun happening. There was a lot less on the shelves the last few trips we made to the store. Someone else has been there, taking what they need. It's a matter of time before the food in the stores is completely gone. Then it becomes survival of the fittest, and I'm not even talking about the undead."

"Okay, okay," Barry conceded. "How is option two, expanding our perimeter any better than staying where we are?"

"It's not," Jimbo answered. "But at least we stay busy and maybe help more folks stay alive for just a while longer. There are problems with expanding too, though, so we need to consider how we can expand safely before we take that step. Not many neighborhoods have a solid perimeter wall like we do here. If anything, they're surrounded by flimsy privacy fences at best. Those won't hold back the creepers for long."

"Drummer Park neighborhood has strong walls," Toad offered. "They don't have a concrete barrier like we do, but they have iron fencing around the entire subdivision."

"Yeah," Judy agreed. "It's a couple of miles from here, but that neighborhood would be as secure as this one if we wanted to go with expansion. It's a place to start anyway. When do we have to decide?"

"No real rush," Cody said. "But the sooner we can decide amongst our group, the better. If we decide to leave, we'll need to get buy-in from the rest of the community."

"I ain't leaving," Kotter reiterated.

"Noted, Kotter." Cody looked at the rest of the group to assess where the others stood. He knew Toad would follow the lead that he and Jimbo set. Barry probably would as well. Judy had Mel's influence to consider. Kotter was firmly entrenched. "How about we take a look-see at this Drummer Park subdivision tomorrow and go from there? Jimbo, you up for taking a drive out that way tomorrow?"

"Hell yeah, Sarge. I'm sure I can find a volunteer or two who'd like a change of pace. Toad, you want to join me?"

"Sure!"

"Great, let's plan on heading out right after breakfast."

"Sounds good to me." The excitement was etched plainly across his features and Cody was glad to see him excited about the excursion. Jimbo had a tendency to disregard the teen's abilities and, for the most part, still treated him like a boy. Toad probably viewed this as a chance to prove himself to the young soldier. In a world where you have to fight for your life and for the lives of your peers on a daily basis, age isn't all that important; what matters is an individual's ability to perform and the capacity to contribute.

"Anything else we need to discuss?" No one had anything so the meeting dissolved and the group headed out,

most to rest for the evening. Cody still needed to visit the
guards posted at each entrance before taking a short break.

He was adjusting his gear and about to set off when
Jimbo intercepted him.

"Sarge, we're fighting a good battle here, but it's one
we can't win."

Cody wasn't ready to give up the fight, but he had to
acknowledge that Jimbo's arguments made a lot of sense.

"Let's take it one step at a time, Jimbo. If we have to
leave, what's our deadline?"

"We don't have a firm deadline, Sarge. But ideally,
now's the time—early summer. We want an area that's not
too remote but away from large population centers. A small
town would be best; one with a large water source nearby and
that could accommodate farming. Whether we like it or not,
we're gonna be back to life like it was when this area was first
settled. Subsistence farming, no electricity, outhouses to shit
in."

"Hmm. And instead of Indians, we're gonna have to
deal with creepers."

"Well, there is that."

"Okay, thanks Jimbo. Get some rest. Tomorrow's
not going to be any easier than today was."

"I hear you. You gonna check on the guards, or
should I?"

"I got it," Cody adjusted the Mossberg and set off
toward the far entrance. "See you in a while."

Cody thought about Jimbo's predictions and felt they
were spot on. If they remained in place, sooner or later,
they'd end up fighting with other humans for the limited
resources available. That would be bad, but it wasn't what

concerned Cody the most. What bothered him was that no matter how many creepers they eliminated, it wouldn't be enough. They would just keep coming. They weren't smart, and their top speed wasn't faster than a jog, but they more than made up for those weaknesses with their non-stop, single-minded determination to *feed*. Eventually, they would arrive in a group large enough to push past their defenses, or human error would show its ugly face long enough to allow them entry into the safe zone. Either way, staying in any large metropolitan area was a game of Russian roulette. It was just a matter of time until the hammer fell on the bullet.

Of course, moving such a large group over nearly a hundred miles of creeper-infested roads wouldn't be easy either. There were any number of dangers that could strike—mechanical failures, run-ins with hostile survivors, washed out roads or bridges. If they could keep rolling, the chances of success were good. Creepers were no match for a rolling vehicle, and Cody planned to keep the Humvee firmly at the front of their modern day wagon train, spearheading the charge. But any problem that stalled their movement, for even a short period of time, shifted the advantage to the undead enemy.

Success or failure often comes down to making a choice between two imperfect options. That's what Cody and the community were faced with—staying put meant they were relatively safe, but their ability to survive long-term was questionable. Leaving meant putting their lives into immediate jeopardy in exchange for potential long-term survival.

Neither choice was perfect, but he knew where his vote would fall when the time came to decide. But he also knew he had to put that decision off for a while longer. He still hadn't found Daisy and Cheech. That failure continued to gnaw at his spirit.

I'll find them Mom, he promised.

Chapter 24

It's often said that good things come in small packages. As the smallest breed of dog in the world—usually weighing between four and six pounds—Chihuahuas are thought by many to be an excellent example of this thinking. The dogs are intelligent, fiercely loyal and courageous.

Chihuahuas are descendants of the Techichi, an ancient dog that was first bred and raised by the Toltecs in what is now known as Mexico. The animals were often celebrated by their owners through carvings and paintings that accurately depicted their small bodies, round heads and large, erect ears. When the Toltecs were defeated by the Aztecs in the 11th century, the diminutive creatures were absorbed into the conquerors' society. Thought by the Aztecs to possess spiritual powers—including the ability to heal sickness and see into the future—they lived in temples and were routinely used in Aztec religious ceremonies. Unfortunately for the small canines, they were also highly valued as a ready source of food and pelts. It was also common for the dogs to be sacrificed and cremated upon the death of their owners so they could guide their human through the afterlife. Although they were important members of the society, when all was said and done, it was a hazardous proposition being a Techichi under the Aztecs.

When the Spanish conquered the Aztecs in the late 1500's, the Techichi were lost to history until the 1850's, when their descendants were "discovered" by Americans visiting the Mexican state of Chihuahua. Hence, the name of the breed.

Although the history of his ancestors was long and colorful, Cheech didn't know—or care—about any of that. All he cared about was the well-being of his pack and all that went with it. Having food and water, giving and receiving affection, and finding safety from the dangers of the world were what drove him. Those few concerns were more than enough to keep him occupied, especially since Mama had died. Since then, things had become complicated—first with The Boy, and now with The Girl and her family. He and Daisy were the core, but he was confused on where the others fit into the pack. He felt a strong tie with The Boy. He was a part of the old pack and an offspring of Mama, which meant his primary allegiance lay in that direction. But The Boy wasn't around and hadn't been for a long time. Cheech remembered where they had last seen The Boy and had no doubt he could find the place again. That had been days and days ago, but the drive to return was still strong.

The Girl, on the other paw, was *here*. She had taken Mama's role as the provider of food and water. Without her, he and Daisy would be left to fend for themselves. Because of this, he also considered her a member of the pack.

The decision before him now was very difficult. Stay with The Girl or seek The Boy?

The door to the back yard always remained open just enough to allow him and Daisy unrestricted access to the fenced area. They were properly civilized dogs and had been educated to relieve themselves outside of the pack's living space, after all. However, for the first time since The Girl had led them on the walk to The Boy's location, the gate that allowed exit from the area stood open. He didn't know why it was open, or how it had opened. He checked it daily—it's just what he did as a member of the pack. Perhaps the wind blew it open, or it was broken. Again, the little dog didn't know, nor did he care. The important thing was that he could leave, and he had a decision to make.

If he was going to find Mama's offspring, he would need to go now, before The Girl or the two males found and secured the opening. He knew from living with Mama that humans disliked open gates, and shut them quickly.

Daisy was inside the den sleeping. Cheech briefly considered retrieving her but the urgency of the open gate and the need to find The Boy drove him through the opening. His eyes and ears scanned the neighborhood as he moved cautiously through the tall grass toward the street ahead. He didn't see any monsters, nor did his nose pick up any strong scent of the hunters. Encouraged by the lack of immediate danger, he picked up the pace and was soon trotting along the sidewalk.

*   *   *

Proceed north on Cloverdale, past the creeper disposal pit at the bottom of the hill. Drive two miles until you reach McMillan Road, then take a right. Half mile further, on the left. Drummer Park subdivision. Can't miss it. Simple directions, even for someone who wasn't familiar with Boise.

For the most part, Jimbo drove slowly. He cautiously navigated the armored vehicle around and through the pile ups and bodies that were scattered liberally along the route. He stomped the gas pedal only when a creeper was foolish enough to put itself in his way—or when he could swerve safely enough to plow over one or more of the slow-moving eaters. There were more than a few of the dirt bags willing to trade their bodies for a potential bite of the two men—a man and a boy, really—nestled inside the moving vehicle. For the living, it was a good trade. For the undead... well, not so much.

Another burst of speed and a slight pull on the steering wheel was quickly followed by the now-familiar *bump-bump* as an older male creeper in jean shorts and a tattered polo shirt was dispatched.

"Nine," Toad announced from the passenger seat.

"You counting?"

"Sure, why not. It helps distract me from the fact that those... those *things*... used to be people."

Jimbo nodded his head. It was a tough thing to get one's mind around. Even for him, a long-time aficionado of zombie culture, the fact that the world was actually populated by the living dead was a strange thing to acknowledge.

Bump-dum-bump.

"Ten."

The former soldier looked at the teen on his right and searched for some sign that the boy was mentally breaking down. He saw none. Instead, he saw Toad perched high in the passenger's seat, trying to look over the empty racks that separated them. He seemed focused on the instrument panel, gauges and knobs that covered the vehicle's dash and driver's compartment. Jimbo tapped the brake pedal, slowed the behemoth to a steady twenty miles per hour. The youngster's attention soaked in the movement.

"You know how to drive, right?" For some reason, Jimbo had assumed that the teen knew how to operate a vehicle, but reminded himself that Toad was only fifteen.

"Sure. My dad had a pickup. He let me drive it a few times when we went camping."

"Automatic or stick?"

"It was an automatic, but the gear lever was on the steering column, not on the floor."

"Gotcha," Jimbo said and pointed to the gear select lever between them. "This works the same way as your dad's truck, it's just in a different location."

He demonstrated by pushing lightly on the fuel pedal, which increased their speed. A light tap of the brake pedal slowed the Humvee. He spotted movement ahead and stepped on the gas again. *Blong-bump-bump.*

"Eleven."

Bum-bum-blump.

"Twelve."

"See? Just that easy. The major difference between this beast and your dad's truck is the weight. It takes a bit more fuel to get this beast up to speed. And it takes longer to stop it once it's moving."

"What are those for?" the teen asked, pointing to the buttons and switches.

"Running lights, windshield wipers, parking brake." Jimbo ran through the entire series of dials gauges, knobs and switches, pointing to each and describing its function as he went.

"Seems easy enough. Can I try?"

"Well...let's not get ahead of ourselves." Jimbo
wanted to encourage the boy and was prepared to teach him
the mechanics. But there was no way he was going to let him
drive the armored vehicle. He tried to lighten the weight of
the denial. "Maybe when you're sixteen and get your license."

"Ha ha. You are so funny." The shake of head and
monotone voice let Jimbo know that the teen thought he was
anything *but* funny. *Asshole*, was probably closer to what Toad
actually believed him to be at that moment. "McMillan is the
next intersection."

Jimbo fought to keep a straight face, but he was
smiling inside.

The kid reminded him of himself at that age.
Intelligent. Eager. Utterly disregarded by adults. The cycle
of life as a young man in America, no doubt. *Hell, he's only six
years younger than I am.* They were sobering thoughts, and the
truth of the situation—the *entire* situation—crystallized into
an epiphany of understanding; one which quickly worked to
erase the internal smile.

The reality was that Toad had already proven himself
a valuable member of the community. He worked on body
removal and burial, had ventured out on several supply runs,
and stood regular guard shifts—first on top of the barriers,
then as a member of the z-trap kill teams. He always pulled
his weight. Not to mention that the z-traps had been his idea.
The teen was a contributor and clearly understood the
circumstances in which they found themselves, usually to a
degree that many of the adults within the community did not.
Hell, Jimbo would take one Toad over ten Mel Thompsons
any day—former Marine or not.

The fact that Toad's parents had been on vacation in Mexico when the shit hit the fan no doubt contributed to his constitution. He had confessed to the two Rangers that he had argued with them against going on the trip, wanting to remain home alone instead—his first attempt at being "an adult." They had grudgingly relented, his mom finally being convinced by his dad that he was mature enough to handle a week on his own. That one week had now stretched into six, and he was fighting to prove that their confidence in him hadn't been misplaced. The story had solidified his status as a trusted associate for both Jimbo and Cody.

And now Jimbo was treating him like a kid. He sighed, now actually *feeling* like the asshole Toad no doubt believed him to be.

"How about I let you drive part of the way back?"

"Really? You mean it?"

"Hell yeah, man. You earned it with that z-trap idea. That was freaking genius."

"Sweet!"

Blong-blumpbump.

"Thirteen."

"But I get to do the counting on the way back."

*   *   *

Cheech's legs ached and his paws throbbed. The empty knot of pain in his gut cried out for food and water—especially water. He ran through streets that he didn't recognize and crossed lawns that offered no familiar smells. He was lost, lost, lost.

But the two monsters that had been chasing him for the past fifteen minutes allowed him to ignore those minor aggravations.

His choices were limited. He couldn't fight them, they were too large. And he knew instinctively that facing them down with on a brave front of bared teeth and wild barking wouldn't slow them or make them re-think their chase. That would just get him eaten. No, his choices came down to running or hiding.

Running—because of the fear racing through his body—had seemed like the only option just minutes before. However, as his short legs grew weary and started to cramp, the *desire* to run was quickly being overridden by the *need* to hide.

He scanned his surroundings for a spot where he could hunker down safely and pressed onward.

Chapter 25

Jimbo understood why Cody was putting off the departure from Boise. They both knew it had to happen at some point, if not now, then in six months or a year. It was likely they could survive the winter in Boise—perhaps as many as two or three. But at some point, immigration would become a necessity. It was those damn dogs. Sarge was loyal to a fault—it was one of the traits that drew others to him—but his loyalty to his mother's Chihuahuas was a shortcoming. He didn't want to say it to his leader, but it was likely that the dogs had already become creeper chow. They were nowhere to be found and the entire neighborhood had been cleared and searched. No dogs anywhere.

Now, here he was, investigating another potentially defensible subdivision. Expanding the scope of their community was just putting off the inevitable, but orders were orders; and even though the US Army had ceased to exist as a fighting unit, Jimbo was still a soldier at heart. So he pushed on. Even if this neighborhood had strong walls, it might not be a good place to take on. Hell, it was over two miles away from their current base. Why couldn't they find somewhere closer? The neighborhood that sat across Cloverdale from them—even though it didn't have anything more than wooden fencing as a perimeter—might work.

The neighborhood across Cloverdale...

"Damn," he muttered and slapped the steering wheel.

"What's the matter?"

"Toad," Jimbo announced in a whisper. He was amazed that the thought hadn't occurred to either him or Cody before. "I think I know where those damn dogs are."

Before either had a chance to pursue the issue, Jimbo stomped heavily on the brakes. The armored vehicle shuddered to a stop and Jimbo pointed out the front windshield. A quarter-mile ahead, a crowd of creepers, numbering in the hundreds, clamored against a barricade of large, metal storage units that had been erected at the entrance to what *had* to be their destination, the Drummer Park subdivision.

"What the…" He didn't know how to process what he was seeing. Someone had enough ingenuity to protect the entrance to the neighborhood, but no one seemed to have enough brains to keep it clear of creepers. Eventually, the crowd would grow too strong for the barriers and it would be overrun or pushed aside by the hungry mob of undead.

"Holy crap."

"Holy crap is right, Toad. What are these people thinking?"

"May be they don't have guns or ammo to fight them off," the teen offered.

"Yeah, right." Jimbo countered. "We're in freaking Idaho. *Someone* in there has guns and ammo."

"Hell, they could whittle the ends of wooden rakes and shovels, if they needed to," Toad exclaimed. "All they'd have to do is stand on the other side of those metal fences and shove the sharp end into the creepers' brains one at a time."

Despite the seriousness of the situation before them, Jimbo grinned and eyed the teen with appreciation. Creativity went a long way with him, especially when it came to killing zombies. The boy—*young man*, he corrected—had a gift.

"Or, they could duct tape kitchen knives to the end of those shovel handles," Jimbo replied.

"Pruning shears."

"Ice picks."

"Screwdrivers."

"Scissors."

"Hmm," Toad thought for a moment. "Molatov cocktail?"

"A bit messy, and more difficult to achieve than it looks in the movies, but I'll give you the point."

"Z-trap?"

"Okay, I give. You win."

"Sweet," the teen pumped his right arm and hooted his pleasure.

The elation was short lived. A small group of creepers had peeled away from the mass at the barrier and were headed their way.

"Looks like we've been spotted."

Jimbo shifted into reverse and hit the gas. The Humvee retraced its path back up McMillan to Cloverdale, only this time it moved ass first. When they reached the intersection, he turned to the left and pointed the nose north. There was a series of brick, office buildings on their right. Behind them, he could see the metal fencing that made up the western perimeter of the subdivision. He considered his options and quickly turned into a parking lot on his right and drove toward the back. As expected, there was an access lane that ran behind the row of buildings. He took a left into

the lane and drove toward the center of the building, where
he stopped and turned off the engine.

The subdivision fence was to their right, an eight-foot
tall enclosure made up of a six-foot high stucco wall, topped
with a series of upright metal bars spaced four inches apart.
Each bar appeared to be nearly an inch in diameter and was
tipped with a decorative but daunting arrowhead-like point.
This fence was sturdier than the one protecting their own
neighborhood, and he had to give props to the designers.
The message they wanted to send was crystal clear and easily
understood: Stay the hell out.

If only I could, Jimbo thought.

He searched the area around them for any sign of
creepers and saw none. If anything, they would come from
behind, but he was confident that none of the small break-
away group could have seen them enter the parking lot, or
drive behind the row of buildings. They seemed as safe as
they could hope to be while parked in an unknown location
during a zombie apocalypse. It would have to do.

"Okay, here's the plan, Toad," he announced while
looking into the teenager's eyes. He tried to simulate the
Sarge's ability to outline a danger-filled strategy in a manner
that made the proposal feel like he was discussing a simple
walk in the park. It was harder than he would have thought,
and Jimbo struggled to speak calmly and slowly, while his
mind raced ahead at a hundred miles an hour. "I'm going to
scale the fence and find whoever's in charge on the other side.
You wait for me here. If I'm not back in an hour, I want you
to drive back to the others and tell them what we've seen.
Can you do that?"

"Um, yeah," Toad answered. "But why can't I come with you?"

"Because we don't know what we're going to find inside this fence. It looks like the folks may be safe for now, but we won't know for sure until I take a look. If anything goes wrong, I need you to get word to Sarge—to Cody. Can you do that?"

Toad looked nervously at the dials and gauges surrounding the steering column for a moment, before looking directly into Jimbo's eyes and nodding.

"Good," the soldier clapped him on the shoulder, retrieved his AR15, and put his helmet and goggles on. "Stay low and stay quiet. Those things can't get to you in here unless they've learned how to open doors, but a low profile is best. Remember, they're drawn by movement and sound. So make as little of each as you can."

"Got it."

"One hour, Toad. If I'm not back, you drive the Humvee back up Cloverdale and report to Sarge."

Jimbo receive a nod of understanding, then scanned the surrounding area once again for creepers. Seeing none, he exited the vehicle and adjusted his weapons and gear.

The early summer heat was in the low-80's which wasn't too hot for the Damascus Gear he wore. In a month or two, though, when the heat hit the 90's and 100's, the protective suit would be nearly unbearable. He took another moment to look around once more, eyed the wall before him, and crossed the alley in four quick steps. On the fifth, he launched his body, grabbed two of the bars extending from the top of the fence and hauled himself up. Once balanced, he swung his right leg carefully over the pointed tips and pushed himself erect so that he stood on top of the foot-wide fence, his feet straddling the metal rods and their arrow-like points. A phantom pain shot through his groin as he imagined the worst.

He caught Toad looking at him from the passenger side window and gave him a thumb's up sign. He then scanned the area inside the fence. It was a large, well-maintained backyard—or at least, it had been. The grass had grown high in the past few weeks from lack of mowing. The single-story home sat a hundred feet away. He saw no movement, living or creepers. Perfect.

He gave a final wave to Toad, swung his left leg over the fence, and lowered himself quietly into the yard. After a twenty-second wait to see if his entrance drew any type of response, he moved quickly but quietly toward the house. Halfway across the lawn he spied a small lump to his right and curiosity sent him over to investigate. As he neared, the lump revealed itself to be a mangled mess of fur and bones. He couldn't tell if the animal had been a large cat or a small dog, but it confirmed that there had been a creeper here at one time, and perhaps still was. He scanned the yard and windows ahead of him, and still seeing nothing that screamed "zombie", sprinted to the back of the home. When he reached the patio, and the set of French doors that led inside, he peeked inside. It was a kitchen. He didn't spy any movement but a pet food dish, half filled with uneaten kibbles, grabbed his attention and reminded him of something important. He had forgotten to tell Toad his idea about where the Sarge's dogs could be.

"Dammit!"

Jimbo debated retracing his steps so he could pass the info to the teenager, but discounted the idea almost immediately. There was no need to overreact. He could pass it along later.

He reached out and tested the handle on the door. Found it unlocked. Stepped into the house.

*   *   *

The water was warm, stale. But it soothed the ache in his throat and he lapped at it greedily. The monsters weren't far behind and he didn't have much time. The two that had been trailing him had been joined by three other members of their rancid pack. They weren't fast. He could easily outrun them, and had—over and over. But that was the problem. They didn't stop coming. He was at the end of his endurance. The brief rest and the water in this tiny pond would keep him going for a while longer, but eventually, he'd have to hole up under one of the cars he passed. The thought made him shiver as he recalled the previous attempts to escape the monsters in that way. The space offered short-term protection but he couldn't hide there forever. They'd simply surround the car and trap him.

He dipped his snout back into the landscaping pond, drew in three more mouthfuls of the tepid water, then lifted his head to view the crowd approaching from his left. They were two houses away and the distance was shrinking rapidly. It was time to move.

Cheech raised up from his prone position and managed a single, weary step before his right flank convulsed.

An all-consuming spasm of fire seized the cluster of muscles and dumped his body back to the ground. The immediacy and intensity of the hurt shoved aside the other aches that had previously tormented his small body.

His body was wearing down. The cramp was an indicator that his muscles needed water—which he'd just provided—and rest. Unfortunately, rest was out of the question. The group of monsters had halved the distance; only a single, overgrown yard separated them now. He pressed himself off the ground and attempted to stretch the offending leg, but the muscle group remained frozen in place, unwilling to relax, unwilling to push further.

Movement from his right captured his attention. Another monster was approaching from that direction. A car to hide under suddenly seemed like an ideal option. Unfortunately, the closest one was across the street. He'd have to scamper between the group approaching from the left and the single monster on his right to reach it. Knowing it was futile, but refusing to give up, Cheech forced his body to move toward the car and began an awkward *hop-drag-hop* gait.

The familiar sound of a door opening behind him was added to the moans of the advancing hunters and Cheech struggled forward, anxious for escape. It was no use. In his current state, the distance between him and the car across the street wasn't closing nearly as quickly as the distance between the monsters and him.

"Little dog!"

The little dog didn't recognize the voice, but he recognized the words and the beckoning tone. He ceased moving and looked back over his shoulder. A man was waving at him from the front door of the house. Was this a

potential rescue? The door gaped open behind the stranger
and he quickly weighed his options.

"C'mon, little dog. Hurry up, now."

Something about the man seemed...off...strange, but
Cheech had little choice. He turned around and *hop-drag-
hopped* past the small pool of stale water, toward the offered
sanctuary.

"That's it. Come on."

He reached the porch, but couldn't climb the first
step with his cramped leg. He struggled to push upwards, but
it was no use. His body had reached its limit. The monsters
were only steps away when the man scooped him up, stepped
inside and slammed the door. The house quickly filled with
sounds of moans, scratching and banging. It was a sound
Cheech knew well, but would never get used to.

The first thing Cheech noticed about the house and
the man who held him was the smell. It was the smell of
monsters. He wriggled in the man's grasp, suddenly
desperate to be free of the stranger's clutches, but the hands
tightened around his body like steel bands. The
overpowering stench and the powerful grip made it extremely
difficult to breath.

"Now, now, little dog," the man crooned softly in his
ear. "No struggling. It's not polite, and you're just in time for
dinner."

The man's breath offered tiny whiffs of onions,
medicine and soap, but those scents couldn't mask the stench
of rot and decay that wafted off the rest of his body. The
stink—combined with the crushing grip, tone of voice and
fevered stare in the man's wide eyes—informed Cheech that

this person wasn't a monster like those trying to get inside.
He was another type of monster altogether.

Cheech couldn't help himself. He issued a low,
menacing growl and released a warm stream of piss on the
man holding him.

Chapter 26

Jimbo made his way through the house slowly, checking each room and corner he passed for zombies. He didn't expect any. He had called out upon entering and waited with his baseball bat cocked and ready, but no creepers came running... or stumbling, to be more precise. But that didn't mean he wouldn't be careful. Every z-movie he'd ever seen had a scene where the actors let their guard down, thinking the coast was clear. Inevitably, that's when a zombie tumbled out of a closet or snuck up from behind to take a great big honking bite out of your ass. He liked his ass just the way it was—sans bite marks, thank you very much.

He cleared the ground floor and debated checking out the second floor, but thought twice. He had told Toad to give him an hour and, having already spent five minutes of that allotment, didn't want to waste the remainder unnecessarily. This house wasn't his goal, just a path to be taken. He took a moment to scan the street through a narrow window beside the front door and, seeing nothing out of the ordinary, turned the knob and stepped onto the front porch. He carefully closed the door behind him, content in the knowledge that, if there was a creeper inside, it couldn't sneak up on him from behind.

The neighborhood he faced seemed normal, quiet. Three bodies, in various states of decay and disposition, were in view. None appeared to pose any danger, but their presence alerted him to the fact that no one here seemed interested in clearing the streets—at least not of the non-walking dead. Whether there were any creepers about was an unknown. The fact that the entrance to Drummer Park was blocked gave him hope that the residents were on top of the creeper infestation within their gates. Resigned to the fact that he'd find out soon enough, he stepped off the porch and headed for the sidewalk.

To his left, the street ended in a cul de sac. The half-dozen homes in that direction showed no movement or life. Their occupants could be hiding away inside, but he elected to turn right and proceed further into the subdivision. The street took a sharp turn to the left just ahead and he set off in search of survivors. So far, the place looked deserted.

Ten minutes and two streets later, the neighborhood still looked deserted. Jimbo had even stopped to knock on several doors, without luck. Where the hell was everyone? So far, all he had seen were a score of dead bodies. Dead bodies, not undead creepers. That was a good sign, wasn't it? The growing crowd of creepers fighting to get past the front gates indicated that *someone* was here. He pressed on. A glance at his wrist showed he had forty minutes of the sixty left.

Jimbo paused to think and an idea came to him quickly.

The clubhouse.

These types of high-end subdivisions often had neighborhood pools or clubhouses. Funded through high-priced monthly association fees, they were places where groups could congregate and feel like members of the community. If he wanted to find a group of survivors, what better place to look than a large building designed to accommodate a crowd? He tried to picture the layout of the community in his mind and oriented himself to where the front entrance—the one with the growing creeper colony—lay. The clubhouse would probably be located near there. With this destination in mind, he jogged forward. Even while running, his eyes never stopped scanning for movement or signs of trouble. As before, he saw none.

The number of dead bodies seemed to increase the closer he got to his destination. Something seemed... *off*...about the bodies as well, but he couldn't put his finger on it. They lay scattered randomly across lawns and in the street. As he rounded a turn in the road and saw what had to be his destination a block ahead—a large stucco building, painted tastefully in several shades of yellow and brown—he spied more than a dozen dead on the sidewalk to his right. The bodies were carefully aligned and facing in the same direction. The red and grey splatters that surrounded them showed the cause of death. These people—all men, he suddenly noted—had been executed with carefully placed shots to the head.

He slowed from a jog to a walk, then came to a stop. Almost all of the bodies he had passed had been men, older women or young kids. That's what had been bugging him. There was a distinct demographic missing from the death toll.

Something wasn't right in Drummer Park. Something *other* than creepers at the front gate.

Jimbo considered calling off his search, turning around quietly and retracing his steps. But he was a curious person by nature. Coupled with an exceptionally strong desire to do the right thing, his curiosity demanded that he investigate the clubhouse first.

He glanced at his watch—thirty-two minutes left. He'd have to be quick. That settled, he checked his weapons, did a quick scan of the area, and moved out.

As a result of the executions, he was now on alert against a living enemy, so changed his tactics accordingly. Instead of moving down the street, hoping to draw creepers to him, he went into stealth mode, hoping to evade the attention of whoever had killed the men living here. He hugged the homes along the street, keeping diligently to the shrubbery and shadows that offered concealment. He would have preferred to move slowly and quietly, but time was not on his side, so he settled for a combination of quick bursts of speed coupled with an occasional pause to evaluate his surroundings. The Sarge wouldn't have approved, but it was the best he could do under the circumstances.

A final sprint across thirty meters of parking lot delivered him to the side of the clubhouse building. He dropped to a knee and flattened himself against the structure, partially hidden by a row of spruce trees lining a concrete walkway. He silently counted off thirty seconds to see if his approach garnered any unwanted attention. When the self-imposed time passed he checked his watch. Twenty-nine minutes left. Time to move again.

A row of windows sat halfway between his position and the front of the building and he crouch-walked to the nearest one. He inspected the area around him, then raised his head up to take a peek inside.

"What the..." The scene inside showed a large, open room. The floor of the space was covered with blankets, chairs, cots and other various odds and ends that you might expect to see in any refugee center. Food, water bottles, trash. Scattered among the detritus were several dozen people—women, he corrected; he didn't see any males. They sat and lay around the space as individuals and in scattered bunches. Some cried, some stared straight ahead, some leaned against each other for comfort. All of them looked like they had been through hell.

Jimbo was on the verge of deciding that they were survivors who just needed help when a doorway at the opposite side of the room slammed open. Two rough-looking men, wearing leather vests and jeans entered. Between them, they dragged the naked, limp figure of a blond female. The man on the right carried a shotgun perched over his shoulder. The man on the left was younger, had a scraggly beard, and wore a pistol on his hip. They roughly flung the woman into the middle of the room and looked around. The women inside began crying and were scuttling away from the two. Only one woman, a redhead dressed in a white tank top and jeans, moved forward to help the woman that had just been delivered. Fear, angst and loathing were written clearly across her face.

The bearded man spit a wad of phlegm in her direction.

"Well, hell. I guess we know who's next then," he announced and moved toward the redhead. To her credit, she turned to face him and squared her shoulders.

"Over my dead body," she exclaimed. She looked at each of the men in turn, her demeanor one of clear defiance.

"As you wish, sweetheart," Beard said. He gave a gap-toothed smile, looked at Shotgun and nodded.

Shotgun calmly lifted his weapon off of his shoulder and pointed it at the woman.

The pull of a trigger, followed immediately by a loud clap and a resulting splatter of blood and gore, caused the women in the room to scream and duck. The redhead wobbled, remained upright.

A second round pierced the portion of the uni-brow that ran directly between Beard's very surprised eyes. He was no doubt still wondering what had happened to Shotgun before tumbling backward and landing next to his partner.

Jimbo scanned the room for additional targets. Saw none.

"Hey, asshole!"

Oh shit. Someone's behind me.

He had no time to react. Before he could turn his head, an explosion of light and agony filled his head. The last thing he saw before darkness dragged him away was a confused look of surprise, horror and relief as the redhead's green eyes locked onto his.

*   *   *

Toad dropped to the ground and tried to become a part of the landscaping in which he lay.

It hadn't been his intention to follow the Ranger through the neighborhood when he exited the Humvee and scaled the wall only minutes after the other man. His only concern, at that point, was watching Jimbo's back in case he ran into any creepers inside the house. The top of the wall offered a good view of the house and neighboring properties. He might have only been fifteen, but he understood that going alone into an unknown situation wasn't the best way to proceed. Even more needling to Toad, was the fact that the soldier was still treating him like a kid. The offer to drive on the return trip was a start, but he doubted Jimbo would have made an older person stay behind in the vehicle while he scouted alone. No, they would have proceeded as a team, watching each other's backs against the zombies. The understanding gnawed at Toad's ego and—when he watched Jimbo enter the home—propelled him from the top of the wall into the back yard. He had been trailing the soldier ever since; staying a hundred yards behind, hugging the houses on the left side of the street for cover as they ventured deeper into the complex.

Now, all hell had broken out. Toad had watched in wonder as Jimbo fired his AR15 through the window at targets he couldn't make out. Moments later, the wonder turned to horror as a large man rounded the corner of the building and ran at Jimbo from behind.

"Hey, asshole!" The giant announced his presence at the same time as he slammed the butt of a large hunting rifle into the back of Jimbo's neck. Toad hoped the Kevlar helmet and other padding he wore helped absorb some of the blow, but the soldier collapsed at once. Toad lifted his own AR15 from the prone position, settled the large man's head into his sights and—

—removed his finger from the trigger.

Three other men—all armed with an assortment of weapons, and dressed in similar outfits of jeans and leather— appeared from the front of the large building.

"What the fuck, Dink," one of the newcomers asked. His voice carried clearly to Toad across the yards that separated them.

"Found this guy shooting into the window," the man with the hunting rifle—Dink—answered. He stepped to the window and peered inside. "Shit, Bill. This guy killed Leif and Little Stone."

"Let me kill him, Bill!" Another of the newcomers, a thin, nervous-looking man hopped anxiously from foot to foot. He pointed a large, stainless revolver at Jimbo's head. Toad lifted his weapon and acquired his new target.

"Put the gun down, Slacker," Bill ordered. "This one's well-armed. And check out that gear he's wearing. Shit, we could use some of this stuff."

Slacker lowered the gun and offered a weak shrug. "We ain't gonna kill him?"

"Oh, yeah," Bill nodded. "We're gonna kill him all right. We just need to find out where he came from and see if he has any friends first. Drag his ass into the rec center and we'll see what he has to say when he wakes up."

Two of the men grabbed Jimbo by his arms and began dragging him to the front of the building. Bill reached down and collected the dropped AR15. He looked through the broken window and shook his head.

"Fucker's gonna pay for this." He then followed the rest of his crew.

Toad trembled and found it hard to breathe. He hadn't done anything to help Jimbo and questioned what he should have done. Wondered what he should do *now*. The only scenario that seemed even minimally plausible was to retreat and bring back reinforcements. Knowing he had very little time if he wanted to save his friend, he waited until the coast was clear, then lifted himself from the ground and ran back the way he had come.

Ten awful, slow minutes later the Humvee was racing along Cloverdale as fast as the teen dared to push it.

Thunk-whomp-thunk.

"One."

Chapter 27

The Bitch entered his life on a Sunday morning. It was springtime and the day was perfect. Not cold, not hot. Sunshine crisped the air in a way that put you on notice that winter had been left behind, and the over-hot days of summer were just around the corner. Birds sang, flowers bloomed, lovers walked hand in hand. Blah, blah, blah. It was a nice damn day; you get the fucking point.

His mother had dragged him to church that day; not exactly kicking, but definitely screaming. There was a lot of screaming and yelling during those years—the years that followed his father's escape from his badgering wife, and the overbearing mother's subsequent attempts to reconcile her place in the world as a single parent. She had never been successful as a dual parent; when left alone to manage a 16-year old boy, she became an absolute horror. Screaming was the grease that coerced the rusty contrivance of their dysfunctional lives to press forward. And press forward they did. PTA involvement, church on Sundays, a never-ending multitude of volunteer activities were their agenda. Anything she could do to present a front of normalcy to the outside world—to prove that she didn't need a man, a husband, a father for the boy—was done and she dragged the son along with her, despite his unceasing protests and tantrums. Yes, behind closed doors, yelling and screaming was the order of the day.

There was screaming on the Sunday before he met The Bitch. Church was the last place he wanted to be in the world. A stuffy building filled with self-righteous show-offs and holier-than-thou hypocrites, the institution represented everything his mother wanted, but didn't have the intestinal fortitude or self-discipline to attain. The hours of boring monologue that he never actually heard and the God-awful (*pun intended*) singing of the posers around him acted as giant hammers pounding against the tender meat of his brain. He left service each Sunday feeling weak and battered.

But the distress of another wasted Sunday morning quickly evaporated when a blond, blue-eyed beauty sauntered down the center walkway and passed his standard Sunday perch—aisle seat, fifth row from the rear, on the right. By the time she settled into her chosen pew, two rows ahead, on the left, his headache has disappeared. Suddenly, church was where he wanted to be.

Of course, he still didn't hear the non-stop prattle being spouted by the pastor. Why would he? He was too closely focused on the hair, the shoulders, the neck—*oh my, what a neck*—of the woman seated across the aisle. Early twenties, he guessed. Older, but not *too* old for a 16-year old who was mature for his age, he decided. His palms grew damp and the tie circling his neck became too tight. The briefs he wore underneath his Sunday suit also became uncomfortably tight, and he shifted in his seat to accommodate the growing bulge. The maddening constriction continued as the service progressed, but the discomfort turned to excitement at the thought that he had a hard on in church. Overall, it was an incredibly pleasurable— though irritatingly unfulfilling—experience.

Then the service ended.

He sat unmoving for a few seconds as the reality of his predicament set in, and people began moving toward the center aisle and the doors at the rear.

"Move it," his mom poked him in his ribs and whisper-screamed in his right ear. "Let's go."

"Um...I..."

"Stop dawdling. I want to speak to the pastor before he gets mobbed by the crowd."

"I want to sit here for a minute."

"Not on your life, buddy boy," she threatened so only he could hear. She poked him again, then pushed against his shoulder roughly. "Move your ass. Now!"

The traffic along the aisle was picking up. Maybe no one would notice the lance he carried in the front of his dress slacks. The blond was forgotten and he stood, bending forward at the waist in a useless attempt to hide his predicament. His mom propelled him from behind and he stumbled forward into the aisle—

—where he immediately slammed into the reason for his current state of arousal. Dick first.

"Oh, I'm so..." he managed to mumble before losing himself in her large blue eyes.

"Eww!" The blond exclaimed loudly and extricated herself from the embrace he didn't even realize they were sharing until that moment. "Yeah, I can feel," she said, looking down at his erection, "and *see* that you are so... so creepy!"

"I didn't mean—"

"Jonathon Samuel Sweeney," his mother screeched. The recitation of his full name was rare, and only employed in public when one of her standard "pet" names for him, like asshole, idiot, lazy, and the like, couldn't be used. "What do you think you're doing to this young woman?"

"I'm not doing—"

"This little perv has a hard on and he's rubbing it on me," the blond, who had lost much of her attractiveness, accused. She pointed at the tent—now somewhat deflated—in his trousers. "Look."

Despite being mortified and far from ever being considered pious, Jonathon's immediate thought was: *Who talks like that in church?*

He had little time to ponder the question. Before he could react further, his mother had grabbed his tie and led him away from the large portion of the congregation who had witnessed the exchange. Several of the crowd pointed at his crotch and shared sidelong whispers with their neighbors. The screaming began as soon as their car peeled out of the parking lot and continued for several days.

A rational person might have thought an incident like that could get you out of church duty for the rest of your life, but it wasn't to be. The very next week Jonathon was seated in his perch, head and eyes cast down to avoid the stares and whispers being exchanged at his expense. To make matters worse, Summer Anderson, the blond-haired, blue-eyed vixen pranced into the place of worship like she owned it and headed for the same seat she had taken the previous week. This time though, she offered a dismissive toss of her perfectly-shaped nose as she passed the young admirer. Jonathon, not as fully entranced by Summer's presence as the previous week, glanced around to see if anyone noticed the slight. That's when he realized that few heads were turned in his direction. Instead, Ms. Anderson had captured the attention of most of the assembled males—and was gaining more than a few scowls from the women gathered here to praise God. Suddenly, it dawned on Jonathon that she undoubtedly realized the affect she had on those around her. Based on her seeming eagerness to demean him the previous week—not to mention her willingness to use terms like "perv" and "hard on" inside a church—it seemed like a strong possibility that she even sought out and enjoyed the attention.

She was just another manipulator, similar to his mother, but with altogether different methods of gaining what she wanted. No screaming for her, no sir. Her body did the talking, and if the reactions of the men around them were any indication, it spoke loud and clear—demanded to be heard. This revelation brought understanding. He grew lightheaded and his vision dimmed while his consciousness struggled to absorb the concept. The knowledge of who and what The Bitch represented was an epiphany, and a sudden cascade of realization filled the previously empty core of his soul. Minutes passed before he the last drop of understanding was ingested, but as soon as his mind fully grasped the kernels of wisdom, his vision returned. With renewed vision came a new philosophy—one born of years of mental and spiritual abuse. It was time for him to become the manipulator, the controller; the one who got what he wanted. Jonathon's plotting began and the blonde tease was given a new, more appropriate moniker. He mentally christened her "The Bitch."

With a clarity of thought that was refreshingly exciting, he cast his eyes boldly to where The Bitch sat just ahead of him, and to the left. At the same moment, she turned to glance over her shoulder and caught him staring.

She rolled her eyes dismissively and waited for him to look away, no doubt shamed by the previous week's events. Instead, he curled the corners of his lips into a comfortable smile and nodded his chin in a casual way, as if to say 'hey, *you* looked at *me*.' The Bitch's eyes widened and her mouth gaped. Unwilling to be humbled or influenced any longer, Jonathon offered a quick wink and pursed his lips in a kissing motion. The blond snapped her head around to face the front and sat ramrod straight in the pew. Over the course of the next ninety minutes, he caught her looking in his direction three more times. Each time, he was ready with a nod, a smile or a tiny kiss. When the sermon finally concluded and the assembly began filing out, Jonathon planned his departure from the hall to coincide with The Bitch's. When she passed, he fell into step just behind her and closed the distance between their bodies. He wasn't hard this week, but when the crowd gathered at the door waiting to exit, he pushed his crotch against her ass—this time on purpose—and spoke softly so that only she could hear.

"Hi, I'm Jonathon." He felt a slight, almost imperceptible return push and he felt himself begin to stiffen.

"Um. Okay." The previously self-assured tease suddenly seemed less confident. She seemed flushed and out of breath. He liked the change.

"I'll see you again next week."

His hands reached out, grasped her waist and gave a quick, but firm, squeeze. The touch lasted no longer than a half second, but it felt exhilarating and she offered no resistance, voiced no objection. If anything, she seemed somewhat disappointed when Jonathon broke contact, moved past her and walked away.

For the first time in his life, he felt powerful, in charge. It was a heady feeling and he vowed to never again allow others to dictate his feelings or to allow their views or norms to control him. He laughed in anticipation at how his mother would react to his new outlook.

"Let the screaming ensue," he mumbled as he marched to their car.

He sat down in the passenger seat and waited for her to make her social rounds. She missed out last week, what, with her bad son and all. She swore she wouldn't miss out a second week and had instructed him to be on his best behavior in her typical high-pitched, high decibel fashion.

"Well, at least it will be the last time."

Later that evening, his mother learned her first lesson at the hands of her teenaged son. It took two broken ribs, a black eye and three loose teeth before the screaming and yelling ceased and the message was driven home. They told the doctor she fell down the stairs. It was only after learning that the husband had left the household years before, and only she and her soft-spoken son lived at home that he even attempted to believe it. The injuries looked like a classic case of spousal abuse, but without a husband or boyfriend to hang any charges on, the woman was released without police involvement.

From that point forward, at least while in public, the pair acted as they always had. She was the tireless volunteer, eager to please and anxious to fit in. At home, she was the tireless subservient, eager to quell her son's rages and anxious to stay out of his way. She was intelligent and quickly learned to accept their new roles. She was the mother of a very deranged, very unstable young man. He was the son of an apprehensive, fearful woman that had been taught to obey

While the situation at home improved remarkably for Jonathon, the relationship with The Bitch became even more satisfying. He was delighted to learn the following Sunday that not only was she a new member to their church, but she was also a new neighbor. A month earlier, she had purchased the small home just down the street and moved in without fanfare. Alone. He stopped by her house unannounced one afternoon, less than a month after they first met. He applied his new-found persuasion techniques and, as they say, one thing led to another, which led to another. Before the sun rose the next morning, he had found his first girlfriend, lost his virginity, and dug his first burial hole in the flower bed behind his house. For the teen, it was a banner evening that gave his life purpose and set the tone for his future existence.

The following morning he ran across a like-new Monblanc, Agatha Christie Edition, fountain pen selling on Craigslist. The interesting find provided inspiration, and he promptly emptied out his mother's savings account of the two thousand dollars and change that it held. He offered cash, plopped down his stack of hundred dollar bills and began documenting his History that evening.

The following day, Jonathon's mother confronted him about the damage to her flower beds and the unexpected zero's that made up the new balance of her savings account. To his surprise, the two items were apparently egregious enough in her mind to overcome her new-found reticence at angering her son, and the yelling commenced—as loud and hurtful as ever.

It wasn't a problem for the teenager, though. A second hole was quickly dug and filled. Good riddance to the both of you.

Over the next few days, the Montblanc sailed across page after page as the first journal was consumed.

Chapter 28

"What's that smell?"

Maria looked away from the view outside their front window at her brother. Estevan was lying on the sofa in Mrs. Clark's family room. A book was propped against his knees. Little Girl was perched on his chest with her eyes half open. It was a position that both the boy and the dog had come to enjoy over the past few days. With little to occupy his mind, he had taken up reading to fill the hours, and she was glad her brother was developing a taste for the activity. Her father, on the other hand, had little interest in books, and spent his time inventorying their dwindling supplies and creating dishes from the ingredients left behind by their departed benefactor.

"What? I don't smell anything," she asked, fearing the worst. Zombies were rank, rank, rank.

"Dunno. Smells like rotten eggs and… liver."

"Hah," their dad kidded. "That dog probably farted, Mijo."

Maria laughed. "Dang, little brother. Little Girl gave you a cup o' cheese!"

"Ugh. No way." Estevan raised up and pushed the dog away. Maria noticed that he did so carefully, gently. Like her, he had come to appreciate the presence of the two Chihuahuas in the house. They added a satisfying element to the boring existence that had become their lives. Although she had posted the notice in the front yard, Maria had begun to hope that no one would ever claim the dogs.

Thinking about the two canines made her realize that she hadn't seen Little Boy in a while. Quite a while.

She left her perch by the front window and walked through the house, checking the usual spots where the little guy hung out. When he wasn't in a lap, he was usually curled up in a blanket or on a pillow on one of the beds—most often hers. A quick search of the house came up empty, so she scanned the fences of the backyard for zombies, then exited onto the patio. Little Girl, having been dumped from her spot by Estevan, joined her outside. Not wanting to call out or make any unnecessary noise, she scanned the yard and, not seeing Little Boy, walked to the side of the house.

When she saw the open gate, her stomach dropped.

"Oh, no."

*　　*　　*

For Daisy, it was obvious. The sight of an open gate is an invitation to a dog, and Cheech never let that type of invitation go unanswered. Her nose quickly confirmed his passing along this stretch of ground within the past hour and, not having seen him in that space of time, she knew he was outside. With the monsters.

Her tail tucked itself between her legs and her body released a long, intense shiver.

Unable to do otherwise though, she put her nose to the ground and followed the scent of her pack mate. He was alone among the monsters and he needed her.

*   *   *

Maria debated going back inside to let her father and brother know what had happened, but quickly discounted the notion. Her dad would forbid her to leave the house. But leaving the little dog to fend for himself against what waited outside the gate wasn't an option. It also didn't appear to be an option for Little Girl. The little blond female was already crossing the threshold that separated the relative safety of the yard into the danger zone beyond; her nose was pressed to the ground, scanning for scents.

Without questioning the dog, Maria followed closely behind. She made sure to pick up the shovel from where she had left it at the end of their last adventure—resting against the house, just inside the gate. She said a silent prayer, stepped through the gate and hurried to catch up with Little Girl. The tiny Chihuahua was moving quickly and had already reached the street.

"I hope you know where you're going, little dog." She scanned the neighborhood for zombies and found the coast clear. "Thank goodness for the folks across the way."

*   *   *

The sense of smell is the most highly evolved sense a dog has. Like all dogs, the olfactory cortex of a Chihuahua's brain is designed for smell. In some dogs—primarily bloodhounds—the olfactory cortex is forty times bigger than in humans, and up to one-hundred million times more sensitive. While humans are capable of detecting between

four-thousand and ten-thousand smells, dogs can sense
between thirty-thousand and one-hundred-thousand. Dogs
can detect odors in parts-per-trillion. This means that while a
human might detect a squeeze of lemon added to a glass of
water, a dog can detect a similar amount of lemon added to a
million *gallons* of water—or roughly the size of two Olympic-
sized swimming pools. Pretty darn incredible.

Daisy's cortex was at the upper end of the doggie
range, which was quite remarkable for a Chihuahua. Even
more importantly, her sniffer was fully attuned to all of the
smells emitted by her pack mate. Her wet nose easily
determined the direction Cheech took upon leaving the yard
and led her easily along the same path he had so recently
taken. The ability to use each nostril independently from the
other allowed her to follow Cheech's path while also keeping
a smell out for any monsters.

After five minutes, Daisy had a good idea of where
Cheech was headed. He was taking a direct path back to
where they had seen The Boy. She picked up the pace, eager
to reunite with the two pack mates.

Moments later, she lost the scent.

Backtracked.

Found it and followed slowly.

His path turned away from the direction she expected
it to follow. Instead of heading for The Boy, Cheech had
stopped briefly, then crossed the road. Halfway across the
road, she picked up the stench of a monster, then a second
one.

Their scents overlaid the track of smell left behind by
Cheech. And he had been running.

Daisy lifted her nose, searched for movement ahead, saw nothing. She wasn't brave but her brother was being chased by monsters somewhere ahead so she pushed on. The Girl followed closely behind and that helped the dog focus on where the trail took them, versus what they might find at its end.

*   *   *

She jogged to keep pace with the dog. For a tiny little thing, the girl could cover some ground with those short legs. When Little Girl crossed the street and headed back in the direction from which they had just come, Maria felt a pinch of doubt. Were they on the right track? But when the Chihuahua turned left and scuttled quickly down a new street five minutes later, the worry dissipated. This Chihuahua knew where she was headed.

Chapter 29

"You spent time in Afghanistan?"

Cody knew the answer. Judy had already filled him in on Mel's background—she cried when she told him how her considerate, loving husband had come back from his second tour a different man. It explained a lot, and Cody was embarrassed and ashamed that he hadn't considered this possibility before. He had all the facts; in hindsight, he recognized all the signs. Leading his own platoon of soldiers through three tours had provided more than adequate training. On two separate occasions, he had been forced to seek help for a brother in arms. In both cases, the men were removed from duty and placed into care. Not all scars are visible. When facial tics, vacant stares, and long bouts of silent withdrawal begin to alter a man's personality and twist his moral character into something foreign, an invisible, mental injury is often the cause. War can alter a man's soul quicker, and with more permanence, than just about any other experience.

"Yeah," Mel answered, squinting at them through the closed screen door. A glint of wary suspicion flashed across his face before settling into the snarling frown that Cody had come to expect. "So?"

"I need your help." Simple, direct, no bullshit. It apparently wasn't what Mel expected. The snarl turned into a questioning look. The look was directed at Cody, then turned toward Toad, who stood at Cody's right. Together, they took up most of the area on the Thompsons' small, front porch.

"Why me?" The voice delivered its apathy, the dull blue eyes offered cold indifference. The face offered no reprieve, showed no signs of acceding to any request.

"We've got a problem and I need someone with..." Cody paused for a breath before continuing. "Someone with a certain type of experience to help me take care of it."

Curiosity across the eyes. Just a hint, but it was there.

"Toad," Cody nudged to the teen standing next to him. "Tell Mr. Thompson what you saw."

Toad nodded, then began. Cody listened to the story for a second time. He was pleased to hear as the youngster's initial nervousness was quickly replaced by an iron resolve to gain help for the man he had left behind an hour earlier. The young man was growing into his own. The level of maturity he showed in knowing to seek help and driving the Humvee back to their location was impressive. And it was growing again as he replayed the events leading up to Jimbo's capture with confidence and conviction.

When Toad returned without Jimbo, the teen had found Judy Thompson at the barrier and—after being calmed down sufficiently—had relayed the events to her. Together, they scoured the neighborhood before finding him talking with the guard at one of the rear set of RV barriers. When he heard what had taken place, Cody knew he needed a small but able crew who could assist in a rescue effort. He had already settled on himself and Barry Evans. As a Navy veteran, Barry wasn't an ideal choice for a ground-assault rescue mission, but he had proven himself to be a trusted commodity, and his experience with weapons was a plus. As much as he disliked the idea, he knew Toad would have to come along also. Time was critical and he could quickly lead them to where Jimbo was being held.

Cody was debating on who else to select—he was leading toward Jeremy, the third leg of his creeper-infested, house-clearing trio—when Judy suggested Mel. Previously mum on the topic of her husband, she offered apologetic explanations for his behavior and explained that he hadn't always been this way. She was certain he would help if he knew one of their own was in trouble. For Cody, it was a no-brainer. A trained Marine with combat experience was exactly the type of individual he wanted beside him when they went in to get Jimbo.

He stood silently as Toad finished retelling the events and waited for Mel Thompson to decide on whether he would join their rescue party. With or without the man's help, in five minutes Cody was going to pass through the barrier that kept their neighborhood safe from the creeper-world outside and rescue his friend from a group of armed murderers.

Mel shook his head and rubbed his eyes. He released one of the heaviest sighs Cody had ever heard from another human being. The slow exhalation escaped the man's body like a death rattle and appeared to deflate the angry man's large, muscular frame. The snarl that had become a permanent fixture on the Marine's face dissipated. In its place, a fatigued countenance—resigned to whatever actions and fate waited just ahead—remained.

Ten minutes later, the four men—three veterans and a young, untried teenager—left the compound. All were armed to the teeth and ready to deal with whatever lay ahead. Although they had been fighting a life-or-death struggle against a horde of undead creepers for weeks, the upcoming battle against a thinking, human foe, seemed like a much more dangerous ordeal.

*   *   *

He fought the darkness and the ocean of pain that hurled giant breakers of agony against the inside of his skull. The relentless *thung...thung...thung* offered a convincing argument against his desire to seek and find the light of consciousness.

A cool, damp sensation joined the strident booms of pain, and he turned his attentions eagerly toward the small relief. He struggled against the powerful current of pain that threatened to whisk him back into the darkness and stroked furiously toward the coolness.

"Are you okay?"

The whisper pierced the darkness like a lighthouse beacon and revealed a path. He swam for the surface; broke into the light and—

—moaned with anguish. The torture of sudden brightness gouged his eyes and struck his head like a blacksmith's hammer against the anvil.

Jimbo took a deep breath and clamped his eyes shut against the brightness while he took stock. How did he get here? He couldn't remember. His upright position and the hardness beneath his body informed him that he was seated in a chair.

Again, he struggled to recall the events that had delivered him to this place. Creepers. Toad. Community Center.

He suddenly remembered.

The force of the recollection caused him to thrash wildly. The movement was an invitation to the darkness that he had fought so hard to overcome. It reached out and gripped his consciousness once again. Pulled. Too exhausted to struggle any longer, he allowed the demanding riptide of pain to sweep him back into the ocean.

Chapter 30

Jonathon Samuel Sweeney sat at his desk and put the Montblanc through its paces. The afternoon light pouring through the large window before him filled the room with a wonderful, golden glow. His mind was overflowing with inspiration since bringing Wanda into his home days earlier. She was a godsend. His needs were being met in a way that none of his previous lovers had ever been able to match. She didn't protest that he was too rough, or that he didn't take his time, or—as one of his less tactful conquests had once imparted—that he scared the living shit out of her. No, there was none of *that* nonsense with Wanda. She did what he wanted, when he wanted, and for as long—or as little—as he wanted to do it.

Of course, he had to be careful; it was necessary for his well-being. But he had learned quickly that the act of overpowering and tying her up served a purpose besides keeping him from being bitten. It was a thrilling aphrodisiac and intense session of foreplay, all in one. The act was so integral to the experience that he untied her (carefully) when they finished, just so he could do it all over again prior to the next round. And the rounds came often. Just writing about it caused a reaction, and Jonathon reached down with his non-writing hand to delicately adjust a growing, but very sore bulge. His writing hand moved even quicker across the page, the anticipation of another bout urging him onward, despite the soreness. He was never one to let a minor ailment get in the way of a major pleasure.

Steven L. Hawk

The only negative attribute that he could apply to Wanda was her inability to communicate more fully. The frustrated grunts and moans were pleasurable *during*, but left him less than satisfied *after*. But no one is perfect and it was a minor flaw, one he could easily forgive. His next thought, which he dictated directly into the journal of his History was: *The best life partner is one whose minor quirks and imperfections somehow transform themselves into tender endearments over time.*

*   *   *

Cheech lay curled up on the carpet, huddled quietly under the relative safety of a chair that had been placed in the corner. The sun's rays reached into his hiding spot, and his dark fur soaked in the heat. At any other time, the sensation of sunshine bathing his body would have been a supreme comfort. But the strange man seated across the room—and the creature he kept in the next room—scared him. Despite the heat soaking into his body, he shivered.

The stranger had helped him escape the monsters outside. He was the lesser of the two bad choices that had been offered. But he was still a bad choice, Cheech now knew.

The hot dog he had been offered sat untouched (mostly) a few feet away. Despite being his favorite meal in the entire world, Cheech couldn't eat more than a bite. The rumble in his stomach and the taste of hot dog on his tongue could not outweigh the assault on his nose. The stench of the monster on the other side of the wall disallowed any sense of appetite.

He had always tried to be a good dog. He listened (most of the time) when Mama told him to Sit, Stay or Getdownoffthecouch. He didn't bark much, he did his business outside, and he didn't bite other dogs, strangers or little kids—though it was hard not to bite little kids, especially when they chased you around the room, tried to pick you up, and squeezed too tight. But he was struggling with being a good dog. In fact, being a good dog was the last thing he wanted him to be at the moment.

He wanted to bark. He wanted to piss on the floor. Most of all, he wanted to bite the man across the room in the worst way.

A low growl escaped his body.

*   *   *

The Montblanc ceased its forward movement and lifted from the page.

Jonathon thought he heard a sound coming from the little pooch *(I'll call him Buddy)* behind him and started to turn. A flash of movement from outside the window drew his attention before he could complete the move. He had placed his desk here—at the window of his mother's former room—because it offered an excellent view of the entire street that fronted his house. The same view that had allowed him to spy Wanda as she stumbled by, and Buddy's frantic race away from the pack of zombies chasing him, now showed something equally as interesting.

A young woman—fully alive, not like Wanda—had just come around the corner. At her feet was another little dog. *A dog like Buddy.* The mutt's nose was to the ground, weaving back and forth. He had no idea a small dog could track scents, but it was apparent that this one was doing just that. And he knew what scent was being tracked.

A shudder of annoyed frustration ran through his core. That was the bad thing about taking in a stray. More often than not, the owner will eventually come around looking for the little shit. The back yard was sprinkled with holes that had been filled with the bodies of neighborhood cats, dogs, and—in one instance—a rabbit that had somehow found its way to his front porch.

The girl stopped moving forward and stepped suddenly behind a car parked on the street three houses away. She had obviously spied the small contingent of undead that still lumbered outside the house. Unfortunately, they hadn't had time to disperse yet, which meant the girl knew exactly where her former pet (*he's mine now*) went.

The frustration of being found by Buddy's former owner was short-lived. In its place, a wonderful idea began to take shape.

"My, my," he muttered, putting down the Montblanc and pushing his chair away from the writing desk. He stepped past Buddy and exited the bedroom. He made sure the dog remained inside before closing the door securely. "I absolutely *love* this new world."

He stopped at Wanda's door on his way to the staircase and knocked. An immediate increase in the urgency of the moans coming through the door let him know she was paying attention.

"We're going to have company, Wanda."

*   *   *

Maria ducked behind the car and peeked out around the rear bumper. None of the zombies were headed in their direction, which was excellent. Apparently, they had spotted the danger ahead before it spotted them. She pulled Little Girl into her chest for a quick hug.

"You did it," she cooed to the small blond dog. "You led us to your brother."

She had no doubt that Little Boy was just ahead. Something had obviously drawn the zombies to the house. The rancid creatures didn't congregate anywhere for long, at least not without a good reason. She counted four in total. One, a balding thin man wearing torn jeans and a tattered blue t-shirt, was ambling slowly away in the opposite direction. Two more—one an overweight male in faded boxer shorts and an off-white undershirt, the other a middle aged woman wearing a tattered business suit—milled aimlessly on the front lawn. The fourth and final hurdle between her and Little Boy was a thin male cadaver. His shirtless torso was covered in tattoos. He stood shirtless and unmoving on the porch, facing the front door of the two-story house.

"Now, how are we going to get past these things?"

*   *   *

If zombies could feel surprise, Jonathon figured the one on his doorstep would have toppled over with it when he opened the front door and calmly stepped outside. The thin young zombie was shirtless; the greyish skin on his chest, back and arms was covered by intricate patterns of ink. The once-colorful torso had faded into a pallid dullness with the man's turning. It took two seconds for the inked up zombie to comprehend that a meal had just presented itself. By the time it tried to move in for a bite, it was too late.

Jonathon slid the six-inch serrated steak-knife into the right eye, spearing the brain beyond. He continued pushing even after the entire blade disappeared into the undead's socket and the inkster toppled backwards. As planned, he released the knife and reached for another—he carried four more in his left hand.

The *crump-squish* splat of Inkster's head connecting with the concrete walkway drew the attention of the two other undead freaks that occupied his front lawn. The business woman was the closer of the pair and came forward with a silent, open-mouthed glare that would have been frightful if Jonathon felt such things. His fear of others—alive or otherwise—had evaporated years ago while seated in church. He hopped from the porch, sidestepped around Inkster's unmoving form. The hand holding the blade passed between the woman's outstretched arms and found its target. He released the knife and she dropped; the blade firmly lodged in her left eye socket and the brain matter beyond.

Neither his girth nor the absurdity of his attire saved the fat man in his underwear from a similar fate. When fat man toppled over with a knife in his eye socket, Jonathon looked across the street where the young woman and the other dog waited. The woman stood, and from the look on her face, understood she had just watched him take out three zombies in less than fifteen seconds. He hoped she recognized the feat for the heroism it demonstrated, and made a mental note to highlight the accomplishment in his next journal entry. He gripped the remaining blades in his left hand and raised his right in silent greeting.

*   *   *

"What the—"

Maria didn't know what to make of the scene she had just witnessed. The man had taken out three zombies with a set of steak knives, and he hadn't displayed a single emotion. No fear, no anger, no disgust—just a matter-of-fact performance that got the job done. The guy was either super-awesome or super-crazy. It was frightening as much as it was impressive.

And now he was waving at her.

She shook her head and scooped up Little Girl from her side, where she sat shivering. Then she noticed the balding, jean-clad zombie. Attracted by the noise, it had turned around and was retracing its steps. It had its sights set firmly on the man who had taken down his... friends? She pointed at it and watched as the man—a pudgy, pale figure who looked to be in his early thirties—moved forward to meet the zombie. Like before, he showed no emotion. When the undead creature reached out to pull the man into his embrace, he casually stepped to the left, pushed the reaching hands away from his body and stabbed the knife calmly into the thing's right eye. The blade reached the brain inside, and they both watched as it collapsed to the ground.

Again, the man looked her way and beckoned her
over.

"Let's go get your brother," she whispered to Little
Girl. She leaned her shovel against the car and jogged across
the street to meet the man. He still held one blade she noticed
as she got closer and was able to confirm her suspicions—the
weapon of choice was a set of matching steak knives.

"That was impressive," she said when she reached the
edge of his yard. She stopped just inside and waited for a
response or invitation.

"Yes! Yes, it was!" A broad smile filled the man's face
and Maria had a feeling that he was more pleased with her
praise than with his own accomplishment.

"I'm Maria. This is Little Girl."

"Little Girl? I've named the other one Buddy. I hope
you don't mind."

Maria relaxed and felt the weight of concern she had
been feeling since finding Little Boy gone dissipate. He was
here.

"No, I don't mind," she waved the concern away. "I
can't even tell you what their real names are. They showed up
in our garage a while back. "Buddy" is just as good a name as
what I've been calling him."

"Let me guess," the pale man said, stepping toward
her. He held the last knife tightly. Again, his body and face
gave away no sign of any emotion or feelings. It was creepy.
"Little Boy?"

"Um. Yeah," she muttered, not liking the vibe she was
getting. She took a step backward, felt the concrete sidewalk
under her feet. "Not very creative, huh? Little Boy and Little
Girl."

The stranger stopped suddenly, turned around and headed toward his house.

"Creative? No, not really," he called over his shoulder. "But I suppose you'd like him back, so come on in and we'll get him."

Maria watched as the man passed the bodies on his lawn, stepped onto his porch, then entered the house. He didn't say another word, but left the doorway open. Telling herself she was being paranoid, she disregarded the sense of unease that had sprouted and followed behind. There was really no alternative anyway. Her dog was in the house.

It didn't make her feel any better when she stepped into the house and Little Girl—who was still tucked tightly to her left side—growled menacingly. The dog's instincts had proven correct in every instance so far; it would be foolish to discount them at this point. She quickly retreated to the walkway outside and, bracing one foot on the dead zombie's head, tugged the steak knife out of the socket. It took more effort than she would have guessed, but a couple of firm tugs—all the while still holding Little Girl—drew the weapon out of the head with a sickening *sluuurp*. She quickly passed the sticky-black blade across the jean-covered thigh of the dead man, then tucked it carefully into a back pocket. She would have to be careful not to sit on the blade less she impale herself, but its presence gave her a level of comfort as she re-entered the house.

"Hello," she called.

"Up here," she heard, and looked up. The man stood at the top of the stairway on her right. "Buddy's up here."

He turned to the left and disappeared. She checked the knife in her back pocket and, gritting her teeth against the fear, began the ascent. As soon as they reached the top of the staircase, Little Girl loosed a loud growl and began to wriggle in her grip. Afraid she might drop the dog, she set her down right away. Instead of running away as Maria expected, Little Girl put her nose to the ground and moved forward slowly. The hair on her back—what little there was—stood up in a pronounced ridge of canine aggressiveness.

Before she could take another step, the man reappeared at the end of the hallway. Held out in front of him, carried in a two-handed grip that showed how little he knew about dogs, was the writhing form of Little Boy.

The relief and excitement at seeing the dog was immediate and overwhelming. Maria cast her uncertainty aside and rushed to greet the little guy.

"You're safe!" She plucked the Chihuahua from the man's uncomfortable grip and hugged him to her breast. She turned to show him to Little Girl. "See? He's safe!"

She was about to put the dog down so he could be reunited with his sister when a sudden reverberation off the door to her right surprised her. The noise was followed by a rapid *bump-bump-bump* as something banged into the door again and again. The *bump-bump-bump* was joined by an insistent, haunting moan. She looked over to find a grayish-blue eye staring at her through a 3-inch hole that had been drilled into the door at eye level. Less than five feet and a flimsy hollow-core door stood between her and an angry zombie. She recoiled away from the door, gripping Little Boy tightly. Recognition of the danger she was in landed upon her consciousness just as a hand snaked itself around her face and landed firmly over her nose and mouth. The hand held a small bunching of cloth that smelled both foul and medicinal. The act took her by surprise and she gasped—the involuntary inhalation of breath immediately at odds with the panicked command that she issued to her lungs. *Don't breathe!* But it was too late. As so often happens, the subconscious *need* overruled the conscious *want.*

She shook her head to dislodge the grip, but she was already growing weak. Maria had just enough awareness to turn to the side as she fell. Her last though was to spare the small dog in her arms from being crushed by the weight of her body.

Chapter 31

Toad had described the situation well. The crowd of
hungry undead pushed and strained at the metal storage units
that—if properly policed—should have offered more than
sufficient protection. But the inability or unwillingness of the
humans inside to keep the creeper population under control
meant it was just a matter of time before the walls were
breached. As some point, the static weight and mass of the
barriers would be overcome by the ever-increasing weight of
the growing horde. Unfortunately for those inside—Jimbo
included—that point looked to be getting nearer by the
minute. The barriers rocked back and forth with the ebb and
flow of the undead. It wouldn't be long before the flow
pushed the metal blockade backward enough to allow the
hungry creepers entry. Cody could already envision the
event. It would start slow, with one… two… three of the
undead squeezing through a tiny gap. But it wouldn't take
long for the trickle to become a torrent. Within minutes of
the initial breakthrough, the neighborhood on the other side
would be filled with hunters.

"We got company," Mel stated with a nod of chin. A
dozen or more of the crowd were headed towards them.

"On it," Cody replied. He stepped on the gas, pulled
a tight u-turn and sped away from the small group of
creepers that had spotted the Humvee. Most of the hungry
mob were too fixated on reaching the meal waiting on the
other side of the barrier to notice them.

Cody briefly considered trying to attract the attention of the main group so he could lead them away from the barrier, but quickly discounted the idea. Pulling them away from the barrier might give those inside more time before the inevitable happened, but it would put the pack firmly on their tail, and they couldn't risk taking on that problem. Rescuing Jimbo was their primary mission. That meant getting in quickly and getting out safely. If the mob followed them now, getting in wouldn't be an issue, but getting back out might be. The last thing Cody wanted was to grab Jimbo and make their way back to the vehicle only to find it surrounded by a few hundred biters.

"Right at the intersection?"

"Yes, right at the intersection," Toad confirmed from his seat in the back. He then led them to the alley behind the brick storefronts and directed them to the area of the fence that he and Jimbo had scaled earlier. "This is the place."

Cody parked the Humvee where Toad indicated, making sure to leave just enough room on the fence-side of the vehicle for the passenger door to open. If they encountered creepers on the way out, they would use the vehicle as a shield. Two of them would position themselves at the ends of the vehicle—one at the front, another at the rear—and provide cover while the others entered through the passenger door. The two providing defense would then work back to the passenger door, with the person at the front going first, then using the door as a shield to protect the person entering from the rear. With luck, it might work.

The Ranger did a quick three-sixty scan and, seeing no sign of creepers, stepped out of the vehicle. He continued scanning the alley while systematically checking his weapons and equipment. Without the need for instruction, the other three men extricated themselves and began making their own preparations. They had discussed their entry into the neighborhood on the drive over and each knew what to do. So far, the plan was progressing as it had been drawn up, with no unwelcome surprises. Cody felt a smile cross his face and he nodded a mental "thanks" to whatever God or Gods watched over the battles of man since the dawn of human-kind. History and his personal experience showed them to be cantankerous, wishy-washy bastards who routinely scoffed at the plans of mortals and created unwanted hurdles for their own puerile amusement. So far, so good, but it didn't matter to Cody. If the Gods were on their side, great. If not, oh well. Rangers are experts at reacting, adapting and persevering.

"Time to get this thing steam cleaned," Mel observed. The front of the military vehicle was liberally caked with splattered gore and various broken pieces of the undead— some identifiable, but most not.

"I've heard they give discount car washes at Albertson's every Tuesdays. I'm waiting until then."

"What? You take it to a place for cleaning? I pegged you for a 'do-it-yourself' kinda guy."

"You ever try to get tufts of hair and brain splatter out of one of these grills?" Cody grinned and shook his head side-to-side. "No way I'm gonna do that when I can hire it out to a professional for ten bucks."

It was the inane ribbing of two soldiers mentally preparing themselves for battle, and Cody felt his nerves settle as a result of the banter. A quick glance at Toad and Barry, however, revealed two nervous-looking warriors. Toad seemed especially on edge; his eyes were wide, he swallowed repeatedly and his hands showed a minor, but perceptible tremor. Barry seemed to be holding things together for the most part, which was a testament to his maturity and former life in the Navy. But this was still the first time he might be pitted against another living person in battle.

Cody looked each man in the eye, nodded and spoke calmly. "Okay, listen up. We're going to move out exactly as we discussed. Any questions before we go?"

No one had any questions, so Mel moved into position and braced his back against the tall fence. His legs were bent slightly at the knees and extended—a step to be used by the other three. He interlaced the fingers of both hands and waited. Cody took two running steps, stepped onto Mel's right knee with his left foot and pushed upward. His right foot stepped into the step formed by the former Marine's hands and—using the offered boost—used his momentum to carry his body to the top of the fence. He quickly readied his shotgun and surveyed the yards beyond the fence. He saw no sign of danger, so gave a thumb's up signal to Barry, who quickly made his way to the top of the fence. Barry stepped over the metal prongs that formed the top of the fence, then dropped noisily into the back yard. Two minutes later, he was joined by the rest of the team.

"Toad, you follow me," Cody instructed. "Stay three meters behind. Move when I move, stop when I stop. If you see me take cover, do the same. Most importantly, make sure I don't take any wrong turns."

"Got it," the youngster acknowledged. He held the AR15 in a tight grip that turned his knuckles white. Cody considered warning the 15-year old not to shoot him by accident, but decided that would likely increase the boy's nervousness when he was doing his best to quell it. He moved on.

"Barry, you're behind Toad. Mel, you take the rear. I don't want any creepers or hostiles sneaking up on our asses."

"You got it," the Marine nodded. Cody was both amazed and pleased that the man—who up to now, had been nothing but a royal pain in the ass—seemed to have turned over a new leaf. He had witnessed it before, and often heard it characterized as a form of PTSD—post traumatic stress disorder. Regardless of the name or the formal diagnosis, he knew that some men conditioned by war sometimes find dealing with the reality of battle a lot easier than dealing with the reality of "normal" society. Mel apparently fell into this category.

Satisfied that they were as ready as they could be, Cody set out in the direction that Toad pointed out. He set a quick pace.

*   *   *

Jimbo's first real thought was that his head was exploding. The throbbing beat a steady, insistent rhythm against the inside of his skull and threatened to drag him back into the dark abyss at the slightest provocation. Unable to escape the pounding, he did the only thing he could do… he gave himself over to the agony, accepted it as an extension of his reality and swallowed it whole. Acceptance delivered just enough relief to keep him moving upward.

The second thing he felt, and the only counterpoint to the incessant pounding, was a touch of cool wetness to his face. He struggled toward the gentle, soothing touch and at last pushed through the final patch of darkness into the surface of light. He managed a weak groan and opened his eyes.

Bad idea.

"Shhh. They'll hear you." The voice was the lifeline he needed and he grabbed for it with all of his will—hung onto it.

He felt another pass of wetness and recognized the sensation of a damp cloth being gently rubbed across his brow. It reminded Jimbo of how his mother used to mop his forehead with a wet wash cloth whenever he got a fever as a child. He steeled himself and once again tried to take in his surroundings. This time, he took it slow and managed to open his eyes against the light.

"Don't move. You've got a concussion, maybe even a cracked skull."

Well, that explained the *thrung-thrumg-thrung* inside his noggin.

It didn't explain why he was bound to a chair though. Duct tape fastened his arms securely to the arms of the chair in which he sat. A quick test of his legs proved they were equally secured. *Shit.* He played back the last things he could recall and promptly put two and two together. The large room, the women being held inside, shooting two of the assholes. Then... nothing until now. It didn't take a genius to realize that someone had clobbered him from behind. Then they dragged him to this room and tied him up.

He lifted his head and saw that the woman standing next to him was the red-haired woman he had seen through the window. They were in a small kitchen-like room. Directly ahead, a single window provided a view of a single pine tree positioned in front of the ever-present cedar privacy fence. Along the right side of the room, Jimbo spotted a long counter with a sink, cabinets and a small fridge. A small table with two chairs was pushed against the left wall. He couldn't see a door, which meant it was behind them.

"Where are the assholes?"

"They're worse than just assholes," the red head offered by way of a whispered reply. The intense look of anger and hatred that crossed her face spoke volumes. "They're a sadistic bunch of *murdering, rapist assholes.*"

"So I gathered," Jimbo groaned. The bodies strewn along the streets of the neighborhood—most lined up and dispatched execution style—attested to the fact that they didn't mind killing. And the private harem they had collected here in the rec center gave credibility to the rapist claim. "Who are they?"

"The rumor is they're convicts who were released when the shit hit the fan," the woman answered. Her green eyes misted over as she spoke. "At least that's what they've been telling some of the girls."

"Damn. Any idea which prison?"

"Someplace in Colorado," she clarified. "ADS Florence, or something like that."

"ADS... you mean ADX? ADX Florence?"

"Could be," she offered with a shrug. "I've never heard of it. At least not until these guys came along."

"Ever hear of the Unibomber? How about Timothy McVeigh or Zacarias Moussaoui?" Red Head nodded. Of course she had heard of them. "Well, those are the kind of folks they keep at ADX Florence. How the hell did they get out though? That's probably the most secure prison in the U.S."

"I don't know anything about that. All I know is they showed up outside the gate a week ago, offering to help fight those monsters in exchange for a place to stay." The woman turned her head away, but not before Jimbo saw the pain in her face and a spill of tears. The strong woman he had spied through the window earlier had been replaced with a paper-thin version of her previous self. "I voted to let them in."

"Yes, you did, sweetheart!" The gravelly voice boomed across the room from the doorway behind them and Jimbo knew his time was up. "And we thank you for your support. If I recall, your hubby wasn't a big fan of ours, but you convinced him we could help. It's been a helluva party ever since!"

Three men walked around the chair and into Jimbo's line of sight. The red haired woman—he realized he still didn't know her name—stood tall and wiped the stream of tears from her face. With the arrival of the men, the stoically brave front he had spied earlier settled back across her features. The crying was quickly replaced by a stalwart resolve. She obviously was refusing to display weakness before her husband's killers.

"Tate, get her out of here. We need to speak with this young fella."

"Yessir, Bill." A fourth man stepped forward, grabbed the redhead's right elbow and pulled her forcefully from the room.

"And Tate?"

The man stopped and waited. "Sir?"

"Get her ready for me," Bill, the obvious leader of the crew, said. He reached down, adjusted the crotch of his jeans and offered a malicious grin to the woman.

*   *   *

The four men lay prone in the same spot where Toad had lain two hours earlier when he watched Jimbo get taken down. The community center was directly ahead. There was no sign of guards or any type of patrol. Except for the occasional glimpse of movement through the line of windows facing them, the building looked empty, inviting.

The same couldn't be said for the metal barrier that currently held back the crowd of hungry creepers. Situated in full view, and less than a half-block from the building they now faced, the wall of storage containers seemed to pulse under the assault being waged by the mass of undead on the far side. The chorus of moaning that came from that direction was a buzz of white noise that produced a current of fear in Cody. He felt a need to get moving quickly and wondered if Toad, Mel and Barry felt the same sense of urgency. From the way they kept glancing toward the barrier every few seconds, he was pretty sure they shared his concern.

"That's the window," Toad pointed. "He shot through that one before they took him."

Cody nodded and raised to one knee. "Okay, let's go. Follow my lead. I'm going to try to stay behind cover as much as possible, but I'm not gonna dilly-dally."

"Screw the cover," Mel countered. "Let's just haul our asses over there as fast as we can."

"Just follow me." Cody took off toward the building at a quick trot. He hugged the front of the homes he passed and tried to keep a bush or tree between himself and the windows facing them as much as possible. Within thirty seconds, he had reached the end of the row of homes and crossed the road separating them from the community center. He sprinted the last thirty feet and came to a halt with his back against the near wall. On his heels, the other three men plastered themselves to the wall. They took a moment to regain their breath and waited for any response that might be coming. A full minute passed without incident or challenge.

When it felt safe to do so, Cody pushed away from the wall, and keeping his head low, made his way to the set of windows on his left. From his pocket, the Ranger removed a small mirror attached to a long retractable rod. Taking care to make no sudden movements, he extended the rod and slowly lifted the mirror into place. Thirty to forty women were crowded into a single large room. In better times, Cody supposed it was used for a dance floor or a large dinner hall. Now, it was a refugee camp—no, that wasn't quite right—it was a prisoner camp. The sole man seated on the far side of the space, even though he appeared to be sleeping, was obviously guarding the others.

One man. Toad had spotted a larger group, so the others must be in another part of the building.

"There's a large room on the other side of these windows. Thirty to forty female hostages, one guard," he relayed to the rest of the team. "Mel and Toad, stay low and watch for any movement from the front of the building. If you're spotted by an armed male, shoot to kill. Barry and I are going to scout around the back to see if we can find the others. We'll be back in ten or less."

Cody noticed Toad glance toward the besieged barricade a half-block away. He knew what the teenager was thinking.

Hopefully, we still have ten minutes.

*   *   *

Jimbo struggled to reach the safety of the darkness, but another dousing of cold water dragged him back into the light. Not that he could see much of it. His left eye was swollen shut and his right was quickly following suit. He sputtered out the mouthful that had found its way past his busted lips and peered at the men around him.

The large, bear-like man stood over him, waiting for Bill to approve another punch to the face. His knuckles were showing signs of swelling, which was good. *At least my face can give out punishment as well as receive it,* Jimbo thought.

The third man was at the sink, filling the water bucket for another round. He seemed bored with the task he had been given. *How'd you like to change places, asshole?* Jimbo wondered how bored the man would be if *he* was the one sitting in the chair.

"Slacker, you take entirely too long to fill that bucket," Bill chided. *The guy's name was Slacker? How appropriate.*

"Well, shit Bill! Why can't I hit him for a change? Let Dink fill the damn bucket."

"Because you hit like a little girl! We'd be here all day if you were tapping his noggin' with those soft hand of yours." Bill rubbed his eyes and shook his head. "Hell, you're just lucky you're my brother."

Dink grabbed a handful of Jimbo's hair—it had grown out quite a bit in the past weeks, he realized—and drew back his right fist. He looked to Bill for approval.

"No, Dink. That ain't working." He drew a knife from his belt and waved it in front of Jimbo's face.

Hey, that's my Gerber.

"He's not talking. I think it's time we tried something a little more extreme."

"Hell yeah, Bill," Slacker added from his place by the sink. He hopped back and forth on the balls of his feet like an excited kid who needed to take a piss. "That's what I'm talkin' about!"

Bill's left hand flashed out and seized the top of Jimbo's right ear in a vise-like grip. His other hand calmly fitted the Gerber's blade into the V-shaped notch between Jimbo's ear and head.

"Where'd you come from boy?"

Jimbo clamped his swollen lips together and stared daggers at the man holding the knife. He knew he'd talk eventually, but the time hadn't come yet. *Screw you, asshole.*

The smile on Bill's face grew and the carving began.

Chapter 32

Maria awoke to the feeling of wetness on her face. Her head pounded and she could taste the residual essence from whatever chemical she had been forced to inhale. She no longer had any doubts about the man who had so calmly dispatched the zombies in his front yard. He wasn't a hero. He was a psycho. Another flash of warm wetness crossed her left cheek.

She moaned against the throbbing inside her head and strained to open her eyes. It took a moment, but when her vision cleared, she found herself face to face with Little Boy. The dog was standing in her lap, his feet planted on her chest. He immediately greeted her with another series of moist licks across the nose, eyes and forehead. She tried to pull away from the warm, insistent lashing, but found she couldn't move. Several bands of thin, nylon cord held her securely tied to an office chair.

"Oh, no."

The chair she was tied to sat in front of a large desk. Across the desk, two large windows provided good views of the street outside. On the far side of the street, she spotted the car that she and Little Girl had hid behind earlier.

A quick swivel of her head showed she was in a bedroom converted to a type of study or office. There was no bed—the desk she sat at was the focal point of the room. The door behind her was closed. To her right, a large bookshelf showed an array of black and white journals—

more than a hundred, if her estimate was correct. To the left, more of the journals sat on the floor.

Several of the notebooks—six total, she counted— were arranged on the desktop in front of her. Each was open and Maria guessed that their placement directly in front of her wasn't an accident.

She was expected to read them.

*   *   *

Buddy could stay, but this growling little bitch had to go. He held the struggling little tan-colored dog away from his body as far as he could. Although she showed them angrily, the sharp, needle-like teeth she displayed were neutralized by the hold. Unfortunately, her tiny claws—badly in need of trimming, he noticed—had raked bloody grooves along his right arm and neck before he had a chance to gain a good grip of her body.

He was considering how to dispose of the feisty canine in the most interesting manner—he had his written History to consider, after all—when Wanda slammed into the doorway beside him. Her once blue, now gray, eyes took turns looking at him hungrily through the spy hole he had drilled in the door of her bedroom. That was what he loved most about her—after the obvious physical aspects, that is. Despite the things he did to her, regardless of how he treated her, she never stopped wanting him.

The eye peering through the peephole turned toward the wriggling mutt he carried and the *snap-groan-moan* of Wanda's need filled the hallway.

Her need gave sudden clarity to his thoughts and provided a wonderful surge of inspiration.

*   *   *

Jonathon Samuel Sweeney.

What kind of creep writes about himself in the first person?

...screamed and begged...

...skin peeled easily away...

...glorious sexual release...

"What the hell?" She read passage after passage from the pages presented carefully across the top of the desk where he had left her bound.

At first, Maria couldn't fathom what she was reading; couldn't get her mind fully around what the words and phrases actually *meant.* But slowly, as the minutes passed, a picture of her captor began to emerge—a picture that horrified and disgusted her to the core. If the words scrawled across the pages in front of her were true, this man was... evil... a demented creature who was more of a monster than the zombies outside could ever be.

The scrawled words and phrases shined a light on the dark horror that had taken over the man's soul. Torture, rape, murder. His own mother, killed and then buried in the back yard. Just when Maria didn't think the horror could get any worse, she read about Wanda, his pet zombie—his pet *female* zombie. She suddenly recalled the undead eye staring through the hole in the hallway door, and realized that she had already met the object of his most intensely disturbed scribblings. And this sick man now had her bound up tightly in his study. She shivered, despite the afternoon heat pouring in through the large windows. The overwhelming need to get away from this man—this place—overtook her being, and she began worrying at the tight bindings that held her wrists to the chair.

Flex-pull-flex.

Flex-pull-flex.

*   *   *

Cheech had jumped from The Girl's lap minutes before and lay curled up in his spot under the table. Noticing her anxious movements, he trotted over, sat at her feet and released a single, worried whine. He was glad she had found him, and pleased that she was awake now; but she was still unable to move—unable to help Daisy.

His concern for Daisy's safety gnawed roughly at his being. The Bad Man had taken her from the room and Cheech could hear the monster nearby, as well as Daisy's occasional menacing growl. It was her real growl—not the pretend one she used when they were playing—and the fear that it conveyed passed easily through the door.

*   *   *

He waited patiently at the top of the stairs for Wanda to settle down. From previous experience, he knew it took between ten and fifteen minutes for her to forget that someone was on the other side of her door. Her

forgetfulness was accompanied by quiet and calm and—right
on time—the moaning and her beating against the door
slowed, then stopped.

It was time, and he moved toward the door.

His shoulders ached with the effort of holding the
little blond bitch at arms' length. She had tired herself out
with the angry growling and constant struggling, and now
hung limply in his grasp. But he refused to relax his grip for
fear that she would get a second wind and sink her teeth into
his hand or use her nails on him again. The damage was
mostly superficial—a few bloody gashes and scrapes along his
hands and arms—but he preferred to be the one dispensing
the pain, not the one receiving it.

A peep into the room showed Wanda facing away
from the door, her focus fully on the window on the far side
of the room and the street and houses beyond. He usually
found her this way, with her attention on the outside world
and her back to him. It made his task easier. Because she
was drawn to noise, he had oiled the hinges on the door early
on to facilitate a noiseless entrance.

He worried that the mutt would give them away. She
was obviously well aware of Wanda's presence—she
squirmed and growled each time they passed her door. But
he only needed a moment to do what was required on this
visit, so quickly dismissed the concern.

Without delaying another moment, he gripped the
tiny dog in his right hand, quietly released the deadlock he
had installed on the outside of the door with his left, and
twisted the handle. He pushed the door open just a crack and
tossed the mutt inside. He was pleased to hear her land

noisily as he pulled the door shut and flipped the deadbolt back into place.

A rush of raucous movement and Wanda's excited moaning filled the air and he put his eye near the 3-inch peep hole.

Success!

He watched Wanda pull the squirming dog to her mouth. He delighted at the shrill squeal of fear and pain when Wanda took a mouthful of tiny ear and bit down hard. Began to chew. For such a tiny dog, she certainly had a set of lungs capable of the loudest cry.

Beautiful!

His friends next door were no doubt listening to the commotion so he rushed over to observe their reactions.

Chapter 33

The reconnaissance of the Drummer Park
community center ended promptly and successfully. Using
the hand-held mirror to check every window, Cody and Barry
quickly determined the layout of the building and the location
of five men inside. One side of the large building was the
open area where the women were being held captive by a
single guard. A hallway separated the larger area from a series
of five smaller rooms on the far side. The two rooms
farthest from the front entrance were packed with food
supplies and bottled water. The middle room was a small
kitchen. It was in this room that they spotted Jimbo and
three of the men. The young Ranger didn't look good, but
he was alive. The next room used to be a small gym, but had
been turned into a sleeping and living area. A single man and
a woman occupied that space, and it was easy to tell that the
woman wasn't there willingly. The room at the front of the
building doubled as a reception desk and lounge area. The
front door opened directly into this room.

Cody described the layout to Toad and Mel, then laid
out his plan.

"Mel, I want you to enter through the front, while I
enter through the rear. If we're quiet, we should be able to
reach the second and third rooms before they know we're
inside. Once we're in position, I'll move first on the three in
the kitchen. You take out the man in the gym."

"Got it," the former Marine stated simply. Cody had no doubt that he did have it.

"Barry, I want you outside the window to the large room. Wait until you hear us firing. The guard inside will probably turn to investigate. When he does, take him out. Shoot him in the back if you have to. We're not here to be noble, just to get our asses out alive."

"I can handle that," the Navy man nodded.

"What about me?"

"Toad, I want you to keep an eye on that barricade." All four men looked toward the metal storage containers just down the street. The rocking back and forth had intensified since they had arrived. They all knew it wouldn't hold for long. "When we start shooting, the natives are bound to get even more restless. If they're gonna break through, it'll be then."

"Okay," the youngster agreed. "I'll follow Mel to the front and watch from there."

"Makes sense," Cody acknowledged. He'd have a better line of sight from the front and could provide backup against the men inside if needed. He looked at each man in turn. "Any questions?"

There weren't any.

Cody watched as Mel and Toad crouch-walked under the windows toward the front of the building. He withdrew the 9mm pistol from his thigh holster, clapped Barry on the shoulder and then turned to make his way to the back entrance. He waited at the entrance for a count of ten, then slowly twisted the knob on the exterior door. As before when he first checked, it was still unlocked. He quickly ran through what might happen in the next sixty seconds, and considered his reactions to each potential scenario. Ideally, when he opened the door, the hallway would be empty except for Mel, who should be entering from the front at any moment. The Ranger NCO drew a deep breath, readied his weapon, and opened the door.

Screeeeech!

Of course the door had to squeal like a banshee. Couldn't be helped now. Cody stepped through quickly, released the door, and quick-stepped down the hall, his weapon pointed at the third door.

Screeeeeech! The obnoxious squeal repeated its announcement that someone had just entered the building as the door was pulled shut by its automatic closure mechanism.

Dammit!

*   *   *

Screeeeech!

Bill stopped slicing. Was that the back door? He mentally counted his men and where they should be. None of them should be anywhere near the back door.

Screeeeech!

Definitely the back door.

"Dink, go see what the hell is going on."

*   *   *

Cody was almost running as he passed the first storage room and gave a quick glance inside. He repeated the process as he passed the second storage room. Because of his noisy entry, he had no time to investigate the rooms properly; all he could do was assume that the men were still in their previous positions. He spied Mel moving toward him from the front of the building. At least that part of the plan was going well.

He slowed his forward movement as he approached his objective, the third doorway that led to the kitchen. The pistol was held up and out, ready to remove any target that might present itself. Without warning, one did.

A large man exited the kitchen and turned toward him. Cody didn't hesitate. Before the man had a chance to register the first glimmer of surprise, a 9mm round tore through his chest and destroyed any chance his heart had of ever pumping blood again. The second and third rounds that Cody delivered to the falling torso were merely insurance.

Without pausing to consider his handiwork, Cody vaulted over the body and turned into the kitchen. Two targets. One was directly ahead, armed with a knife. The other, a thin man fumbling awkwardly with a large caliber revolver, stood off to the right.

Two pulls of the trigger removed the immediate threat, and the thin man—minus a large portion of skull and brains—dropped to the floor. Cody nudged the barrel left toward the man with the knife. Only he no longer held the knife. Instead, his hands—bloody hands—were held high. Cody eased off the trigger just a smidge.

For the first time since entering the building, the Ranger relaxed and allowed his thinking-self to step forward and regain jurisdiction over the instinctual-self that had been in control to this point. Without taking his eyes or weapon off of the man standing in front of him, Cody allowed his senses to take in what was happening elsewhere in the building.

He heard Mel's "All clear" announcement at the same time as he heard a bark of fire from behind him. That would be Barry taking out the guard in the large room. The sudden outburst of screaming and crying that drifted over from the room informed him that the women there were upset and surprised about what had just happened. All normal noises; ones that he expected to hear.

Then he heard the sound that he hadn't expected. It was the bark of Toad's AR15 coming from the front of the community center.

He knew what that sound meant.

"Unnhh." Jimbo moaned and Cody dropped his eyes to his friend for the first time. He could only see him from behind, but a heavy wash of blood covered his entire right side. These clowns had been torturing him.

"I give up, man," the man standing over Jimbo said. He lifted his bloody hands even higher in the air. "You can't shoot me. I'm unarmed."

"Yeah, well so was he," Cody stated before pulling the trigger of the 9mm once more. The round entered the man's right eye and punched a large hole out of the back of his head. He collapsed in a heap next to his partner. Neither would be joining the creeper ranks.

Two more barks from Toad's AR15 announced a new danger.

Chapter 34

The door opened behind her. Maria's emotions boiled as the pudgy psychopath entered the room.

"Buddy, why don't you wait in the hallway?"

She watched over her shoulder as the male Chihuahua was booted toward the door. To his credit, he showed his full set of teeth and tried to bite the foot that moved him out of the room. When the door closed, he began scratching to get back in.

"What did you do to Little Girl," she demanded. The sound of pain and hurt that had come through the thin wall just moments before made her want to cry with anguish. Jonathon stepped beside her, then moved closer. She shivered with involuntary revulsion as he placed his body fully against her. Was that an erection poking into her shoulder?

"Let's just say that little bitch gives new meaning to the term 'dog food'."

"You...you didn't!"

"Oh, but I did," he insisted. He rubbed his groin against her again and she struggled to move away from the contact. She was only moderately successful; the binds that held her did their job quite well. "Wanda was quite hungry. It's been some time since she ate."

Maria clamped down on the tears that threatened to flow. The pain of losing the little Chi was almost more than she could stand. She wanted to bawl at the loss, but knew it would do her no good. Instead, she focused on the ember of fury that had begun to form in her chest. She channeled her thoughts toward this monster and fanned the ember into a ball of heated rage. She wanted to hurt Jonathon Samuel Sweeney. Badly. She imagined raking his eyes with her claws, stomping his pudgy cheeks into mush, kicking him repeatedly as he rolled on the ground. Her hands pulled helplessly at the cords that kept her from acting out her aggressions. Unable to act against him with her fists, she lashed out with the only weapon she had—her words.

"So, is Wanda your girlfriend? I'm not surprised the only girl you could get would be a dead one."

The grinding against her shoulder stopped.

"My girlfriend? I guess you could call her that," he replied. Instead of being offended, he seemed to accept the question at face value. "She has advantages over most females. Present company included."

"Really? And what would those be? Rankness? Inability to converse?" The fury bubbled over and Maria tried again to push a button or two. "Don't tell me… she's great in bed."

Still, Jonathon either didn't recognize that he was being goaded or didn't care.

"You got two out of three. Not bad," he stated with an air of approval. He followed up with a chuckle. "Unfortunately, she *is* getting a bit stale. It may be time for a replacement."

His fingers reached out and stroked tenderly through Maria's hair just as she began to comprehend the statement.

*   *   *

"Nooo!"

"Oh, yes," Jonathon calmly reaffirmed to the struggling teen. This was his favorite part. The moment when his prey realized that they were his to play with as he wished. The Bitch had begged and pleaded with him—promising all sorts of unconventional pleasures in exchange for her release. But he had seen through those false promises. It was good while it lasted, but like all good things it had to end. And he had taken his pleasures anyway. This one would be no different.

He seized the girl's hair and pulled her head roughly toward his straining erection. He humped against the side of her face. Her crying and pathetic struggling only added to the experience and he quickly found release. He pushed her head away from his body but maintained his hold on her hair while he regained his breath.

The unplanned act sated him momentarily, but it wouldn't last. He needed to get her to Wanda soon. A quick nip in an out-of-the-way spot—on the hand, or perhaps on the foot—should do the trick. Then he'd have to wait for her to turn, of course. But after that...she would be all his.

"Buddy, stop scratching at the door!" The little mutt issued an angry growl in response, and Jonathon Samuel Sweeney began to reconsider his desire for a pet. Male or not, the dog was rapidly becoming a disappointment.

Chapter 35

"Mel, get Jimbo and the women and take them out the back door," Cody directed. Toad's AR15 barked again, then again. Either he was missing the mark, or more creepers were beginning to push through the opening they had made. "Jimbo's injured so you won't be able to move fast, but head north so the building stays between your group and the barricade. Hopefully, none of them will spot you. We'll draw the Z's through the front to buy you some time."

"Got it," the Marine replied. "We'll head north until we're out of sight and then cut west. Meet you back at the house where we came in?"

"It's as good a rally point as any. We can hold out there while we arrange for transportation." The distinctive *craaack* of Barry's hunting rifle joined the AR15. Not good. "Quick, go!"

Cody didn't wait for a response. He turned and sprinted for the front of the rec center. He arrived to find Toad kneeling inside the front door, his rifle barrel pointed toward the barricade. Barry was crouched behind a window on the right; his weapon pointed in the same direction. A quick glance outside showed a half-dozen creeper bodies sprawled between their location and the metal barrier. The right side of the metal wall showed movement as more of the undead tried to push past. The sheer number of creepers trying to force themselves through the small opening was acting as a bottle neck, and worked to the defenders' advantage. But for how long? As an answer to the unspoken question, three of the staggering forms burst through the congested opening. They paused momentarily to look around, then headed directly for the three men.

"Watch my back," Cody ordered. "Save ammo if you can."

The Berretta 9mm was back in its holster. The Mossberg was still looped over his right shoulder. From the scabbard he had slung over his left, he drew the dented Easton XL1 and trotted toward the three figures heading his way. He met the first creeper at a near-sprint. The emaciated corpse was little more than a walking scarecrow of bones in a pair of baggy gym shorts but the swing connected with his forehead and bowled him over backwards. The cracking sound as aluminum slammed into bone let Cody know that this one was down for good. He turned with the swing and did a full three-sixty loop. At the end of the loop, his weapon rained a vicious blow to the crown of the second moaning deader. It too dropped. He was facing off against the third when double shots rang out. He completed the trifecta and looked toward the barricade.

Holy crap.

The dam had apparently burst. More than a dozen creepers were headed his way, and more were pushing through the ever-widening gap between the container on the right and the fence against which it had been placed.

He elected to initiate a strategic withdrawal and began dropping back slowly. His pace allowed the quickest of his pursuers to catch up, which was exactly what he wanted. Whenever the lead stumbler got close enough, he paused his retreat just long enough to deliver a head blow. In a zone, Cody no longer recognized individual details of the creepers.

His only concern was swing, retreat, swing, retreat. The plan worked great until he mistimed a swing and missed. Instead of connecting with his target's head, the tip of the Easton merely grazed the undead man's cheek. The miss threw off his balance which allowed the creeper to reach out and snag the right arm of his leather jacket. The undead hunter was about to take a taste when a crack of Toad's AR15 punched a hole in the center of his forehead. It was highly unlikely the bite could have broken through the thick leather covering his arm, but Cody felt relieved to know he was being protected from behind. The close call caused him to abandon his slow retreat. He took out one more of the growing trail of undead, then turned tail and ran back to the center. He tried to catch a glimpse of Mel or the group he was leading, and was pleased that he saw no sign of them. If all was going to plan, they should be well on their way.

He, Toad and Barry now had to conduct their own escape.

*   *   *

Jimbo leaned against the red head and did his best not to move his head as they shuffled-walked along the street. It was an impossible task, though, especially with his left arm thrown across her shoulders for support, his inability to see more than ten feet ahead, and his need to carry his retrieved weapons and gear. He was full reliant upon her and she seemed fully prepared to accept the job. For that he was grateful. He wasn't capable of moving on his own and, from the sound of gunfire behind them, he knew they'd have creepers on their ass if they didn't get away from the rec center quickly.

Despite the circumstances, he couldn't believe that Sarge had somehow conscripted Mel Thompson—the asshole of the neighborhood, of all people—to the cause. That was a story he was anxious to hear, though he'd probably have to listen with his left ear. His right was still lying on the floor of the small kitchen, probably hidden beneath Bill or Slacker's bodies. His ear for their deaths—it was a good trade. The young soldier laughed and received a questioning look from the red head.

"What could you possibly find funny in all of this?"

"Long story," he explained. Talking made his head hurt worse. "When we get out of here, I'll fill you in."

The woman nodded in silent agreement and trudged resolutely onward, trying to close the distance between them and the next small group ahead. They were at the rear of the pack, which is where Jimbo had asked to be placed. Even injured, he could hold and fire a rifle if the need arose.

"By the way," he began, wincing with each word. "What's your name?"

"Monica," she replied. "What's yours?"

"James. But my friends call me Jimbo."

"Well, it's a pleasure to meet you, Jimbo."

*   *   *

The front of the center was filling up quickly. At Toad's suggestion, they had pulled a table across the hallway and lodged the ends in the doorways leading to the large

room and the gym. Being directly across the hall from each
other was a boon because it provided them with the perfect
short-term barrier. The pressure of the creepers held the
table in place long enough for the trio to use their hand
weapons—Cody's Easton, Toad's kukri machete, and Barry's
ax—to slow the tide. Putting down the first line of undead
proved effective at increasing the size of the barrier that
stood between them and the masses that were pressing
forward through the front door.

Unfortunately, the room on the far side of the table
was rapidly diminishing, which meant the overflow would be
forced to bypass the front door. Once that happened, the
enemy would be behind them.

"I think it's time to beat a hasty retreat, guys," Barry
offered. Cody had to agree. They had slowed the advance as
much as they could. Hopefully, it would be enough to allow
the women and Jimbo to escape.

"We're heading north," Cody indicated with a nod
toward the back door. "When we get far enough away from
any prying eyes, we turn west and meet the other group at the
house by the Humvee. Any questions?"

"Do we stay together on the way, or just haul ass as
fast as we can?" Toad posed a good question.

"We haul ass as fast as the slowest man can move."
Cody forced himself not to look in the retired Navy man's
direction, but Toad had no such filter.

"Kid, before the shit hit the fan, I was running two
marathons a year," Barry replied. "You may get out in front
at the beginning, but I'll be carrying your ass over the long
haul."

Toad laughed and nodded. "Sorry, man."

"Don't be sorry. Just be safe and keep up."

"You two done?" Cody asked. He was quietly glad that he hadn't been the one to push Barry's buttons. Otherwise, he might be the one with something to prove. "We've got chompers breathing down our backs. Let's move."

Screeeech! Once again, Cody was caught off guard by the obnoxious squeal. Noise was the last thing they needed. He waited for the other two to pass him before gritting his teeth and leaning into the door. He made sure it was closed securely before he turned and gave chase. As he crossed the parking lot, he couldn't help but notice he was in the rear as they raced away from the building. He increased his pace and pushed to catch up.

The mob of overflow creepers was just making its way around the building when they turned left at the first intersection.

A line from *Jurassic Park*, one of his favorite movies as a child, popped into his head.

Must go faster. Must go faster.

Chapter 36

"How do you think this all come about?"

The question caught Maria off guard. One moment,
this psycho was humping her face; the next he was asking her
strange questions as if the previous three minutes hadn't
taken place. He seemed totally removed from the fact that he
had her tied to a chair; and that he had basically informed her
that she was being prepped to be his next zombie girlfriend—
though she'd prefer that fate over being his real one. The
only thing creepier than having to put out for him as one of
the undead was the thought of having sex with him while all
of her senses were intact.

To say that she was utterly freaked out was like calling
the Grand Canyon a hole in the ground. Her legs trembled
with trepidation and she fought to hold back her tears. She
was worried for her life, but the emotions didn't stop there.
A white-hot rage threatened to bubble free, and she gritted
her teeth against the accusations and curses she so badly
wanted to hurl in his direction. The abuse that this pudgy
little excuse for a man had heaped upon her, his previous
victims and—perhaps most appalling to Maria—the little dog
she had brought into this house, was almost too much to
bear. The painfully insistent throb that heralded an over-full
bladder didn't help. But she refused to let him see the affect
he was having on her. The few pages that she had read of his
journals showed just how demented and vicious he could be.
Maintaining her composure—if only on the outside—was
her only option.

"How did *what* come about?" The retort left her mouth with more testiness than she had intended. He didn't seem to care or pretended not to notice.

"Don't play dumb," he replied casually. "How did we suddenly find ourselves in this wonderful new world?"

He was talking about the zombies. As if *she* knew how it came to be that the dead no longer stayed dead. Fine, she'd play along. She had kept up with the on-line conversations and reporting that had shepherded the downfall of society. The fact was that no one—at least no one that was talking, or that seemed credible—really knew how the end of the world started. Rumors were rampant, of course, and everyone espoused their own theories and accusations, dependent largely on their previous personal beliefs. Conspiracy theorists claimed biological warfare as the cause. Evangelicals cited God's wrath, and laid the blame on man's sinful ways. The more scientific-minded wondered if a mutated flu virus was the cause. Still others blamed aliens, Communists, ancient curses, a shift in the polar magnetic field, tainted seafood, evolution, solar flares, poisoned Girl Scout cookies, yadda, yadda, yadda. Except for the poisoned cookies—Maria was partial to Tagalongs—she felt it didn't really matter. Just pick one and run with it.

"Aliens."

"Excuse me?"

"You heard me," she stated, putting a serious face on the bullshit she was spinning. "Aliens did this. They want our planet for themselves. What better way to get our natural resources than to have us eat each other? Once we're all dead…or undead…they'll swoop down in their giant motherships and take over."

Jonathon Samuel Sweeney stared down at her, mouth agape.

*   *   *

You. Little. Bitch.

And to think he had wasted time trying to make conversation.

He wanted to slap her, but couldn't. He needed her face in pristine condition, otherwise she'd be marred when she underwent the change and keep the mark forever—or at least for as long as he decided to possess her. That wouldn't do, so he bit back his anger, swallowed his pride. Instead of reacting to her blatant patronization, he ignored the slight. Thoughts of what he would do with her later acted as a salve to his wounded ego, and he smiled. Decided to lay along with her idiocy.

"Aliens. Yes, that's a definite possibility."

"Then again, maybe it's the poisoned Girl Scout cookies."

"No, no," he grinned. "I'm sure it's the aliens. I'll have to thank them when the motherships arrive."

The girl—Maria—offered a slight nod and a grunt in reply.

It was time to take the next step. Enough time had passed for Wanda to have eaten her snack, though he hadn't heard another peep from the pooch since the first bite, which seemed strange. Regardless, he had no doubt Wanda had done her job. He also had no doubt that she'd be hungry for more. A dog that size couldn't be considered a proper meal.

The question was "how" to best accomplish the task. He put his mind to the problem and quickly had the solution.

Maria sat in a rolling chair. He'd roll her to Wanda's door, push her hand inside the room, and wait for the inevitable to take place. Fortunately the door opened inward, so Wanda's urgency to get at the snack would put pressure against it, and keep her contained during the process. The real trick would be retrieving the offered hand before any serious munching could take place. Oh well, he'd just have to cross that bridge when he came to it.

"Are you ready to meet Wanda now?"

*   *   *

Maria shuddered as the rolling chair was shoved toward the study door.

Her bladder ached mightily and she labored to keep her screams and her piss from escaping her body.

Little Boy scratched furiously at the other side of the door but stopped when the psycho bumped her knees against the wall beside it. He turned her sideways so he could reach the handle and the little Chi sprang into the room as soon as the door cracked open.

"Stay back, Buddy," the creep ordered as he opened the door fully. The hallway beyond was dark and smelled rank. The room next door would smell even worse.

"His name's not Buddy," Maria announced. Knowing his plans for her, she was no longer concerned with not trying to piss him off.

"Of course it is," he countered. "He's my dog now, so I get to name him. I might even re-name you, once we make you better. I never really liked the name Maria. How about... Rhonda?"

"Really, asshole? Wanda and Rhonda? Is that the best you can do?"

In response, he rolled her through the door and slammed her knees roughly against the far wall once...twice...a third time. The third slam caused her right knee to punch a hole in the drywall and a sharp pain flashed through both legs, but Maria felt a small twinge of victory at getting under his skin. He turned her to the right and pushed her along the carpet until they stopped directly in front of the door where he kept Wanda. Maria wondered briefly what the girl's real name had been when she was still alive.

"Stay here," Jonathon grinned. "I'll be right back."

He moved to the stairway at the end of the hallway and disappeared down the steps.

She released a long sigh and dropped her chin to her chest. She was screwed. Little Boy took the opportunity to jump into her lap and she felt a hint of comfort at his presence.

"Hey, little guy," she cooed. The dog gave a small whine and pasted two quick licks to her forehead. Maria felt as if the dog understood her plight. For sure, he could feel her apprehension. "I don't suppose you can chew through rope, huh?"

Maria's relief was short-lived as her tormentor returned two minutes later. He carried another one of the steak knives he had used on the zombies outside earlier. The sight of the weapon reminded her that she had shoved a

matching implement into her back pocket before she entered
this hellhole of a house. She couldn't tell if it was still there;
not that it did her any good anyway.

Before she had a chance to wonder what he planned
to do with the knife, he set to work on the binding that
secured her right hand and arm. He was cutting her loose.

Bumpf!

The door rattled in its frame as Wanda slammed
against the far side.

Bumpf! Bumpf! Bumpf!

*   *   *

The loud banging noises pounded inside his head and
the rancid smell of the nearby monster assaulted his sensitive
nose. Combined with the waves of fear pouring off The
Girl, the mixture pushed Cheech past his breaking point. He
had been trained against aggression, but the need to *growl-
bark-bite-attack* was upon him—consumed him. The monster
in the next room was out of reach, but the Bad Man was not.

Without a shred of fear, he launched himself at the
large figure.

*   *   *

One moment, he was kneeling beside the chair, the
task of sawing through the girl's bonds nearly complete. The
next, he had a savage, growling dog attached to his cheek.
The side-to-side ripping motion of the dog's maw didn't hurt
so much as it surprised him. The anger and ferocity of the

attack caused him to fall backwards onto his ass, and his back
slammed heavily against Wanda's door. With his back pressed
against the hollow core door, he easily could feel the thumps
of her insistent beating on the other side.

His first reaction was to stab the little mutt, but his
hands were empty—the knife dropped in the attack. His
second thought was to yank the small body from his face.
With a grunt of anger, he pulled at the raging dog and tossed
him into the far wall. It obviously wasn't enough to deter the
little shit, because he hit the ground and immediately
launched a second attack.

Jonathon pushed backwards against the door in an
attempt to retreat. He heard the door reply to his actions
with an ominous cracking sound.

*   *   *

There!

The knife was still in her back pocket and she
struggled to free it. Little Boy's attack had given her a chance
to save them both and she was determined not to waste it.

She watched in horror as the man threw the small dog
against the wall. Her horror turned to amazement as the little
Chihuahua ignored the abuse and launched a second assault.
The initial skirmish had left a deep gouge in Jonathon's right
cheek that dripped blood down his face and onto his neck. It
was unlikely that a second attack would be as effective now
that the man was ready. Despite his ferocity and
perseverance, the canine was no match for a grown man—

which made her efforts to retract the knife all the more important.

With a final tug, she freed the blade and, without any second thoughts, drove it downward into the man with all the strength she could marshal with one arm. She aimed for his chest but was off target and the knife sank deeply into the man's left shoulder.

He howled with the new wound and, ignoring the dog, grabbed for the knife's handle.

"You are so gonna get it now, you Mexican *bitch*!"

The remark sent Maria's anger over the edge; she had passed her daily limit of physical and verbal abuse. She reached out and snatched at the handle, fighting with the injured man to win a better grip. Little Boy took that moment to leap at Jonathon's injured face once more and delivered another wicked bite. Jonathon reacted instinctively. He gave up on the knife and delivered a powerful swat. The small canine was tossed into the wall of the hallway for a second time. The action provided Maria with the opening she needed and she reached the handle easily. She gripped it tightly in her free hand, then gave it a violent twist and a strong pull. The twist caused Jonathon to cry out in renewed agony; the pull withdrew the blade from his shoulder.

She didn't hesitate.

*   *   *

Jonathon Samuel Sweeney felt the blade slice into his neck, but the pain was minimal. The powerful jet of red that splashed across the hallway, however, was not. He reached up

to investigate the damage and found a long slash stretching
from his right ear to his left. Another heartbeat sent a second
geyser of blood onto the carpeted floor.

His vision clouded and he struggled to staunch the
flow.

You bitch.

I can't die now. This is my *time. My world.*

The encroaching cloud grew darker and darker, while
the circle of light through which he viewed the world grew
smaller and smaller.

At least my History will survive…

*   *   *

She cut the cords securing her left arm, then worked
on releasing her legs. Once free from the restraints, she
pushed with her feet to roll herself and the chair away from
the red puddle that had begun to surround the dead body of
her kidnapper. She also wanted as much space as she could
get between herself and the undead body of Wanda, who
continued to beat against the door.

Bumpf! Bumpf!

The Chihuahua lay a few feet away, staring at her and
panting.

"Little Boy, you okay?"

In response, he lifted himself gently and walked
toward her. He was moving slowly, but he wasn't limping and
he wasn't making any "I'm hurt" noises. All things
considered, those seemed like good signs.

Bumpf!

"That's a good boy," she called while kneeling down to his level. "You're a *very* good boy."

His tail wagged twice, then he was at her side. She reached down to pet the little wonder that had saved her life and was rewarded with several warm laps of tongue.

Bumpf!

"Just a minute, Wanda," she called out to the poor soul behind the door. "Let me thank my friend. Then I'll take care of you."

The dog and the young woman shared a few quick moments of each other's company. When Maria finally couldn't take another *Bumpf!* she released the dog from her embrace and made her way to the door. She was careful to not step on Jonathon's body, but she couldn't avoid making prints in the blood pooling around him. The fact that she was treading in the sticky redness didn't affect her as much as it would have only hours before.

Wanda's eye stared malevolently from the hole that had been drilled in the door. The blue-gray gaze locked onto the brown eyes looking back at her and the *Bumpf! Bumpf! Bumpf!* of the zombie's attack on the door escalated to a fevered pitch. Maria no longer feared the creature behind the doorway. Now, all she felt was an intense sadness at how this... *thing*... had once been a living, breathing person. She had been someone's daughter, someone's friend, a sister perhaps.

The now-familiar moaning sound joined the banging and the eye pressed closer to the hole. The blade, still slick with the blood of their kidnapper, entered the hole...then Wanda's eye... and then her brain, smoothly and without pause. Moments later, the undead was made dead and dropped loudly to the floor.

A thin bark from the other side of the door announced another's presence inside the room.

"Little Girl?" Maria squealed, her surprise overpowered only by the sudden elation she felt at the dog's apparent survival. Little Boy yipped beside her and she quickly pushed her way into the room.

Chapter 37

It took twenty minutes for Cody and his two partners to find their way back to the home where they were to meet Mel, Jimbo and the women they had rescued. Their route through the twisting turns of the unfamiliar neighborhood took them down two dead end cul-de-sacs before they finally found the street they wanted and made it to the rally point. As a result, they arrived at the home at the same time as the tail end of the large group, which included Jimbo and the woman helping him.

Unfortunately, the mistakes also allowed the leading edge of the creeper pack to keep them in sight. Cody guessed they had a two- to three-minute lead on the closest followers and quickly ushered everyone into the house.

Jimbo looked to be in bad shape. His face was nearly unrecognizable, and blood from the severed ear covered his right side. On a positive note, he held his weapon firmly and seemed in control of his senses, which meant the damage probably looked much worse than it really was. At least that was Cody's hope. Someone had wrapped a bandage around his head, which was good, but they needed to get him back to their neighborhood for a full evaluation and some real treatment.

"What's the... plan... Sarge," Toad panted as they pushed inside the home. Mel had most of the women settled in the back portion of the large house, and had re-joined the soldiers in the front room. "We're not all... gonna fit in the... Humvee. We need... transportation."

Despite the teen's earlier claims of physical superiority, the run through the neighborhood—Cody guessed they had covered about two miles—had worn the youngster out. Cody felt like he could go another six miles easily, and Barry, who was watching for creepers through the front window, didn't even look winded. *So much for youthful exuberance*, he thought before turning his mind to the problem at hand.

"Toad, take over from Barry and watch the front. Make sure none of those creepers breaks in. A handful shouldn't be able to get in, but if they assemble in mass, alert Mel and Barry and do what you can to slow them down.

"Barry, I need you to find a couple of ladders. Try this garage first. If you don't find two here, go next door— but make sure you cross the fence between the houses so you stay out of sight from our friends outside. Once you've got the ladders, set one on the near side of the fence where we came over. The other one goes on the far side. We need to make sure we've got an easy exit point so that everyone can get over the fence quickly. Got it?"

"Got it," the Navy man acknowledged, then set off on his assigned task.

"Mel, you and Toad—" Cody glanced at Jimbo who was reclined backward, but paying close attention, on the staircase at their right. "—and Jimbo, I need you guys to hold out here until I get back."

"Where you headed, Army?" Mel asked. Good question.

"I'm going to lead our friend down the street, then circle back here and see if we can't get some transportation."

"You just gonna take 'em on a chase in the opposite direction? That your plan?"

"Unless you've got a better one, yeah."

"Modified z-trap, Sarge" Jimbo offered weakly. All heads turned toward the injured man who—with the help of the red head—pushed himself into a seated position. He spoke slowly through bloody, cracked lips, but focused on the enunciation of each word so his idea was clearly understood. "Lead them to a house down the block. Make sure they see you enter it and leave the front door open. Exit through the back door. Just be sure to close the back door behind you. Then get your ass back here using a backyard route."

Cody ran the scenario through a quick, mental review and nodded appreciatively. It was a good plan.

"That's my zombie expert," he said. Then he stood up, adjusted his gear, and prepared to leave the relative safety of the house. "Anything else?"

"Good luck," the woman helping Jimbo offered. "And be careful."

Cody nodded his thanks. He could use all the luck he could get. Being careful was a bit wishful, though. He was heading out to engage a group of creepers on a mixed game of tag and hide-n-seek, after all.

Sixty seconds later, he was being chased—albeit slowly—by a group of half a dozen of the enemy. He scanned the street ahead for a good house to use for the plan and spied a tan, two-story behemoth just ahead. He turned to gauge the distance to the undead posse on his tail and slowed his momentum. He wanted them anxious and eager when he led them into the home. Satisfied that they were

following, he jogged onto the home's front porch and tried
the door.

Locked, of course.

He debated trying to kick the door open, but quickly
dismissed that approach. He didn't want to pit the strength
of his leg against the strength of the dead bolt. He might
win the contest, but he needed both legs in good working
order, so he couldn't risk the potential injury. Besides, noise
at this point wasn't a bad thing. A blast of two from the
Mossberg would help draw the hunters to his location. He
took three steps back, put the weapon to his shoulder, and
fired a single blast into the door. The lock held, but just
barely. An easy kick with his right boot pushed the door
inward. He glanced backwards to make sure he was still
being trailed and—seeing the first of the creepers only a
house away—stepped into the house.

And right into the arms of one of the undead.

The attack was immediate and Cody knew the creeper
must have been standing right inside the door. *How stupid can
you be, Cody*, he asked himself as he was knocked sideways and
got pinned against the wall to their left. The proximity of
snapping teeth and that God-awful insistent moaning
informed him that the creature was doing its best to rip a
chunk of flesh from his neck. Fortunately, the neck guard
that Jimbo had insisted he wear was doing its job. On the
down side, the face shield on his helmet was in the open
position, which allowed the creature's rancid breath to wash
over his nose and mouth.

The sudden urge to vomit was strong but Cody
swallowed the bile out of necessity and struggled to free
himself from the close contact. The arms circling his torso

prevented him from bringing the shotgun into play, so he
released it and reached for the 9mm pistol on his thigh. He
couldn't reach it.

Quickly abandoning an armed response, he ignored
the evil snapping of teeth against his neck and concentrated
on reestablishing his footing and center of balance. He
shoved away from the wall with his left elbow while thrusting
against the monster clinging to his side with his right. The
movement put him back on the balls of his feet and gave him
a chance. He pushed aside the thought of the creepers now
approaching the house and focused on ending the current
battle as quickly as possible. He brought his right arm up and
levered it between his body and the creeper's until it was
pointed at the ceiling. He then twisted his torso to the right
and stretched the raised arm to the rear, going for a head
lock. The move offered the right side of his body to his
opponent's hungry maw, but he trusted the leather jacket to
hold up against the angry biting. He felt the uncomfortable
pressure of teeth biting into his lattisimus dorsi muscle where
it met his underarm. He completed the headlock maneuver,
and without pausing, he lifted onto his tiptoes and twisted the
captured head with all of the strength he could muster. The
cracking of the creature's neck was followed by a release of
the bite's pressure and a sudden limpness in the creeper's
body. Cody released the head and the body dropped to the
ground.

A quick pivot showed the first creeper just reaching
the porch. Cody drew his Beretta and fired. The 9mm round
hit its mark and the undead—a thirty-ish woman wearing a
blue blouse and white capris—fell backwards. Two more
rounds found two more creeper heads and Cody had a

moment to reach down and retrieve his fallen Mossberg. That's when he saw his attacker had been a middle-aged man—and that he was still not fully dead. While the broken neck prevented his body from moving, his eyes still tracked its prey and his teeth still clacked in an angry, biting motion. The former Ranger dispatched the poor soul with a single shot from the Berretta.

He took a quick glance outside the home and saw a larger crowd headed in his direction. Not wanting to push his luck, he turned and made for the back of the house in search of the back exit. His Mossberg was held ready but he reached the sliding glass door and let himself out without encountering other surprises.

He waited outside the rear door until the first creeper arrived. It was quickly joined by two others, and they began beating against the glass. Satisfied that his work here was done, Cody turned on his heel, ran toward the back fence and scaled the high wall. It was the same wall the group had crossed to enter the community. From the top, he looked left and spied the Humvee a short distance away. He didn't see any hostiles surrounding it, which was a positive sign. With a final glance backward—the hungry group on the other side of the glass had grown significantly—he lowered himself down the far side of the fence and jogged toward the Humvee.

Moments later, he was using the ladders that Barry had placed against the fence to re-enter the yard behind the house where the others waited.

*   *   *

"There, right there." Barry was pointing down a side street, and Cody slowed the vehicle and stopped. "What do you think?"

"A definite possibility," Cody admitted. They were scouring the roads for an RV or some other type of vehicle large enough to carry thirty-seven woman and an injured Jimbo. The vehicle Barry had spotted was a white, older model school bus. A beach scene with the words "Ohana Shaved Ice" was painted in bright colors on the side. Additional advertising lined the top of the bus' side and gave notice that snacks, drinks, shaved ice and candy could be purchased inside.

"I could go for a shaved ice when this is behind us," Barry confessed.

Cody thought the idea of a lemon-lime shaved ice was a great idea. It was something to hope for anyway. He turned the Humvee down the road, and cruised slowly past the white bus. Both he and Barry eyed the surrounding area for signs of movement or unwanted guests. Neither spotted anything of note. A quick u-turn later and they were parked behind the white bus.

"Someone had a sense of humor." Cody pointed out the words "Cool Bus" painted on the back of the vehicle. "Let's hope they left the keys in the ignition."

"Fat chance of that," Barry stated what they both were thinking, then pointed to the home where the bus sat. The front door stood wide open. "But I'm sure we'll find them in that house somewhere."

He was correct. The keys were hanging on a hook just inside the door. To make things even better, they didn't encounter any creepers and Cody gave silent thanks that things seemed to be going their way for once. Their lucky streak seemed in jeopardy when they tried starting the large vehicle. It took Barry several minutes of fiddling under the hood and coaxing the engine to get it going. Once it finally started, though, the Cool Bus ran just fine. With a growing sense of relief, Cody pulled in front and led the way back to the folks waiting for them while Barry followed at a safe distance.

The subsequent loading and return to their home base went off without a hitch. Toad—from his vantage point in the front passenger seat of the Humvee—counted thirteen creeper kamikazes on the ride home.

Chapter 38

The first thing Jimbo felt when he awoke was a blinding flash of white sunshine burning into his eyes. He fought to lift his head and spotted the single, offending beam as it sneaked through a slit in the RV's curtains. It entered the otherwise dim interior at just the right angle to hit him in his face. He dropped his head back to the pillow and that's when the pain hit. The pounding inside his head was a reminder of what he had been through, but as pain went, it wasn't nearly as bad as it could have been. In fact, he hadn't felt this good in... at least a few hours. The last thing he remembered was sitting on the stairs and watching Sarge leave the Drummer Park home.

His hand worked its way to the side of his head and the fingertips brushed against the bandage where his right ear should have been. Someone had patched him up and put him to bed; and he'd slept through the entire ordeal. He wondered how long he had been out and considered moving from the bed. Before he could decide on whether to get up or go back to sleep, the front door opened and footsteps approached.

It was the redhead. Monica.

"So, you're awake."

"How long have I been out of it?"

"You've been sleeping for about eighteen hours," she announced with a smile. "The older gentleman, Kotter, had some morphine, and we gave you a healthy dose before we cleaned and bandaged your ear."

"Not sure I'd ever put Kotter in the 'gentleman' bucket," he replied. "But tell him I said thanks."

"Ha," the smile on her face made her green eyes light up. "I know what you mean. But you can tell him yourself. It's time you got out of this bed and rejoined the rest of the living. People have been asking about you. Cody has been beside himself with worry, despite me telling him you were fine."

Jimbo relaxed his own worry at hearing that the Sarge had made it back okay. The realization that his friend was fine tripped an internal switch, though. There was something he wanted to ask the man… or tell him… he couldn't remember which. His thoughts still seemed somewhat scattered.

"You okay, Jimbo?" Monica reached out and put the back of her hand on his brow. The touch was light and reminded him that she had helped him while he was tied to that chair by wiping a cold towel across his brow. "You don't feel hot. Does anything hurt besides your ear?

"Just my head, but I'll be fine."

For the first time, he really, really looked at the woman standing over him. She was a bit older than him, but he could easily see falling for a woman like this. Then again, there was the issue of her husband's recent death, so that was likely out, at least for a while. And, what the hell was this, anyway? Who the hell had time to think about the opposite sex when it was all they could do to keep one step ahead of the undead? He shook his head to clear the strange thoughts; was hit by another wave of pain.

"At least, I think I'll be fine," he admitted. He turned his body and lowered his legs to the ground, fighting through the *thump-thump-thump* to sit up. "I just need to get moving."

She gripped his elbow and helped him stand. He managed it fairly well, and that's when he knew he was going to be fine. The upright position even helped relieve the thumping inside his head. He shuffled slowly to the front of the RV and carefully managed the three steps. By the time his foot hit the pavement, he was feeling almost normal.

"Well, well. Lookee what the cat dragged in," Kotter declared. "Boy, I thought you wuz gonna sleep for a week with the amount of pain juice we put into you."

"Is that why my mind feels like mush," Jimbo asked. "Too much morphine?"

"Well, son. I'm not sure we can blame that on the medication," Kotter replied with a smirk. "I think that's just the natural way your brain is, to be honest."

"Thanks, Kotter," he acknowledged the comment with a wave and a return smile. He knew the old man was messing with him and he refused to continue the back and forth. "Where's the Sarge?"

Kotter spat a dark stream to his left and jerked his thumb over his shoulder. "Went thattaway, last I saw. Trying to get a count of how many folks want to leave and how many want to stay."

That grabbed Jimbo's attention. He had been pressing the 'need to leave now' button hard and often over the past couple of weeks. He knew Sarge was leaning toward leaving, but this was the first solid indication he had that he was serious about the proposition. The need to find his dogs had been holding him back.

And that's when he remembered what he needed to tell the man.

*   *   *

"So, you've decided?"

"Cody, I can't see leaving now," Mel replied. Judy stood close to her husband, her right hand tightly intertwined with his left. She was nodding in agreement. "I understand why you feel the need, but someone has to stay and help the folks here. Someone who can help protect them."

"But eighty percent of the community is on board with the move. As soon as we can get enough RVs and pack them with supplies, we're heading west," Cody argued. "Hell, it'll only be you and handful of others to hold out against whatever comes your way."

"Yeah, but don't forget. We've got *Mister* Kotter on our side," the former Marine chuckled and looked over his shoulder to make sure the older man didn't hear. "He's got to be worth a dozen normal men in a fight."

"I can't argue against that," Cody conceded. He thought back to earlier in the day when he and Jimbo had approached Kotter about the move. The man had turned them down flat, while making it very clear that he wasn't going to be ousted from his home by anything, including a growing army of the undead. Despite his refusal to leave though, the older man's eyes teared up when they announced the decision to leave within a few days. He had blamed it on allergies, but Cody knew the codger would miss them—just as they would miss him. "The truth is, it helps knowing you're going to be here. We've given the folks staying behind a solid start. They're safe for now, but you never know when the shit will hit the fan. Knowing someone capable is here takes a load off of my mind."

"We'll do everything we can to keep things going."

Mel put his arm around his wife and pulled her close. She smiled up at the man she had married and Cody could tell they had begun the process of healing their relationship. He didn't have a crystal ball, so couldn't see where they might be in a year, but it was good to see that Mel was stepping up and taking responsibility. He didn't seem like the same person Cody had met only weeks before.

"Hooah, Marine," Cody smiled and offered his hand to the man who had helped save his best friend.

"Hooah, Army."

The handshake was quick and efficient. The bear hug that Judy gave him afterward was long and hard.

"Thank you, Cody," she said, stepping back to look into his eyes. He knew she was thanking him for giving their family another chance at a life together. "Thank you for everything."

"You two take care of that family. And remember, there's always a place for you and anyone else in the community if things don't work out here."

"We'll keep that in mind," Mel agreed, then pointed over Cody's shoulder. "Look who's up and at it, today."

Cody turned and saw Jimbo—trailed carefully by Monica—approaching at a quick walk.

"You look fit, Jimbo," the Ranger Sergeant called to his former trooper. "What's the hurry?"

"I had an epiphany, Sarge."

"Really? Must've been that head wound," Cody kidded. "What's the nature of this so called 'epiphany'?"

"Well..." The young men hesitated for a moment, then continued. "I can't be sure, but I think I might know where Cheech and Daisy are."

That got Cody's attention and the smile dropped from his face. The loss of his mother's dogs haunted him on an hourly basis. He had failed her, and them. He didn't reply; just held his tongue and waited for the other man to continue.

Chapter 39

"No way," Cody muttered and stared. "It couldn't have been this easy."

"Don't kid yourself, Sarge," Jimbo answered. "With the shit we were dealing with, it wasn't easy at all."

But Cody knew differently. The sign on the lawn said it all:

FOUND:
TWO CHIHUAHUAS
SAFE INSIDE

*   *   *

Cheech's head lifted from the pillow he had been using as his bed and turned his ears toward the rumble that was moving toward them. He knew that sound, had longed for it. The rumble drew closer.

Closer.

It stopped outside.

He jumped from the couch and stood at attention, his entire being focused on the rumble.

*   *   *

His hands shook as he put the vehicle in park and
climbed out of the driver's seat. His palms were suddenly
damp and he wiped them on the front of his shirt. His feet
refused to move as his mind ran through possibilities—none
of them good. Perhaps the dogs inside weren't his, or they
were his, but something had happened to them and they had
disappeared again.

*   *   *

The rumble was joined by the sound of the vehicle's
door opening and closing. The five-pound dog walked
tentatively to the front door, still unsure. His nose began
sniffing at the tiny gap, but only detected the normal scents
of the den. His ears were fully perked, on high alert.
His tail wagged slowly. Once, twice.

*   *   *

"You just gonna stand there and stare, Sarge? Or are
we gonna go get the little guy and gal?"
"Let's do it." He hoped Jimbo didn't hear the doubt
in his voice as he made his way around the front of the
Humvee.

*   *   *

The Boy's voice!

The Boy was outside, Cheech was certain of it now. He offered an excited, eager bark. Then another.

I'm here, I'm here!

"What is it Little Boy?" The Girl called out from the kitchen. Cheech barked again.

He's here! The Boy is here!

*　　*　　*

Cody heard the familiar barking and stumbled, nearly falling. He took half a second to regain control of his legs then rushed forward.

The race up the driveway and to the front porch was the longest five seconds of his life.

Epilogue

The last field of the season had been planted earlier in the day. The final mile of perimeter fencing had been erected by Toad and his fifteen-person crew only a week earlier. There hadn't been a creeper sighting for over a month, and that one had been a gaunt, pitiful straggler who washed up on the bank of the Snake River, their western border. Cody suspected the thing originated from someplace far to the east. Still, putting up the fence, and authorizing a team to patrol it regularly made everyone feel safer.

The first winter had been harsh, and the initial fight to eliminate the local undead, while also uniting the local living, had been tough. They struggled to beat the elements while finding enough to eat. In the spring, they planted their first crops, and for the most part, they were successful.

The upstart village received their first real blessing when their friends from Boise showed up en masse at their southern checkpoint late the next summer. The reunion with Mel and Judy Thompson and the rest of their enclave was marred only by the news that Mary Fitzgerald, the elderly blue-haired matriarch of the community, had passed away in her sleep just as winter was winding down. Upon seeing Cody, Kotter had lodged an immediate and boisterous complaint against Judy, citing assault and kidnapping. According to the former teacher, the hundred and ten pound woman had dragged his sleeping form from his Boise home and physically tossed him into the bed of the pickup truck that carried him west. Cody's only response was "Good for

her" which set off another bout of shouting and demands to
be returned—all of which went pretty much ignored. In
time, the old man eventually found his place and thrived in
his new surroundings. Everyone knew he was happy, despite
his attempts to persuade them otherwise.

Now, after three years, the growing farm community
had a lot to be thankful for. The radio delivered enough bad
news about the rest of the planet to let them know how good
they had things. Their relative safety and bounty made strict
diligence against outsiders all the more important. Those that
didn't have always wanted to take from those that did; and
while Cody and the rest of the community welcomed
newcomers with open arms on a regular basis, it was with one
very strict rule: you had to pull your weight.

Cody collapsed into the old, wooden rocking chair
and kicked his feet onto the porch railing. After the final
planting, his muscles felt like he had pulled everyone's weight
ten times over. Soldiering had never left him this exhausted.

He looked over at the acre of corn just beginning to
sprout to the north. It bordered two acres of potatoes. To
the south of his home, the rest of his six acres was planted
with various plots of mint, onions, peppers, tomatoes and
strawberries. He liked the diversity, and would have grown
even more if he could. But he was comforted by the
knowledge that what he didn't grow himself, he could trade
for with one of the other families. The hundred square mile
section of small farms that had been carved out around
Weiser and Payette offered a lot of variety.

It was also comforting to know that, as head of the
community's defense force, he didn't have to farm. The
position earned them a sufficient allowance of food from the

common stores. But he felt good about his work and enjoyed getting his hands into the soil.

His tired reverie was interrupted by the flash of sun off a vehicle's windshield as it turned into his lane. He put up a hand to shield the late afternoon sun and, as expected, saw Jimbo's pickup truck headed his way.

A single, loud bark came from inside. It was immediately followed by the sound of paws and nails hitting the hardwood floor. *Time to trim those nails again*, Cody thought. When the truck pulled up, the screen door behind Cody opened and the sound of dog nails hitting wood finally found its way onto the porch. Without looking, the former Ranger dropped his right hand to the ground and was greeted by several licks.

"Good timing," Maria announced and placed a hand on her husband's shoulder. "The biscuits are just about done."

"Mmm, my favorite," Cody replied and turned his head to kiss her hand. "Cheech's too."

"Don't I know it. Who knew a dog could be such a biscuit eater?"

"Cheech will eat just about anything. Daisy on the other hand. Picky, picky."

The two dogs raced down the steps and ran to the pickup where Jimbo was helping Monica from the passenger side. The small canines bounced up and down with excitement. The large stomach the woman sported bore testament to a rapidly approaching due date.

Jimbo escorted her to the steps, then helped her sit down where she could reach the little dogs, who struggled to be first in line for her attentions.

"Little Boy! Little Girl!" Maria exclaimed. "Don't bother Monica!"

"You know they aren't a bother, Maria," Monica said. "Besides, this one reminds me so much of Jim. Just look at her!"

"Hey, just because we're both missing an ear doesn't mean we look anything alike," Jimbo complained good-naturedly.

It was a running joke among the friends. Jimbo and Daisy had both lost their right ears, and on the same day. His was taken by a crazed escaped convict before being rescued by Cody; hers was lost to a hungry creeper named Wanda. Fortunately, the little dog managed to escape further damage and hid under a nearby bed until Maria rescued her. The incident provided proof that dogs were immune to the virus that caused humans to turn into creepers.

The perfection of the moment made Cody think about his mother. He thought maybe—just maybe—she might have been satisfied with how things had turned out. He was happy and her dogs were safe, and that was probably enough. He couldn't make up for how he had treated her in her final year, but he finally felt that he had done something good—something right—to honor her memory. The two scrambling forms at his feet were proof.

He shook off the sadness of his loss and made a conscious decision to focus on the immediacy of the here and now. After all, living isn't about what's happened in the past; living is about what's happening around you at *this* moment.

He lifted his tired body from the comfort of the rocking chair and closed the short distance to his wife. He gave Maria a long, tender kiss and stroked her cheek.

"That's how you do it, Sarge!"

"Okay, I'm starved," Cody announced, ignoring Jimbo's playful taunt. "Who's ready to eat?"

Cheech and Daisy recognized the phrase and immediately began turning circles. Cheech spun left; Daisy turned to the right.

The End

Acknowledgments

I've said it before, but it bears repeating: I enjoy the Acknowledgments section. It gives me a chance to tell everyone who helped me finish the book how much I truly appreciate their support.

First, I want to thank you, the reader. Without you, I'm just a guy putting a story on a series of pages that no one will ever read—much like Jonathon Samuel Sweeney, but (thankfully) without the sociopathic tendencies. What a sick bastard that guy was, huh? He was fun to invent, though. My editor wanted me to consider writing a full-on sex scene between him and Wanda, but I nixed *that* idea. Frankly, I didn't want to think through the complex technicalities or intricate planning that such an act with a creeper would require. Can you imagine? Too much "be careful doing *this*" and "how would *that* work" kind of thinking for my personal comfort. Sheesh...

Where was I? Ah, yes... thanking you, the reader. You make it possible for me to keep going when the last thing I want to do is start banging away on the keyboard. Working a full time job and trying to maintain a personal connection with my family often make writing seem like a third job. But writing a book is a labor of love, and I'm reminded of that on a regular basis. Your positive reviews, emails, tweets and posts help me keep the creative juices flowing. Thank you, thank you, a thousand times thank you.

If you've made it this far, the book probably held at least a tiny bit of appeal. If it didn't, I sincerely hope you skipped to the end to see how things ended for Cheech and Daisy and wound up here by mistake. The world is filled with too many good books to spend time with the bad ones. I'm enough of a realist to know my writing doesn't appeal to everyone, but I hope you were at least mildly entertained by the story. Ideally, I hope you enjoyed the hell out of it. Either way—good or bad—I urge you to take a few moments and tell others how you feel about the book by leaving a review on Amazon, B&N, or wherever you purchased it. In addition to helping a struggling writer (that would be me), your review will also help other readers like yourself.

It is important to name some of the key contributors to *CotZA*. This is not an endeavor I could have completed on my own. Just as it takes a village to raise a child, it takes a team to build a book. Some of the key team members for this book include my editor, **Laura Kingsley**; my cover artist, **Keri Knutson**; and my wife and best friend, **Juanita**. Thanks to all of you for your support, encouragement and hard work.

A special thanks goes out to my son, **Taylor** who kept bugging me to write a z-novel, even when I didn't think I had anything new to add to the genre. Fortunately, one night I thought, "hey, what about adding in some Chihuahuas?" The result is in your hands.

Finally, I'd like the real-life **Cheech** and **Daisy**. They are a big part of our family and were the inspiration for the tiny canines in the book. Many of the traits they display in the story are on display in our home every day. Cheech is a tiny little warrior, who loves everyone. Daisy is a shivering little girl who doesn't care too much for outsiders. Both turn circles when we give them a snack: Cheech turns counter-clockwise; Daisy, clockwise. Cute as hell, I tell ya. Cute as hell.

Steve Hawk
10/21/2013

Daisy and Cheech:

CotZA Equipment List

I thought it might be cool to show some of the equipment used by Cody and the gang.

Weapons

Typical AR15:

Customized AR15:

Easton XL1:

TenPoint® Carbon Elite XLT ACUDraw Crossbow:

Berretta 9mm Pistol:

Gerber Mark II:

Mossberg 500 Tactical Shotgun:

Protective Gear

Jimbo's FX-1 FlexForce Damascus Gear:

Cody's Gear:

House of Harley® HCI Screaming Skulls Retractable, Full Face Helmet:

Reflective Evil Triple Flaming Skulls Cruiser Armored Leather Motorcycle Jacket:

Gauntlet gloves:

CCM® U+ Crazy Light Ice Hockey Shoulder Pads:

Easton Power Brigade leg guards:

Shock Doctor ® Ultra Neck Guard:

Miscellaneous

Armored Humvee:

Monblanc Agatha Christie Edition fountain pen:

About the Author

Steven L. Hawk spent six years as a Military Intelligence Specialist with the U.S. Army's 82nd Airborne Division before joining the ranks of corporate America. He has a B.S. in Business Management from Western Governor's University and is a certified Project Management Professional (PMP). He has traveled extensively across the United States and, at various times, has lived in Georgia, North Carolina, West Virginia, Massachusetts, California and Idaho.

He currently resides in Boise, Idaho with his wife, Juanita. Together, they have a blended family of five sons and two Chihuahuas.

This is his fourth published novel. For more information, you can follow him via the following channels:

Website: www.SteveHawk.com

Linkedin: http://www.linkedin.com/in/stevenhawk

Twitter: @stevenhawk

Also by Steven L. Hawk:

The Peace Warrior Trilogy:

Peace Warrior
Peace Army
Peace World

Made in United States
Troutdale, OR
10/14/2023

13714949R00195